DEEP END

ALSO BY GEOFFREY NORMAN:

Midnight Water
Sweetwater Ranch
Blue Chipper

Geoffrey Norman

William Morrow and Company, Inc.
New York

It is the policy of William Morrow and Company, Inc., and its imprints and affiliates, recognizing the importance of preserving what has been written, to print the books we publish on acid-free paper, and we exert our best efforts to that end.

Norman, Geoffrey.
    Deep end / Geoffrey Norman.
      p.   cm.
    ISBN 0-688-11655-8
    I. Title.
PS3564.05645D4   1994
813'.54—dc20   93-37748
                                                                          CIP

Printed in the United States of America

First Edition

1 2 3 4 5 6 7 8 9 10

BOOK DESIGN BY LISA STOKES

For Mark McCaughan

CHAPTER 1

It was not quite six and the sun was just coming up. I had the highway to myself, and I listened to the morning farm report as I drove through the low, wet country on the margin of the coast. Ground fog hung in the big patches of swamp and filled the gaps between the undernourished pines that struggled in the thin soil. I drove with my lights on and had to drift across the center line to avoid a snapping turtle that had crawled out on the blacktop to soak up a little of its residual warmth.

I took it slow and listened as the announcer pitched herbicides, pesticides, tractor parts, and software for the modern agricultural entrepreneur. I'd been paying close attention to the price of feeder cattle. Beef had been low for a few months, long enough for the cycle to have just about bottomed out. I'd done all right in beans over the winter, and was thinking about taking out some new contracts.

It was one of several things I did to keep busy and make a little money, a kind of action, and if I had an incurable weakness for anything, it was action. That's why I'd jumped when Phil Garvey called and asked if I'd like to go diving with him this morning. If he'd called and asked me to help him haul a boat and clean the bottom or pull the engine, I'd have probably said yes to that, too. Things had been kind of slow lately.

So I sat behind the wheel, with the monotonous sound of the tires on wet pavement for background music, while I listened to the announcer run down the numbers in his thick, black-earth drawl and watched the ground fog burn off the road and out of the gaps between the pines. It was a pretty spring morning on the Gulf Coast, and I felt glad to be alive.

With some people, it doesn't take much.

Garvey's boat, *Second Shot*, was moored in a wet slip at a place called the Outrigger, a down-and-dirty working marina in a little cove about a three-mile run from the Gulf. I turned off the blacktop onto an oyster-shell drive and followed it through some scrubby oaks and past a small fleet of old, out-of-commission boats that were resting in wooden cradles, waiting for the maintenance and rebuilding that would never be done.

I parked at the water's edge and got out of the truck. The air was a fragrant blend of mud at low tide, old shells, and diesel fuel. It was quiet except for the occasional off-tune call of a passing gull.

I dropped the tailgate, grabbed the two tanks I'd had filled the night before, and carried them out the dock to the last slip, where *Second Shot* was moored. It was one of the better-looking boats at the marina, a forty-two-foot Bertram whose last owner hadn't used it much because he preferred staying on the beach and drinking. He hadn't paid enough attention to the weather reports and got caught flatfooted by an early-season hurricane that came ashore like a racehorse. When the storm passed and the insurance adjusters came out, the boat was written off as a total loss.

Garvey bought it for next to nothing and had it hauled out and put up on dry land, where he worked on it for six months, spending on it every spare minute as well as every dollar he could put his hands on. When he finished, the boat was in the best shape it had been in since it left the factory in Fort Lauderdale twenty years earlier.

With my gear loaded, I sat at the end of the dock and watched a flock of pelicans glide low over the water in a precise echelon formation. There is something about the way those birds fly, something in their ponderous determination, that I find endlessly fascinating. They remind me of those old bombers that had been designed not to look good but to haul the freight against the Nazis. But utility can be beautiful, too.

Garvey pulled in a few minutes later and parked his pickup next to mine. I walked up the dock to help him unload.

"Good morning, Morgan," Garvey said heartily when he saw me. Garvey always comes on hearty. It isn't temperament as much as a strategy. He believes that a positive approach pays dividends. We used to call it a "can-do" attitude, a million years ago in Vietnam. Did us a lot of good, too.

"How're you, Phil?" I said.

"Got some good diving lined up and a beautiful day for it," he said, showing me a mouthful of very white, very straight teeth. He had shaved close. His face was strong, made up of clean, symmetrical angles, and his eyes were clear and a pale shade of blue. "So I don't see how things could be any better."

He reached into the bed of his pickup and lifted a tank by the regulator at its neck. He made it look easy. Garvey was lean but very powerful. He'd been a Navy SEAL for ten years and still had the look, still kept in shape, in spite of the leg wound that had forced him out of the service. His femur had deteriorated from osteomyelitis and a staph infection and the edge of the scar showed just below the line of his cotton khaki trunks. He limped, just a little, but he would probably fight you if you called him "disabled."

We carried his gear down the dock and loaded it on the Bertram. Garvey took the canvas cover off the controls and stored it below, raised the engine covers, looked the diesels over for leaks, and checked the bilge. Then he fired the engines. They caught right off; he throttled them down to a slow idle and put the covers back down.

He took the radio from a small duffel and attached it to a mount on a console next to the wheel, hooked up the antenna cable and the power, then turned on the set. When the dials glowed, he picked up the handset and keyed it.

"Base React," he said, "this is *Second Shot*. Radio check. One, two, three, four, five. Five, four, three, two, one. How read? Over."

"*Second Shot*," a voice came back through the receiver, "this is React Base. I read you five by. Over."

"This is *Second Shot*," Garvey said. "Roger. Out."

He put the handset back in the cradle and looked around the boat, slowly taking it all in. When he'd finished, he took a small notebook from the duffel, opened it, and wrote a few things on a blank page with a plastic Scripto pencil like schoolkids carry. He put the notebook and the pencil back in the duffel, looked at his watch, and said, "Okay, Morgan, let's dance."

CHAPTER 2

WE RAN EAST DOWN THE LAGOON AND into the bay, where you could see the Navy base with its ancient hangars and seaplane ramps. This was where the Navy had trained all those aviators who had gone off to fly against Japan, Vietnam, and various other enemies actual and potential. But the Cold War had ended in a whimper and now the Navy didn't need so many pilots. The base looked almost deserted.

"Kind of sad, isn't it?" Garvey said.

"Yes," I said. "It is." I suppose just about any vet feels a little melancholy when he looks at an empty parade ground.

"But I'll tell you something," Garvey went on, "if they ever go ahead and close that baby all the way down, it will be some of the choicest real estate anywhere. Can you imagine what that place is worth in today's market?"

"Nope," I said. "I can't count that high." All over Florida, even here, in the furthest reaches of the Panhandle, conversations about landscapes, especially waterfront, came down to price. There's no land in Florida, just real estate.

We were passing across the narrow mouth of the bay now, where the ship channel makes a turn out toward the Gulf. The pass was guarded on both sides by old brick forts. The harbor had been considered militarily important long before the U.S. Navy started teaching young men how to fly airplanes off ships, and the old forts had been active through the Civil War. One of them, Fort Pickens, on the east side of the pass, had been one of the three Federal forts that Lincoln decided to resupply after secession, an action that led to the shelling of Fort Sumter and war.

Pickens had stayed in Union hands. For a while, a fort across the bay, Barrancas, had been held by the Confederates, and the two outposts had exchanged cannon fire; occasionally, one side or the other sent a raiding party across the bay, by boat, to create a little nuisance. These skirmishes probably had no effect at all on the outcome of the war, but they had left a lot of old ordnance at the bottom of the bay.

Phil Garvey liked to dive for that stuff when he had a day off. What made him happiest, as far as I could tell, was a two-cannonball day. But then, I didn't know Phil intimately. We first met when I went into his dive shop with a regulator that had started free flowing on me. We talked a little and we got along. I brought him a little trade. He'd invited me diving seven or eight times. When we were on the boat, we talked about inconsequential things. We'd told each other a few war stories. I'd met his wife, once, when we'd gone out for dinner. And I played with his children when I went by his house. But I didn't know about his secret hopes and fears and he'd never introduced me to his inner child. We were dive buddies.

"Tide is running just right," he said and throttled back on the engines. I moved up to the bow and freed the anchor.

When Garvey shouted, "Drop it," I let the anchor go and watched the line, bleached very white by the sun, angle off into the emerald-green water. When it went slack, I took a hitch on the cleat and shouted, "It's firm."

Garvey cut the engines and everything went suddenly quiet. It was a minute or two before my ears could pick up the sound of the small waves slapping the side of the boat.

We sat in the cockpit, rigging up. There were a few other boats on the bay, mostly fishermen running hard for the pass. The billfishermen had a long way to run, thirty miles or more, to get to blue water. So they were in a hurry.

My eyes picked one boat out of the crowd, and after a second I realized why. It was showing flashing blue lights, just like a prowl car on dry land. The boat was big, maybe sixty feet, and painted red and white. It had a lower, more warlike profile than a sportfisherman, and it threw a huge wake.

"Looks like the Coast Guard is after someone," I said.

Garvey looked up. "Some marlin fisherman with a generator fire, I imagine," he said. "They love it."

We went back to our gear. When the regulator was finger-tight on the tank, I opened the valve a half-turn and then pushed the purge button on my mouthpiece, releasing a blast of compressed air. Then I checked the little knife I carry on my vest. Fishermen have left lots of monofilament line on the bottom of the bay and you can get tangled up in it before you even see it. The stainless blade was plenty sharp.

"Hey, Morgan," Garvey said, "you'd better stand by."

I looked up and saw the Coast Guard boat bearing down

on us, no more than four hundred yards away now, still running wide open.

"You think he plans on ramming us?" I said.

"If he does, he'll miss," Garvey said. "The worst seamen in the world are in the Coast Guard. Bunch of Kansas farmers and Cleveland street punks, joined because they want to see the ocean."

The big steel-hulled boat backed off when it was about two hundred yards from us. I could see machine-gun mounts fore and aft. The tarps were off and the guns were manned . . . and aimed at us.

"Well, son of a *bitch*," Garvey said. "I believe they intend to board us."

The U.S. ensign flew above the bridge of the crash boat and there were marijuana leaves stenciled on the bulkhead below it. Three rows of five leaves. Ten or twelve men were standing on the deck looking at us. They were all wearing black utilities, black boots, black flak jackets, and black helmets with plastic visors. They carried little black rifles with plastic stocks.

"Looks like they got us outnumbered," Garvey said.

"Not to mention outgunned."

"Remember," Garvey said, "nothing but name, rank, service number, and date of birth."

A static sound came over the air between us and the crash boat. Somebody had keyed the hailer.

"To the skipper of the sportfisherman *Second Shot*," a voice boomed.

Garvey cupped his hands around his mouth and shouted back, "You got him."

"This is the United States Coast Guard," the voice said, and Garvey muttered, "Well, no shit."

"Prepare to be boarded for inspection," the voice went on. "Stay topside with your hands in view. Do not attempt to weigh your anchor or start your engines. I repeat. Stand by for boarding. Keep your hands in view and do not attempt to weigh anchor or start your engines."

"Roger," Garvey said. "I got it the first time. What's this about?"

"Just stand by for boarding and follow instructions, skipper," the voice said.

Garvey said nothing.

"Do you understand my instructions?" the amplified voice insisted.

"Roger," Garvey shouted.

"What's this about?" I said.

"Harassment," Garvey said. "I hope you don't have a kilo of cocaine in your bag."

"No," I said. "Just a ham sandwich."

We watched while two of the men in black uniforms laid their M16s on the deck and lowered a Zodiac from a davit at the stern of the crash boat. They had trouble with one of the winches and it took them ten minutes or more. While they struggled with the gear, another man in a black suit, probably a petty officer, yelled at them to "get a fucking move on," and the man at the helm kept kicking the engine in and out of gear to keep the crash boat in position about fifteen yards off our port side. The diesel fumes drifted over us.

"Wonder if it ever occurred to them to get on the downwind side of us," Garvey said.

When the Zodiac was finally in the water, five men climbed down into it, all of them still carrying their rifles. The man in the stern jerked the starter cord on the outboard, and when it kicked over he put it in gear and pointed the little rubber boat in our direction. During all this, the men on deck kept their rifles at an easy port. The mounted M60 machine guns, though, stayed pointed right at us.

The Zodiac bumped against the transom of *Second Shot* and a man threw a line around a cleat, then came over the side. His boots left black rubber skid marks on the gunwales and the oiled teak deck.

He took a position all the way aft in the cockpit, with the stock of his rifle at his shoulder and the muzzle aimed at a point on the deck between us. His finger was inside the trigger guard and his thumb was on the safety. He was a kid, probably no more than nineteen or twenty, with pimples and nervous sweat on his face.

Three more men followed him, also carrying M16s. Then one more man, this one with an automatic in a holster on his pistol belt and a clipboard in his hand. He had a radio slung onto his load-bearing equipment, and a wire ran from it to his ear.

"Okay," he said, "we are aboard. We have two subjects and no weapons in view."

He listened to the instructions that came through the earpiece. He was a little older than the other men, and had the look of someone who enjoys being in charge with no possibility that anyone will question his authority.

"Roger," he said, "commencing search."

He looked at us and said, "This is a Coast Guard search for contraband. If you are carrying any illegal drugs on your boat, it would be to your advantage to hand them over now. Are you carrying any such materials?"

"No," Garvey answered, saying a lot more than that with one word.

The man nodded as though he heard the answer all the time and it was always a lie. "Are you the only personnel on board?"

"Yes."

He nodded again.

"Your names?"

We gave them to him and he wrote them down carefully.

"Let me see your boat registration."

Garvey went to the drawer where he kept his documents. The petty officer took them impatiently and studied them with deep skepticism. He made another note or two and handed the papers back to Garvey. Then he turned to one of the other men and said, "Where are the tools, Johnson?"

"In the Zodiac," the man said nervously.

"Well, goddamnit, they aren't doing anyone any good there, are they?"

"No," the man said.

"Well, get 'em."

The man climbed back over the gunwale, leaving more rubber streaks, and returned with a black cordura bag that he dropped on the deck hard enough to scar it. The man with the clipboard opened the bag and took out a pair of Vise-Grips and a screwdriver.

"Okay, skipper," he said to Garvey, "first we'll make sure you didn't try to flush anything when you saw us coming."

CHAPTER 3

THE PETTY OFFICER WAS VERY METHODI-
cal about his work and he plainly enjoyed it. The search
took over an hour. First he unscrewed the clamps on all
the drains and pulled out the hoses, which he checked
with his fingers. Then he opened every drawer and locker
on the boat and scattered their contents on the deck. He
checked the bilges. He even dumped the ice and drinks
from our fiberglass cooler.

When he had done all this, he stood in the cockpit,
sweating a little because he had been working hard and
was wearing a hot black uniform and a flak jacket. He
spoke to Garvey, who was still as stone. I believe Garvey
would have given *Second Shot* away for ten minutes alone
with the petty officer right then. *I* might have given more
than that, and it wasn't even my boat.

"All right, skipper," the petty officer said, "there are
two voids up forward. If you have some sort of secret way
of getting into them, I suggest you show me now. Otherwise I'm going to have to cut into them."

Garvey said nothing. Didn't even move his head.

"Okay," the petty officer said, cheerfully, "have it your way."

He bent over the tool bag and took out a small chain saw. It started on the third pull.

He carried the chain saw down below, and in a few seconds we heard the sound change as he engaged the chain. Then again as the teeth bit into wood. That happened three times. Each time I could feel Garvey, who was standing a yard away from me, stiffen. By the time the petty officer came back topside, with sawdust on his black uniform, Garvey was quivering.

The petty officer dropped the saw next to the tool bag, denting the deck. He keyed the little radio and said, "Flashpoint, this is flashpoint one."

He waited a moment, then said, "Ah, this is flashpoint one, negative on the contraband. Papers are good. Life jackets and fire extinguishers are also good. We are returning."

He wrote something on the sheet of paper attached to his clipboard, then pulled it free and handed it to Garvey.

"Okay, skipper," he said. "You lucked out this time. If you want to claim any damages to your vessel as a result of the boarding and search, then you need to fill in this form and mail it to the indicated address. For now, remain topside, with your hands in view, until my men and I are back aboard our own ship and are under way. Do you understand those instructions?"

"What's your name, little man?" Garvey said.

The petty officer took a step in Garvey's direction and said, "Do you understand those instructions?"

Garvey said nothing. A knot had formed in the angle of his jaw. It throbbed like it had been touched to a hot wire.

"Do you understand those instructions?" the petty officer said once more.

"My instructions to you, maggot, are to get yourself and these other little babies off my boat before I jam that clipboard up your ass sideways and then make you write your mommy a letter on it."

The man took another step toward Garvey. I looked at the four men on the fantail. Their M16s were still pointed at the deck and none of them had touched a safety. I shifted my weight to my toes and decided to try for the youngest, most nervous-looking of the four, the kid who had come aboard first.

But the petty officer had left the mike on his radio keyed and somebody on the crash boat heard what was going on.

"Okay, Joe," a voice boomed out over the hailer. "That's it. Leave 'em the paperwork and come on back."

The petty officer glared at Garvey, but in spite of himself he looked relieved. He moved to the stern, careful to drag his feet. In a minute or two, he and his men, along with the tool bag, were back in the Zodiac and heading for the crash boat.

They were no better recovering the Zodiac than they had been launching it. After fumbling around for ten minutes or so, they had it back aboard. The helmsman poured on the power and the crash boat left us wallowing in its wake and breathing fumes from its dirty diesel engine.

Neither Garvey nor I said anything. We watched the crash boat leave, then we looked around and surveyed the damage to *Second Shot*. We could have raved and bitched and sworn vengeance, I suppose, but we were both grown-ups.

The boat looked like it had been shanghaied for a party

weekend by a bunch of motorcycle bums. The deck was littered with life jackets, charts, foul-weather gear, and all the other things that Garvey kept carefully stowed. There were ugly holes sawed in the voids up forward, under the vee berths. And all the drains had been left open, along with the hatch to the bilge.

Without a word, I went to work on the drains while Garvey carefully folded and stored all the scattered gear. It took a couple of hours. When we'd finished with that, I went up to the bow and pulled in the anchor while Garvey started the engines. His burned a lot cleaner, I noticed, than the Coast Guard's.

We ran back to the Outrigger, and when the lines were secure, Garvey said simply, "I need to go get some things to patch those holes. Sorry about the way the day turned out, Morgan."

"Your fault, for sure," I said.

He shook his head and marched up the dock to his truck.

I found some abrasive cleaner and fine-grit sandpaper in his locker and went to work on the skid marks while he was gone. I was about half done when he got back carrying a sheet of plywood, a couple of one-by-twos, and a toolbox.

"You don't have to do that," he said.

"I know. You want me to put some primer on that wood while you make your measurements?"

"Yeah. Check the locker over there. You'll find what you need."

So we worked until midafternoon, and when we had finished, you'd never have known we'd been boarded and trashed by a bunch of kids in flak jackets. The work did a lot for the boat, but not much for that feeling of red, impotent rage that had settled on me like a fever. My fingers still trembled when I held a paintbrush.

*   *   *

When there was nothing left to do but wait for the paint
to dry, Garvey and I sat on the transom, eating our lunch
and drinking the beer that had been meant to cool our
throats after we'd been diving and breathing dry compressed air. It tasted pretty good and seemed to burr, just
slightly, the edge of anger.

Garvey finally sighed heavily and said, "You catch that
call sign? *'Flashpoint'?* I wonder if they dreamed that up
all by themselves."

"Goes with the costumes, I suppose."

"I wonder what would have happened if I'd told those
boys to go piss up a rope. You think they would have
cranked off a few from those M-Sixties?"

"Maybe," I said. "But if they had, you think they would
have hit anything?"

"Probably not. Range was a little too much for the Coasties. Jesus . . . "

"You going to do anything?"

"Send that paper in, you mean," he said, "and spend
the next year or two hassling with the government?"

"Maybe you could find a way to make it hot for Joe and
the people he works for."

Garvey shook his head. "Not worth the effort, Morgan.
What they did was perfectly legal. It happens all the time."

Maybe so, I thought, but not to me.

CHAPTER 4

DRIVING OUT OF THE OUTRIGGER, I RE-
lived the entire episode. Felt the humiliation, again, of
having to watch helplessly while someone with nothing
to back him up except the whole authority of the state
strips your pride for the fun of it. I suppose I should have
been able to reconcile myself to it, like somebody who has
been mugged and feels like he has gotten off lightly because he only lost his wallet and some cash. I'd been in
prison, after all, and had been strip-searched. But I'd never
learned to like it. Hadn't even learned to pass it off. I could
still work up a scalding rage just remembering some of
the guards. And I'd rather die than lose that.

You can't always get even. In fact, you can seldom get
even. But I felt like this time I ought to try, and, anyway,
I didn't have anything better to do.

I parked in the visitors' lot behind a complex of three
ugly, mustard-yellow buildings, including the county hospital, the jail, and the sheriff's department. Except for the

razor wire around the jail and the antenna farm on the
roof of the sheriff's department, there was no way of telling one building from the other. I went through the front
door of the sheriff's department, and then through the
metal detector. I asked the woman at the desk if Lieutenant
Pine was in.

"Your name?"

I gave it to her.

"Just a moment."

It took Pine about that long.

It's a funny thing how, in spite of the fact that he has
never changed, I'm always a little shocked by the way Tom
looks when I first see him. Part of it is the sheer animal
size of the man. He's six-four, six-five and probably weighs
265 or even 270. He had been an all-American at 240 or
-50. But the extra weight hasn't made him look soft, or
anything even close to it.

The other thing about Tom I can never quite get used to
is just how *black* he is. When you call him a "black man"
you're speaking a literal truth that still doesn't quite cover
all the ground. Tom is so deeply, flawlessly black that his
skin is the color of freshly poured hot tar. It even glistens
like hot tar.

His size and his startlingly black skin give Pine the look
of a warrior from another world, another epoch, even
when he's standing inside an office building, wearing
pressed khakis and a Sam Browne belt.

"Hello, Morgan," he said. "You don't look much worse."

"Neither do you, Tom."

We shook.

"How you been keeping?"

"Good. You?"

"Fine. And Phyllis?"

"She's fine," Pine said. "And now that we got that cov-

ered, why don't we get out of here and go get something
to eat."

We took my truck about a mile to a place called Billy's,
one of Tom's favorites, a conventional diner with Formica
tables and a tile floor, a long counter with stools, and a
black cast-iron grill where a fat man in an apron, his arms
covered up with watery blue tattoos, was turning
hamburgers.

When the waitress came for our order, Tom said he was
watching his weight, so he'd just have a piece of pecan
pie, no whipped cream, and some coffee. *Black* coffee. I
said I'd have the coffee without the pie.

While we waited, I told Tom about how Garvey's boat
had been boarded. Pine listened without expression.
When the coffee came and Pine picked up his mug, it
seemed to vanish in his large, gnarled fist. The pie came
and I kept talking while Pine worked on it, which didn't
take long. He wiped his mouth with a napkin and pushed
the plate away, then motioned to the waitress for more
coffee. When she had poured it, he said, "Goddamn a
bunch of drugs."

He shook his head, then slapped his leg, hard, with the
flat of his hand. The waitress looked our way. Nervously.

Tom went on, without raising his voice, but speaking
out of a bottomless anger. "I mean, god*damn* all the drugs
in the world. You know what I mean, Morgan. Drugs ain't
nothing but poison in the bloodstream of the world. Man
but I am *tired* of drugs."

I nodded.

"That's why your friend was stopped, like that, because
of drugs."

"I know. That's what they told us."

But Tom wasn't listening. This was his sermon, and he
was going to preach it even if to the choir. "Half my job,

seems like, touches up against drugs. Maybe more. Any night I wanted to make a felony arrest, I could get in a cruiser and drive right straight to a crack house and bust three or four dudes. Get 'em on a paraphernalia charge at least. There's already so many of them doing time that the studs who aren't in there on minimum-mandatory are getting ten days of gain time for every day served. Guy gets ten for killing someone with a butcher knife, he'll be out in less than a year. Another guy gets six for having a crack pipe sticking out his back pocket, he wears the whole suit of clothes."

Tom shook his head and looked at me with an expression that blended weariness, disgust, and bone-deep anger. He'd arrested men he'd played ball with back in high school. And then he'd arrested their sons. When Tom said he hated drugs, it was not merely rhetorical.

"Your friend—this Garvey—any chance he *was* moving stuff?"

"None at all," I said.

"You got to be sure, now," Tom said. "Does your man need money? People get behind and they start thinking that all they need is that one score. I put one guy away, he was a colonel in the Air Force, started thinking that way."

I considered it. I thought I knew Garvey, but I wasn't sure I knew him that well. I wasn't sure I knew anyone that well, except maybe the man who was sitting across the table from me. Then I thought a little more. No. Not Garvey. He was made the same way Pine was made.

"Nope," I said. "There just isn't any way."

"All right," Pine said. "I'll buy that. I know some who would starve before they'd buy their groceries with dirty money. But I'm kind of curious about something, Morgan."

"What's that?"

"How come you wanted to see me?"

"I thought you might know why they picked Garvey's boat. Why now. He's no stranger. Anybody who spends any time on the water around here would have seen him before. Would have known what he does and where he docks."

"You ask him?"

"No."

"I mean, maybe he's been doing some work for somebody who they think is dirty, you know."

"That's possible, I suppose." I said. "How would you find out?"

Pine pinched his earlobe, then ran his hand across the back of his neck.

"I wouldn't," he said. "Fact is, I wouldn't even try. The Coast Guard is part of the federal government, and none of them feds talk to us. Not the FBI, Customs, or DEA. Probably not even the meat inspectors from the Department of Agriculture or the boys from the National Weather Service. They think we're inferior because we're local."

"I see."

"We're corruptible, you understand?"

That was laughable coming from Tom Pine. So I laughed. Plenty of people in his line of work are on the take, and some of them probably work right down the hall from Tom. But Tom has a deep, furious sense of pride. He cannot be bought. He cannot even be rented. It would probably be safer to pull a gun on him than to offer him a bribe—of any size.

"Of course," he went on, "I know some feds who have had their palms crossed. But even so, their attitude is that those boys are the *exception*. In our case, you see, it's the *rule*."

"I see."

"But there's another problem between us and them. Seizures."

"Seizures?" I said.

"Yeah," Tom said, finishing his coffee and motioning to the waitress for more. She filled his cup and looked at me. I passed.

"Few years back, somebody got the idea that the way to go after the big hogs in the drug industry was to take away their toys. Anything used in the commission of the crime was considered contraband. House, airplane, boat, car. Whatever it was, it was *ours* once we'd caught some drug stud using it in the commission of a felony.

"Well, shit," Tom went on, "it was like a yard sale, all of a sudden. Everybody went ape over seizures. You got commendations and promotions based on your seizures. Guys started feeling like they had quotas to fill. If you hadn't seized a car this month, you felt like you just weren't doing your job.

"Lot of that stuff, we got to keep. The best boats the Marine Patrol has, it took 'em off the druggies. Same with airplanes. Weapons. Sheriff himself uses a laptop computer we took off a drug guy who used it to keep his books.

"So, even if the Coast Guard—and any of those feds— thought we were tolerable honest, they still wouldn't share any information with us because they'd be afraid we'd cut in there ahead of them and get the good merchandise, like some mean old lady at a sale, jabbing the other customers in the ass with her umbrella. It's a hell of a way to do business, Morgan, I'm telling you. Just a hell of a way to do business."

"So you can't do much for me with the Coast Guard?"

"Less than that."

I nodded and played with the coffee cup for a moment. Then said, "Well, thanks Tom. Worth a try, anyway."

Pine nodded and said, "There is one thing you might consider."

"What's that?"

"I don't know about the Coast Guard, understand, but with us, when we make a drug raid like that, it almost always starts with a tip. You don't necessarily know if that tip is worth anything. Sometimes people call in and tell you to go bust up a house because of what you'll find there and it turns out they just want to make trouble for the people living in that house. You see what I'm saying?"

"Yes."

"You might talk to your buddy, see if he has any enemies might want to cause him that kind of inconvenience."

I thought about that. Then said, "How would you find out if somebody had called in and informed on someone. With the Coast Guard." I was talking to myself as much as to Tom.

He finished his coffee in one, decisive gulp. Checked his watch, then fished in the pocket of his uniform shirt for a toothpick. When it was wedged between two back molars, he said, "I suppose I'd see if I could get up close to one of the young guys. Catch him at a bar sometime, after he'd had him a glass or two of that old loudmouth, and wanted to tell people what a hero he was."

"You think somebody young and junior like that would know who the informer was?"

Pine shook his head. "You're right. Don't know what I was thinking."

"Tough problem," I said.

"Near about impossible for a civilian, I'd say."

"Maybe," I said. "But I've got a notion."

"Well," Pine said, looking at his watch again, "you let me know how it works out. Right now, I got to get back to the store. It's Saturday night and the weather is nice. Guarantee we'll be busy."

"Sure," I said. "Thanks for your help."

"I didn't do nothing."

"Sure you did."

CHAPTER 5

My HOUSE HAD BEEN BUILT BY AN OLD sea captain who had started small and kept adding on every time he came home from a cruise and found a new baby had joined his family. By the time he was finished, there were twenty rooms.

Over the years, the captain's children had left home, his wife had died, and he had finally gone off to an old seamans' home on the Carolina coast. The children had never been able to settle their differences and the house eventually went derelict. I picked it up at auction when I was just out of prison. My plan was to live in it and rebuild it at the same time. It was an absurd house for one man, but I'd spent too much of my life in barracks and bunkers and cells. I wanted a place where I could bounce around.

The river house was that, for sure, and it was also all mine.

I parked out front, under a big live oak, and walked around back, where I took off my clothes and stood under the cold-water shower I had rigged next to the porch. The water came out of the spring at about sixty degrees no matter what time of year it was, and in a few minutes my skin was tight and I was shivering. I turned the water off, dried myself, went back inside, and dressed in clean khaki pants, a white cotton shirt, and a pair of moccasins. I went into the kitchen and turned on the heat under the last of the morning coffee. While I was waiting for it to warm, I tried Jessie Beaudreaux on the phone. I got her answering machine—probably out playing tennis, I thought—and left a message to call. I poured coffee and took it to the front porch, sat on the steps, and watched the river.

Dozens of red-winged blackbirds were flying among the tops of the cattails, perching for a minute or two, then taking to the air again for reasons I could not determine. Now and then a mullet would jump out of the river, catching the sun with its silver side. Sometimes it would jump as many as five or six times. It's a mystery why.

I drank my coffee and watched the abrupt, pointless activity of the blackbirds and the mullet against the slow movement of the river. I seem to spend a lot of time doing that. An alternative to television, I suppose. Certainly no worse for the mind.

I was still sitting on the step, almost an hour later, when the phone rang.

"Morgan," Jessie Beaudreaux said, "in a couple of hours it's going to be Saturday night. What do you think about that?"

"I think we need to drive into town and hang around down at the Dairy Queen."

"I don't usually think of myself as old, Morgan," she said. "But I am too old for that."

"Then why don't I come pick you up and take you out to dinner?"

"That would be fine, Morgan," she said. "That would be very nice."

Jessie lived a couple of miles upriver from me in a house that was as modern, efficient, and complete as mine was all of the other things.

She was sitting in a lawn chair under a spreading magnolia in her front yard when I pulled up her drive at last light. She had a tall glass of something in her hand and was wearing a deep-green cotton dress that set off her olive skin and raven-colored hair, which she cut at her shoulders and combed high to reveal the strong bones and clean angles of her face.

She's a good-looking woman in a sort of warm, Latin way. There's nothing remote or secretive or detached about her. None of the icy fashion model in her beauty. One look and you know she's a woman with a temper, a sense of humor, and appetites. I liked all of those things and considered myself lucky.

We'd met, after a fashion, while I was in prison. She'd read about me in the papers and wrote me a letter, which I answered. After I got my pardon, we became friends, and then something more.

"Morgan," she said, "I believe you have washed and waxed your truck. Did you do that just for me?"

"Certainly."

"Well I'm touched. Truly."

She kissed me full on the mouth. Her perfume, which smelled faintly of jasmine, and the touch of her body under the soft cotton gave me a sudden, electric spasm of pleasure.

"Ummm," she said. "You feel like a man who's been getting ready for Saturday night. Like one of those roughnecks been out on the rigs all week."

"What's in the glass?"

"Bourbon, lemonade, and bitters. I'm getting ready for Saturday night, too. Want one?"

"I'm driving," I said. "But I'll take a taste."

The drink was cold and sour and strong enough that one sip gave me a fleeting sense of vertigo. Probably it was the combination of the bourbon and the perfume.

We stood there on her lawn, taking alternate sips from the drink and listening to her resident whippoorwill until the glass was empty and the sun had gone down completely.

"We'd better get going," she said. "Or we'll stay here and drink right through dinner."

We ate at a place Jessie liked. It was in one of those old buildings with high ceilings and screens on every side to catch the breeze from any direction, the way it was done before air conditioning. It sat on the edge of a small, shallow bayou in a lot that was grown up with pine trees and live oaks.

We ate the special, which was grilled amberjack. And we drank a wine that Jessie liked. The fish was firm and tasted of some kind of seasoning smoke. Hickory, I guessed.

"Good, huh?" Jessie said. "I used to think amberjack was just a trash fish, but you cook it on the grill and it's some kind of good."

I agreed.

"Hey, Morgan," she said, "you don't seem like you have the Saturday night feeling. You got troubles?"

"No," I said. "No troubles."

"Don't lie to me. You aren't all here."

"No," I said. "I don't suppose I am. Sorry."

"Don't be sorry. Can you tell me about it?"

I told her about the morning with the Coast Guard while we finished eating. She listened carefully and didn't say anything until I had finished.

"That's awful," she said. "That happened to me, I'd still be boiling."

I nodded. "I'm getting over it."

She looked at me. "Are you?"

"Sure. Dinner, a little wine."

"I don't believe you get over things that easy. Matter of fact, I *know* you don't."

"Maybe if I work at it."

"Not you. I'll bet you're working on some kind of plan to get even."

It always surprised me, the way she could do that. Cut right past my evasions and know what it was I was thinking. She was the kind of woman, if you planned to cheat on her, she'd know before you made your first move.

"What is it?"

"I thought I'd write a letter to the newspaper."

"Morgan," she said, "I might have been born at night, but it wasn't *last* night."

For some reason, I was enjoying this. We both were.

"Maybe I'll write my congressman, then."

"Give me just a little break."

I filled both our glasses. "Good wine," I said.

"If you're going to change the subject, you got to do better than that."

"I don't really know what I'm going to do," I said. "Probably nothing. That would be the smart thing."

"But way out of character."

"What would you suggest?"

"Forget about it. Like your friend said, what the Coast Guard did was legal. Wrong, maybe. Outrageous, maybe. But legal just the same. You start going around trying to get even for everything that happens like that, then you aren't going to have time for anything else."

"True."

"And you'll probably just bring more grief on yourself. *Especially* you, Morgan. You don't need to be taking chances with the law."

She was right. No question about it. And I said so.

"But you won't quit thinking about it, will you?"

"I'll try," I said, and I meant it.

"Morgan, don't get yourself in trouble. Okay?"

"Okay."

The fun had gone out of it now and we both knew it. She was right on both counts. I ought to forget about it and I probably wouldn't. I motioned to the waiter to bring us the check, and when I'd paid it I asked Jessie if she wanted to go listen to some music.

"That sounds fine," she said, in a tone that was just a little cool. I made up my mind that the Coast Guard had ruined enough of one Saturday, and that for the rest of the night I wasn't going to think about it. Jessie and I were going to have a good time.

CHAPTER 6

TUCK TUCKER PICKED THE FIVE-STRING with strong, nimble fingers so the notes came out clean and mournful. He had a fiddle player who was almost in his league, and together they were a close match for some of the great old groups like the Stanley Brothers or Flatt and Scruggs. They played "Fox on Run," and "Ginseng Sullivan," and "Paul and Silas." All the old mountain classics. The audience was small but devoted and applauded respectfully during the breaks.

"Thank you," Tucker would say, grinning in a bashful sort of way, like he didn't really deserve it. "We appreciate that. We surely do. Now here's an old number that Doc Watson and some others have played. We kindly think you'll like it."

Then the banjo notes would flow out over the room with the six-string, the fiddle, and the mandolin in close company.

"Cloudy in the east and it looks like rain
Looks like rain
Looks like rain.

Cloudy in the east and it looks like rain.
I'm on my long journey home.

It seemed to me that I'd always liked mountain music for some reason. When I was living out of a rucksack, I'd carried a tape of my favorites around with me from Nha Trang to Khe Sanh, the way some Civil War soldiers carried a battered Bible in their blanket rolls between Paducah and Vicksburg. For me, listening to that tape was as reliable as reading Ecclesiastes.

I hadn't been sure that it would be Jessie's kind of music, but she held my hand while the Black Water Ramblers sang. And after they'd done "In the Pines," one of my favorites, she smiled and said, "Morgan, those boys can *pick.*"

We left after two sets and drove down to the beach. We rode with the windows down and didn't say much. The night air was mild and clean and a moon hung wetly above the horizon, looking like it had struggled to rise out of the Gulf. I turned east and drove until the road ended.

We got out, took off our shoes, and walked. I carried a blanket. The sand felt cool and granular and it squeaked underfoot. There was just enough breeze off the Gulf to make the air moist and taste slightly of salt.

We walked across the dune and down onto the packed wet sand next to the surf. The waves didn't amount to much. Bulges of two or three feet that curled, then broke with a soft slap, scattering sparks of phosphorescence through the foam.

We went a mile or so. The moon had climbed a few degrees and seemed, in the process, to have dried out and lost the sheen of gold. It looked warm and silver now, like a bright bulb.

"Let's sit for a while," Jessie said.

I spread the blanket on the dry sand farther up the beach

and we sat on it, close together, and looked out to sea. There was nothing to see, precisely, except the blended black of the water and the sky, the scattered stars, and the moon.

"Sure is peaceful out here, Morgan," she said. "Reminds me of when I was a kid and liked to look for shooting stars."

"Yes," I said, "I come out here a lot."

"Well, how come you never brought me before?"

"Oh, I don't know," I said. "I suppose it seems a little . . ."

"A little what, Morgan? Sentimental? Quaint? Corny?"

"All those."

"Women aren't supposed to go for those things anymore?" she said, and leaned against me with her arm under mine. We were touching and the pressure of her breast, and the give of it, did something to my breathing.

I shrugged.

"I'm just old-fashioned, I guess," she said. "I like walking on the beach in the moonlight, especially."

"I'm glad," I replied.

"Could we neck, too?" she said. "Or is that just *too* old-fashioned?"

She laughed and her teeth were brilliantly white in the moonlight. I laughed a little with her and then we kissed for a while sitting up. Then some more, lying down on the blanket. After a while, she had unbuttoned my shirt and then it was off and the damp breeze off the Gulf felt good against my skin.

"We're like a couple of teenagers here, Morgan," she said, and before I could say anything back, she added, "And I love it."

I waded through the small breakers, out to where the water came up to my waist, then made a shallow dive. I kept my eyes open and could see the beads of phosphorescence popping in front of me. I stayed under until my lungs burned, then surfaced and tried to stand. I was over my head. I looked back at the beach and could barely make her out. An indistinct, almost spectral shape.

I swam back in until my feet touched, then waded through the surf and walked back to her. She was sitting on the blanket. Her dress was still unbuttoned and her hair was tangled and limp from the salt spray.

"How can you stand it?" she said.

"It feels great," I said. "Not that cold. Come on in."

"No, Morgan," she said. "I may be crazy, but I ain't *that* crazy. What are you going to use for a towel?"

"I thought I'd just drip dry," I said.

"Well, sit down here next to me," she said, "and get warm."

"What about your dress?"

"It's just a dress. I can wash it."

I sat next to her. The water and the wind made my skin tingle and my head felt light. I had no sense, at all, of time.

We stayed that way until she said, "You'll die from the cold, Morgan, if you don't get dressed soon."

So I put my clothes on and we walked back down the beach to the truck and drove to her house, where we showered together under hot water and I drank a glass of Spanish brandy in her bedroom while she dried her hair.

She was wearing a long cobalt-blue nightgown when she came to bed. The color went with her hair, which was combed out and soft. It smelled clean and friendly of some kind of scented shampoo. Apricots, maybe. She was also wearing a little of the jasmine perfume again.

"That was a real, old-fashioned Saturday-night date, Morgan," she said when she eased under the covers and put her head on my shoulder. "I didn't think people knew how to do it anymore."

CHAPTER 7

WHEN I LEFT HER HOUSE, JESSIE WAS
still sleeping. It was barely dawn, with the air still cool
and damp and smelling of pine resin. I drove back to my
house, changed into some shorts, and ran five miles on
the section-line blacktops that cut through the bean fields.
The crops looked green and healthy, and I made a note
of it.

When I'd showered and dressed and had my coffee, I
drove to the Outrigger, hoping to catch Garvey before he
left the dock. There was no sign of him, so I waited. After
an hour I gave it up and drove in to his shop, which was
in an old Quonset hut a mile or two back toward Pensacola.

Garvey's truck was parked out back. I walked in and
found him at the workbench, disassembling a regulator.
The shop was as orderly as a barracks on inspection day.
The tanks were racked neatly on one wall. Wet suits and
vests hung, by size, from a pole on the opposite wall. The
workbench was clean, with all the tools stowed except for
a couple of small screwdrivers Garvey was using.

"Morning," I said.

"How you doing?" Garvey answered. He put the screwdriver down, checked to make sure the parts were set aside in order, then turned to give me his complete attention.

"What brings you around?" He sounded a little suspicious.

"Thought I'd catch you at the Outrigger," I said, which wasn't really an answer. "Shouldn't you have a class on a Sunday morning?"

Saturday morning, too, for that matter, I thought. A big part of Garvey's living came from teaching people how to dive and getting them certified. As long as I'd known him, he'd had students out on the water every weekend.

"Times is tough," he said, and tried to smile like it wasn't worth worrying about. "You had coffee?"

"I could use some more."

He poured two cups. Handed me one and said, "You didn't say what brings you around. Pleasure of my company?"

Garvey seemed vaguely uncomfortable about having me there, as though he were expecting someone and didn't want me to know about the meeting.

"Are you busy—I mean, too busy to take a minute?"

"Don't I wish."

"I just can't get off that business with the Coast Guard yesterday."

"Tell me about it," Garvey said. But it didn't seem like something he wanted to talk about.

"That kind of stuff happen a lot?" I said. I didn't want this to seem like an interrogation, so I talked around the question I really wanted to ask.

"Oh yeah. You saw those guys, Morgan. All tricked out in their black utilities and flak jackets. Just like those Alcohol, Tobacco, and Firearms boys who raided that ranch in Texas. They like those high-profile raids." Garvey's mouth tightened. "They just like to play dress-up," he said. "They don't really expect anyone to put up a fight. One of these days, someone will surprise them, way those Bible beaters did the ATF."

I nodded.

"I could take one man from my old team and take care of every one of the Coasties on that crash boat. Without ever breaking a sweat."

I nodded again.

"But I've got other fish to fry."

Meaning, I thought, a wife and children.

"I wonder why," I said, casually, "out of all the boats in the bay, they picked us."

"Just lucky, I guess," Garvey said and smiled.

I took a sip from my coffee mug. Garvey brewed it strong, the Navy way.

"You can't think of any reason they might have settled on your boat?"

"Hey, Morgan, are you asking me if I ever ran any drugs?"

I shook my head. "I know you better than that. What I was wondering is, did you ever give anyone reason to call the Coast Guard up and *say* you were running drugs? There is a distinction."

Garvey shook his head. "I understand."

"So . . . ?"

"You want to know if I gave somebody the red ass bad enough to sic the Coast Guard on me, right?"

It seemed like he would have been as interested in the possibility as I was. Not irritated at me for bringing it up.

"Just wondering," I said.

"Not worth the strain, Morgan. Ask around; the Coast Guard boards people for no reason all the time. It was just my lucky day."

"I suppose," I said, and finished my coffee.

"Anyway, it was my boat. If I can forget about it, then you should, too."

"You're right," I said. "Absolutely."

I took my cup to the sink and rinsed it. Then I started back out for my truck.

"You got a new class starting up soon?" I said.

"I sure hope so," Garvey said. "See you around, Morgan."

"Yeah," I said. "See you."

I got in my truck and drove back home, not especially satisfied with Garvey's answers.

For some reason, Sunday afternoon has always been tough on me. Probably because it seems so goddamned aimless. Nothing more than a space to fill between the weekend and work. Sunday afternoons are like New Year's Eve. I can't remember a good one.

The worst of them were in prison, naturally. With all the sad-faced visitors getting in their old, shabby cars with the busted mufflers, dented fenders, and cracked glass and heading up the road to another week of waiting for the wasted father or the rotten son to finish doing his time. A week of welfare or dead-end work with this feeling always nagging you that you might somehow be to blame for having close kin in prison.

And the convicts themselves, at supper and then lock-down, with the look that told you how they were feeling. No matter how bad the life those visitors were driving back to, even if it was pure welfare and roaches, at least it was better than this. And with the way time dragged on a Sunday evening, it seemed like it would go on forever, until the sun just burned down to a cinder. Time never moved any slower than it did on those Sunday afternoons.

Well, a Sunday afternoon at the river house was a lot better than that. But I needed something to do.

So I changed into a pair of old Carharts and a cheap sweatshirt, and went to work on the rotting floor in the small corner room downstairs.

I started slowly, testing boards with an ice pick. The wood gave like wet cardboard. I used a chisel to knock a section loose so I could look at it; the wood was so soft I could crumble it with my fingers. The fibers had been broken down entirely by the water. The wood felt like mud in my hand.

It wasn't much anyway. Untreated pine, with no heart. Probably this room had been built when the old sea captain was low on funds. He'd gone with cheap materials, which, judging by the rest of the house, wasn't like him. I was glad to be rid of the floor. In my mind, I'd pretty much settled on cherry to replace the ruined pine. I was eager to see what the new floor, with the rich red wood, all sanded down and oiled up, would look like.

So I put away the ice pick and went for a real tool, a three-foot-long crowbar that weighed about five pounds and splintered those floorboards into five- and six-foot lengths when I applied a little muscle. It was mindless, destructive work, which made it perfect for a Sunday afternoon, and in fifteen minutes I was sweating, swearing, and happy.

It took a couple of hours to tear up the floorboards and pull the old rusted nails out of the joists. And most of another hour to haul the scraps of rotten wood outside and pile them for burning. A few more minutes to take

some measurements and figure out just how much plywood I'd need for the subfloor, and then how much of the
cherry I would need on top of that. I wrote all that information out on the back of an envelope that had come with
a remarkable one-time-only offer on a credit card for responsible citizens like me.

There was plenty of daylight left when I finished what
I could do to the room, so I stripped and showered again
under the cold-water faucet out back. Dried off and put
on a clean pair of jeans and a faded old jungle fatigue shirt.
I stuck a small box of gaudily painted, cork-bodied popping bugs in one of the shirt's many pockets, and put four
cans of beer and a couple of trays of ice cubes in a small
cooler. Then I took down the fly rod I keep on a couple of
pegs on the back-porch wall and started down the trail
that led into the woods behind the river house.

It was a quick walk to the little slough where I keep a
canoe and where I sometimes see the nine-foot alligator I
call Charlemagne. Now and then, when I'm sitting on the
porch, I'll hear him barking down in the water. A big,
territorial sound, which is how I came up with the name.
The gator is the emperor of the swamp—an empire that
is on an inevitable, irreversible decline.

I like having Charlemagne around. He helps me believe
that we're still holding on to God's plan, if only by our
fingernails, in this part of Florida. Down in the south part
of the state, where they can't pour the concrete fast
enough, gators have made a kind of nuisance comeback.
They have a reputation—which the newspapers love—for
scaring golfers and eating poodles.

I looked around the slough for some sign of Charlemagne, his snout riding an inch or two above the surface
or a smooth wake left by the sweep of his big tail. But he
wasn't here on this Sunday afternoon.

I rolled the canoe down from the two lengths of cypress I use to keep it up off the ground and loaded the rod and cooler. Then I slid the canoe across the wet ground and through the lily pads, climbed in the backseat, and pushed off with the paddle. I made a few shallow strokes and eased down the slough twenty or thirty yards to where it opened into a little branch of the main river.

The water in the branch was stained the color of dark tea. Cypress trees grow in the shallow water along the bank like columns, tall enough to keep the branch in a kind of perpetual gloom.

I opened a beer and then let the negligible current carry me downstream, so slowly that I could steer by simply dragging the paddle. The river was a blend of sights, sounds, and smells and I let them carry me along, like the current, while I sipped my beer. It beat, by miles and miles, watching some ball game on TV.

I pulled the canoe up against the shallow, outside bank, grabbed a branch on a small shrub, and sat down on it. When I had finished my beer, I took the fly box from my pocket and selected a dark-green popper with rubber legs and match-head eyes. For some reason it looked just right for this water.

The bug was lying a foot or so from a cypress knee and still quivering from the force of my cast when a bluegill took it. The bug vanished in a decisive little swirl of water.

I set the hook and the plump, game little fish bored down for the river bottom, swimming in furious circles. I could feel the pressure, the desperation, flowing down the rod and into my arm.

It took just a minute or so to land the fish, a bluegill with dark blue flanks, bug eyes, and a red breast brighter than a robin's. I put him on a stringer and made another cast.

In half an hour I had eight, all like him, and that felt like enough. The sun was low and the air had turned suddenly cool. Downstream, a roosted dove made a few mournful calls, then waited for an answer, tried it again, and gave up. The evening colors seemed to seep in through the gaps in the trees, turning the air over the river a soft, washed-out purple. A gator barked, somewhere, and I wondered if it was Charlemagne. An owl hooted. I could stay here like this, I thought, for a long time. If not forever, then at least as long as the beer held out.

But the signal came, the way it always does, this time in the form of an especially persistent mosquito that would not leave my left ear alone. It was time, as the coon hunters say, to piss on the fire and call the dogs.

I hated to leave, but I had eight good bluegill and it had been a good afternoon. I'd saved a Sunday.

I got back to the house just after dark and called Jessie. She wasn't home.

I cleaned up. Ate some chili. Sat on the porch, enjoying the air and putting off bed just like a kid. I was just about to give in when I saw a pair of headlights easing up my drive. I felt, for a moment, like stepping inside so I would have at least a wall between me and whoever was coming to my house. Also, I'd be closer to my gun cabinet.

Jumpy, maybe. Even a little hysterical. But these days everybody is. Even those of us who live out in the safe, quiet country.

I was still thinking about going inside when I realized the headlights belonged to Phil Garvey's truck.

CHAPTER 8

"HELLO, MORGAN," HE SAID WHEN I walked out to the truck to meet him. "Didn't wake you up, did I?"

"No," I said. "Even I don't go to bed this early."

"How you coming on the house?" he said aimlessly. He'd been out before, once or twice, and I'd showed him around.

"Coming along," I said. "I'm in no hurry. Come on in. I'll pour you a beer."

Something about him was different—not quite right, somehow—and I thought, at first, that he might be drunk. I'd never seen him drunk. Never seen him drink more than four or five beers, and then he hadn't showed anything. But there was something different about him tonight. A kind of hesitancy, as though he had to concentrate to steady himself.

"No beer," he said. "You got coffee?"

"I can make some," I said.

"No trouble?"

"I don't exactly have my hands full here tonight," I said, and led the way into the house. He followed, very deliberately.

When we were in the kitchen, I said, "Have a seat. Coffee will take a minute."

He sat at the kitchen table and I looked at him in the light. He didn't look drunk. So maybe, I thought, it was trouble at home. His wife had thrown him out and he'd come here looking for a place to flop. I hoped not.

"Long day?" I said.

"Yeah. A very long day." He was sitting on half the chair, his back perfectly erect, his chin parallel to the floor. Perfect military bearing.

The coffee finished perking. I poured two mugs and said, "Black?"

"Right."

I put the mug in front of him and said, "It's a nice night; we might as well drink this on the porch."

He followed me back out to the porch, where we sat on the top step, looking out at the black space that was the river. I heard him take a sip of his coffee and sigh.

"Morgan, I've got a problem," he said, forcing the words. "More than one, actually. Lots of problems. I need some . . . some *advice*."

"I'll do what I can," I said. This was a new one.

"I know you've been . . . well, in trouble."

I stopped him before he could go on. "I killed a man, Phil. He was married to my sister and beating the living hell out of her. She came to live with me, to hide out. He came after her and was beating her up in my house one afternoon when I walked in. I believe he was dead before I stopped pounding on him. I was convicted of second-degree murder and would have done a pile of time if I hadn't had help. So, yeah, I've been in trouble. Got out of it, too, with a little help. I imagine you can, too."

"It's not that kind of trouble," Garvey said.

"I'd call that good news, then."

He took another sip of his coffee. This was hard for him.

"When you had your trouble," he said, speaking with a kind of formality, as though he weren't quite sure of the language, "there was a lawyer who helped you, right?"

"Nathaniel P. Semmes," I said, "without whom I would still be stacking time at Holman Penitentiary. They broke the mold."

"I might need a lawyer."

"Well," I said. "I could call Semmes and he'd probably see you. In the morning."

"I don't know."

He hated this situation. I could hear it in his voice, which had an extra measure of control in it. That restraint kept him from shouting. From raving. He didn't like telling his troubles and he didn't like asking for help and, above all, he didn't like being put in a position of having to do either of them.

"What you were asking this morning, you know."

"Yes," I said.

"You had it right."

"About somebody calling the Coast Guard?"

"Yeah," he said, wearily. "That." He sipped his coffee and then he told me about it.

It had been a bad week. A real bitch. Starting with last Saturday, when he'd gone out with a group of students. He was taking them down for their first dive, in a shallow part of the bay, near an old crumbling fuel dock where they might see a few interesting fish.

"There were some jellyfish in the water, Morgan," he

said, almost plaintively. "Not that many and, what the hell, all those students were wearing full wet suits. They were a little worried, though, at first. And I figured I had to do something to get them to relax. So I reached over into the water and picked up the smallest jellyfish I could find. And I ate it."

"That would have reassured me," I said, "for sure."

"It's an old SEAL trick. I saw it first at Little Creek. An old chief saw a couple of us new guys rubbing ourselves where we'd been stung and he says, 'Jellyfish?'

"We said, 'Yeah, Chief,' and he says, 'Shit, why didn't you tell me. I *love* jellyfish.' Then he reached down and grabbed one out of the water and scarfed it right down. Then he smiled real big and said, 'Tastes just like a jalapeño pepper.' "

I nodded. It was a new one, but I'd seen others out of the same book. Knew a guy once who ate live grasshoppers.

"So what happened after you put on that show?" I said.

"They came around," he said. "All but one of them."

"And what about him?"

"He was a prick," Garvey said. "A twenty-five-karat prick."

"Didn't see the thrill of diving with the jellyfish?" I said.

"He told me he wasn't going in the water and he wasn't going to wait around on the boat while I took the other people in the water. He wanted me to take him back to the dock. Right now."

"What did you do?"

"I told him he'd have to just wait until I got finished taking the other people down for their dive. Told him I'd give him a full refund. He wasn't hearing it. He stormed around making noise about how he was going to sue. He was a lawyer, naturally."

"Naturally," I said.

"Well, I finally just outlasted him. He could see that I wasn't going to take him in and it was for sure he wasn't going to kick my ass, so he just went below and sulked. The rest of us suited up and made our dive. I had five happy customers and one pissed-off sonofabitch. I figured I could live with that.

"Well, when we got back to the dock, he started in on me again. He got right up in my face, in a way I just don't let anyone do, and started yelling about how he was going to ruin me, take my boat and everything else, leave me without a pot to piss in. I tried to let it ride, you know. I didn't back away but I didn't try to yell with him or sling spit with him. I just kept saying, 'You'll get a full refund. Please get off my boat. I'll send you a full refund.'

"But he kept at it. Finally, I'd just had enough. You know how it is. I'd just had enough. He called me one name too many and that was it. The little shit didn't know anything about real contact. He was a mouth fighter. He turned white when I grabbed him. Looked like he was going to piss in his pants. I felt like I just didn't have to take any more of that shit. You know what I mean. It was dumb. But I'd just had enough. Of him . . . and a lot of other things."

"What did you do with him?"

"I slapped him a few times and then I threw him in the water. That wasn't so bad. But then, I got out of the boat and stood on the beach, where he was going to come ashore, and just waited for him. He was just paddling around out there, afraid to come out. And meanwhile the jellyfish were stinging him. It didn't last that long. Maybe ten minutes. Then I let him come ashore."

I was sorry I'd missed it. But didn't say so.

"He went straight to the cops. They arrested me for

assault. Cost me a couple of hundred with a bailbondsman to get out of jail. And my other customers were so bent out of shape they canceled. That's why I didn't have any classes this weekend."

"You had a hearing yet?"

"No."

"No trial date, then?"

"No."

"So he could still drop the charges."

"Not this guy. More likely he'll sue me."

"He hasn't done that yet?"

"No."

I thought for a moment. This wasn't Nat Semmes's usual territory. Misdemeanor assault. But he might try to help Garvey as a favor to me. I was deeply and permanently in Semmes's debt, but he would still feel like he owed me a favor if I came to him, asking for one. He's made that way.

"I'll talk to Semmes," I said. "In the morning. What's the name of the fellow gave you such a hard time?"

"Loftin," Garvey said. "Frank Loftin." He spoke the words as though he were talking through a mouthful of rancid meat.

"Okay. It doesn't sound fatal to me, if you know what I mean. But I know how it works on your mind."

"There's more," he said, still keeping the stern set to his face and delivering his words with careful, soldierly precision.

I looked at him. "Not your week, is it?"

"Hasn't been. Not since I got out of the Navy. I don't make a very good civilian, Morgan. Don't seem to be cut out for it."

I waited for him to go on. No point in my telling him he was a great civilian.

"Man, I don't know," Garvey said. "I just don't *know*."

It wasn't an answer to any question of mine, since I hadn't asked him anything. More an expression, I suppose, of generalized bewilderment.

"How bad is it?" I asked.

"What do you mean?"

"Are you in real deep," I said, "or just up to your knees?"

"More like my chin, I'd say. And hoping nobody makes waves."

I nodded and said, "Tell me about it."

CHAPTER 9

I WENT INSIDE AND GOT THE COFFEEPOT, brought it out, and refilled his cup. I wasn't worried about ruining his sleep. He was agitated beyond anything caffeine could do, and without knowing him all that well, I was worried about a lot more than how Phil Garvey was sleeping. I read him as the kind of man, accustomed to being in iron control, who could just fall apart—even kill himself—if enough things went wrong and he felt, all of a sudden, like he just couldn't get back on top. He was a total commitment man, a graduate of the all-or-nothing school.

At least he was willing to talk. So I listened, trying to find out how bad it was and if there was any way I could help.

"I didn't have anything when I got out of the Navy," he said. "But they were cutting back and I was—what's the word?"

"*Expendable,*" I said.

"Right," he said. "So I got out and I married Rachel."

He'd met her at the hospital. She was a Navy nurse and they wanted to raise a family. So she got out of the Navy, too. Now she worked in the emergency room at one of the local hospitals and he had his dive business. They had two kids. Garvey was fiercely proud of them. In his mind, "family man" was not a job description; it was a mission.

"We didn't have any money to speak of. I wrapped my fingers around every dime that wasn't nailed down and then . . . then, I went to the bank."

He made it sound like he had gone to a pusher.

"Which one?"

"Sunshine States."

"Uh-oh."

"You got that right."

"What happened to your loan," I asked, "after Sunshine State went west?" It had been, if not the most expensive bank failure in Florida, then certainly the most spectacular. The man who had made Sunshine into one of the most aggressive, high-flying banks in the country, one Vernon Culp, turned out to have been not much more than a common thief and con man who rode from job to job in a leased Grumman instead of a stolen Buick. He knew all kinds of politicians, state and federal, and had given almost all of them money. Not them, precisely, but their campaign committees. This was a legal distinction that the pols piously insisted on after Culp went down in flames.

Of course, it wasn't only the people who were addicted to votes who had been taken in. Culp was good with the press, too. His lean, smiling, surgically modified face had been on the cover of several magazines, one of which had said he was bringing "Solar Power" to the old-fashioned, steam-driven world of banking. All the stories on Culp dwelled breathlessly on his fine fourteen-room home in the horse country between Orlando and Gainesville, his art collection, his hundred-foot boat, his ski condo in Aspen, where he mingled with movie actors, his Ferrari, and his second wife, who was blond and thin but able to carry her own weight in jewelry on her back.

This was no dour, green-eyeshade banker with an extra chromosome for caution, the stories all said. He was a new kind of banker for the new age in which money, like information, moved at the speed of light. All of which, of course, was bullshit. Culp was just a crook.

The bank had been seized. That had been hard—he had a battalion of lawyers to conduct a fighting retreat against the government. And in the early stages, he also had all those politicians, bought and paid for, who dutifully called the examiners into hearings to publicly scold and humiliate them. Why, our public servants wanted to know, were these little men picking on Vernon Culp, who had, almost single-handedly, brought so much to the state of Florida in particular and the country—even the world—in general?

After the seizure was complete and the books were open, these pols said that they hadn't really been carrying Culp's water. Just providing a little constituent service, which was their job, after all.

It was much harder for the bank to pry the art works, the boat, the horses, and the airplane from the death grip of Culp and his lawyers. They were still fighting it out in the courts.

Culp kept the house under Florida's generous homestead protection laws, which had, for fifty years, made the state a magnet for high-rolling flimflam men. When somebody got indicted on Wall Street, the first thing he did, under the instructions of his lawyers, was buy the biggest house he could find in Florida.

The last of Culp's trophies—the wife—was also beyond the reach of the prosecutors and examiners, but in addition to her ability to hump heavy diamonds, she also could sense a change in the wind. Word was she'd left Culp and gone to live in the Aspen condo, where she no doubt felt sure she could find another just like him. Maybe from California this time.

Meanwhile, what was left of Sunshine was bought by another bank. Its management was as stingy as Culp had been profligate.

For the last six months the new team had been selling assets—everything from art to adding machines—and calling loans. I suspected that Garvey had gotten one of those calls.

"I never missed a payment," Garvey said. "Never came in late."

"But there was a problem?" I said, knowing what it was. You heard the story—and variations on it—all the time.

"Bet your ass there was a problem. With the equity."

"Not sufficient to cover the size of the loan, right?"

"You got it."

"Have you renegotiated?"

Garvey looked at me and then back out at the river. Something large splashed out there. A gator, maybe, taking a small animal.

"Morgan, I don't know my ass from second base about this shit. How it seemed to me was . . . I borrowed some money and I told the people I borrowed it from that I'd pay it back a little at a time. Then, the people I borrowed the money from get their asses in a crack. Not my fault, the way I see it. I've been paying them back, a little at a time, just the way I said I would. But they go down and somebody I don't know comes along and takes over from them. This new team says I owe them the money I've been paying the other boys. So I keep writing the checks, only now I make them out to different people.

"Then, after a while, the new people want to talk to me. I go in and we shake hands all around, sit down at a table, and they tell me that things have changed."

"They want more money."

"How did you guess?"

"More than you can afford?"

"I couldn't afford what I was paying them before. Since I started this business, everything has gone up except the number of customers coming through the door. Something about a recession, I'm told. Nobody has any money for anything, much less for learning how to dive from a hard-ass old Navy guy who doesn't know how to be nice to his customers. But insurance has gone up. Dock space for *Second Shot* went up. Gas went up. Electricity went up.

"Everything goes up, Morgan. Everything. Now what I used to pay the bank goes up, too, and I can't keep up with it. But the bank says I have to pay them a little more every month or they want the whole thing, which is like asking an oyster to dance."

He hadn't renegotiated. It was still early in the game and he was just scared of the bankers. He didn't know that the last thing they needed was a dive business and a Bertram boat. The federal drug people couldn't get rid of all the boats they had seized. Garvey had his problems, but he had some room to maneuver.

"I keep remembering when I was a third-class petty officer," he said dreamily. "Made about three hundred a month with hazardous duty pay and I *never* worried about money. If I wanted to go out for a beer, I went out for a beer. Some of the boys wanted to hit Virginia Beach, I went along and bought a round when it was my turn. No sweat.

"Now I don't buy anything unless it's for business. I don't buy toys for my kids or flowers for my wife. I don't have money for anything and money is all I think about."

"You're still building the business," I said, trying to sound reassuring. "These are hard times everywhere. They'll get better."

"I guess so," he said. "They can't get much worse."

They could, of course, but I didn't say so. Instead I said something about no matter how bad it seemed, it was just money. He had his family. And they were all healthy.

"No," he said. "Not quite. That's the real crusher. I've got a kid who is having dizzy spells and headaches and then, the other day, he passed out. They're running tests."

"Any idea what it might be?"

"No," he said, "not yet." For the first time, I realized that what he was feeling wasn't merely self-pity but real fear that his life was running out of control, that he was genuinely helpless.

And, also for the first time, I honestly wanted to help.

"I don't know anything about doctors," I said. "But I know Nat Semmes. And I'll talk to him first thing in the morning."

"I'd appreciate it, Morgan," Garvey said. "I really would. I wouldn't ask except . . ."

"I know," I said. And I did. Perfectly.

CHAPTER 10

Nat Semmes's office was on the top floor of an old ten-story building made of rough quarried stone that had gone gray with age. The building had once been headquarters of the local bank and the most distinguished structure in town. Now the banks were all run out of some other town—or by the civil servants in Washington who had taken them over—and this building was about half empty. Those tenants who remained were mostly lawyers, like Semmes, who stayed in order to be close to the courthouse.

"Come in," he shouted, after I knocked on his private door.

He was sitting behind a vast old partner's desk, with his back to the window. You could see the bay through that window, and beyond it the barrier island, and then miles and miles of the Gulf, until it finally merged with the sky.

Semmes stood up and smiled. He is tall and lean. Not thin from dieting or frailty but from a combination of hunger and anger that burns off any surplus flesh. His face is long and angular, with ridges of hard bone, especially around the deeply set eyes that are dark and unrevealing most of the time but can turn in an instant. Either to anger or the other thing completely. Semmes is a great hater but he also likes to laugh. Strangers and enemies see one thing in those eyes. Friends see something else.

What I saw was genuine delight.

"Morgan Hunt, as I live and breathe." He stood up and came around the desk with his hand out. We shook and he cupped my right shoulder with his left hand.

"Hope I'm not interrupting something important," I said.

He smiled and shook his head. "No; not at all. I'm just doing a little reading before the workweek starts." He nodded in the direction of the desk, where a copy of *The Divine Comedy* lay facedown and open.

"Nothing like a little Dante before breakfast."

As long as I've known him, Semmes has been coming into his office early to read the old stuff. I think he considers it part of his duty as a civilized man. And, also, I think he enjoys it. The stillness of his office in the early morning and the ancient cadences . . . I suspect that's his idea of peace.

"I could come back in a couple of hours," I said.

"Oh, bullshit. Dante will keep. He has for a few hundred years now. I can read him any morning. How about some coffee?"

"Sounds good."

He walked across the room to a small table that held a stainless percolator and a couple of mugs.

While he filled the mugs, I looked around the room. It was not particularly lavish for a lawyer of Semmes's reputation. Mostly bookshelves. Then the wall with the window and the view of the bay. And a wall that was covered with framed photographs of his family. He was intensely proud of his two kids and devoted, as far as I could tell, to his wife. They had been married a long time and when he talked about her, there was always a note of respect in his voice.

What you didn't see hanging on Semmes's wall were any trophies, and he had plenty of them. There were cover stories in magazines, long newspaper articles, awards from various professional associations that he could have had framed and mounted to impress people and remind himself. But he didn't operate that way.

He handed me a mug of coffee and said, "Sit down. Tell me what brings you around. You looking for work?"

"Always," I said. When Semmes got me a pardon from the governor of Alabama, one of the conditions of the deal was that I do honest, civilian work. I'd been nothing much but a soldier. So Semmes promised the governor that he would see to it that I got my private investigator's license, in Florida, and he would also give me some employment. Turned out, I liked the work—or, as I thought of it, the action.

"I wish I had something that required your talents," he said. "I'll call when something comes up."

"I know," I said. "Actually, I wanted to talk to you about someone. Friend of mine."

"In trouble?"

"Yes."

"Serious?"

"No. I mean, he's not looking at a murder charge or anything like that. But he needs help. It's not in your league, though."

"What league is that?" Semmes smiled.

The big league, I thought, but didn't say it. He hated flattery.

"You know what I mean," I said.

"Tell me about it."

So I told him about Garvey and his troubles. Semmes listened, his face blank and detached, giving nothing away. It seldom does, and this fools people—especially other lawyers—and causes them to underestimate him.

"You're right," he said when I'd finished. "That is pretty small stuff. It's a shame you can't just beat on a man like Loftin when he behaves that way. Be good for him. But you can't. It's the law. The law is an ass, as we all know, but that doesn't change anything."

"He was pretty well provoked," I said.

"I understand," Semmes said, leaning back in his chair and putting his feet up on his desk. "It's the way we live now. Civility has been dead so long we don't even remember what it looked like."

"He's a good man," I said, "and he's having a tough time."

"Tell me about him."

I told him what I knew about Garvey. The sick child. The problems with the bank. And how his boat had been boarded and searched. Semmes had finished his coffee and put the mug on his desk. He rested his elbows on the smooth, polished mahogany and propped his chin on his fist. His eyes narrowed as he listened.

"Your friend has been visited by the plagues, Morgan. For certain. Doctors. Lawyers. Bankers. And the government. The man is a modern-day Job."

"He got shot in Panama, too."

"Umm-humm. But he was doing his job there. He volunteered for that. The rest of his woes were just handed to him."

"That's right."

Semmes's eyes were not much more than slits now, and there was a knot in his jaw. The knot seemed to quiver like stressed wire.

"No idea why they stopped his boat and searched it?"

"Nope."

Semmes shook his head in disgust. "Part of the 'War on Drugs,' like your man said. Government likes those high-concept wars, you know. War on Poverty. War on Drugs. Of course, we've got more poor people and more drugs than ever before. Maybe there's a lesson in that. Surest way to get more of something is to have the government declare war on it."

I smiled and nodded.

"Any reason for suspicion? Anything remotely like probable cause?"

"None," I said. "And he didn't fit any kind of profile. Strictly a local boat, cruising local waters. I suspect somebody informed on him."

Semmes studied my face for a moment, then smiled like a man who has just caught on to the joke.

"I see."

"I don't believe in coincidence, Nat. Seems like you taught me that."

"Right. I was so eaten up with righteous indignation there that I missed it. So you think that Brother Loftin might have called the dogs down on Garvey."

"It happened the same week," I said. "And Garvey doesn't fit any of the logical drug-smuggler profiles. So I'd say that there just about had to be an informer. Someone who wanted to cause Garvey a little grief."

"And you'd like to poke around a little and find out if Loftin is the informer?"

"Yes."

"Because," he said, slowly, enjoying the sound of each

word, "if you can prove that Loftin was the informer, then you can turn it around against him?"

"I figure there must be laws," I said. "Maliciously informing, or some such. If nothing else, you could maybe take his ass into civil court for slander and libel. And if *that* didn't work, you could at least let it be known all around that Loftin is the kind of slug who would call up the law and lie about an innocent man just to satisfy a grudge. Shame the sonofabitch."

Semmes smiled. "Morgan, you can't *shame* anyone these days. Don't you watch television?"

"No." There was never a moment in prison when a television wasn't on, somewhere close enough that you could hear the soundtrack and your eyes would register the flickering blue light. It became part of the mix of sensations that you couldn't escape. There was the noise. The smell. And the television.

"Well, check out the afternoon talk shows sometime. They've got folks confessing to things that people didn't even *talk* about a few years ago. Any day now I expect to see somebody talking about how he's a cannibal and proud. You can't shame Loftin just by proving he's a fink."

"Well," I said, somewhat defensively, "he *is* a lawyer."

"You especially can't shame a lawyer," Semmes said happily. "Haven't you heard the one about the research laboratory that switched from white rats to lawyers? Because there were more lawyers than rats; none of the scientists ever got attached to a lawyer; and there are some things a white rat won't do."

"I'll give you that one," I said.

"Nothing cheers me up like a good lawyer joke. Some bar association types want to make them a kind of hate speech. Put people who tell them in jail. *That* will certainly make people more fond of lawyers, don't you think?"

"I don't know," I said. "Myself, I couldn't be any fonder of them."

Semmes smiled. "You lie badly. However, I do like the idea of a civil suit. That's got real possibilities. You know how afraid a doctor is about going into surgery. That's because he *knows* all of the stories about the foul-ups. Same with a lawyer who gets sued. But first you have to prove that Loftin was the informer. Which means that you have to establish that the Coast Guard boarded Garvey's boat on the basis of information they got from an informer. That might be tough."

"I know," I said. "But it would be impossible if I weren't working for someone. On a case."

"Oh . . . right," Semmes said. "Because if you were just snooping around on your own, trying to dig up dirt on Loftin, then he could come after *you*."

"What there is of me."

"And that is plenty," Semmes said. "I know about those bean contracts."

I shrugged.

"So, you're correct. You *do* need to be working for somebody. You knew that when you came in here. And you knew how to get me to take what is really nothing but a low-grade assault and battery case. Bring in the government violating people's basic rights and then add one of those sleazy little fast-breeding lawyers . . . how could I resist?"

I shrugged, again.

"You remember Big Jim Folsom? Governor of Alabama a couple of times, must have run for the job and lost another three or four times?"

"Sure," I said.

"Well, he was in a tight race once. Things got dirty, the way they always do. One of the boys who was running against Jim sent a couple of operators out to get something on him. They hired a blond woman with a big chest and they got her into the same room with Jim. There was a bottle, too. Or maybe more than one bottle, since Jim was a man with big appetites."

Semmes paused in the story and smiled at the thought.

"Well, Jim didn't let anyone down, and pretty soon there were rumors all around the state. Supposedly there were photographs showing him sporting with a woman other than his wife. Jim's opposition figured this would ruin him with the Baptists, who still considered lipstick sinful in those days.

"So Jim had a press conference coming up and he told one of his reporter buddies to ask him about those rumors. When he took the question, Jim sucked in some air and stood up a little taller. He just looked like a giant. And everyone figured he was going to roundly deny ever *looking* at a woman other than his lovely, loyal wife or even *thinking* about whiskey, which everyone knew was Satan's own poison that he brewed up himself, in a special corner of hell.

"But old Jim was smarter than that. A *lot* damned smarter. What he said was, 'Well, boys, you know my opponents, who are in the hands of the big bankers and the mill owners and the other fat cats in this state, are so afraid of old Jim and what he'll do for the working people and the little people that they'll do *anything* to ruin him. Why they'll even go out and try to lure Jim into temptation using the rustle of unholy skirts and the power of strong spirits.

"Now, boys, I want to tell you something, when you go out trolling for Big Jim, and you're using that kind of bait . . . then, *hail*, you're going to catch Big Jim every single time.'"

Semmes laughed and so did I. He liked those old country stories and missed that world.

"So you got me, Morgan," he said. "You were trolling with the right bait. Tell your buddy to call me and make an appointment. He can come in here and talk and sign some papers so it will be on record that I represent him. Meanwhile, you go out and see what you can do with the Coast Guard. It isn't going to be easy."

"No."

"But you can do it. You just have to recall one thing."

"What's that?"

"You got to use the right bait."

CHAPTER 11

It was still early when I left
Semmes's office and rode down ten floors in the old, creak-
ing elevator with its ornately molded red-oak paneling.
There was no one in the lobby, which smelled stale and
dusty. No one on the street, either.

The little downtown park across the street looked green
and fresh, with blooming azaleas and tender young green
leaves opening on the branches of the old live oaks. There
was a statue in the center of the park; the weathered granite
image of a man with a sword. A Confederate hero from
these parts who had survived the battles up in Virginia
and come home to make a fortune in timber, raise a large
family, and hold office after his pardon came in. The lines
of scripture ran through my head:

Let us now praise famous men,
And our fathers in their generations . . .

Three or four men in filthy rags were sleeping on the benches around the statue, their belongings, such as they were, stuffed into paper sacks and cardboard boxes that they kept close to them, as though for protection.

There was a public phone at one corner of the park, and this was one of those rare days when it had not been gutted for a few dimes and quarters. I got a dial tone and called Garvey's shop. He went to work early, too.

"I just talked to my lawyer friend," I said when he answered. "He wants to meet with you," I said.

"Listen, Morgan," Garvey said, "I got to thinking last night. Nathaniel Semmes . . . I may not know the legal scene around here, but I know about him. This stuff of mine is way out of his league. Just chicken shit to a man like him, you know."

"My advice to you on that is, let him be the one to decide."

"I probably couldn't afford an hour of his time."

"Neither could I when I needed him. And I needed him a lot more than you do. Just go see him."

"When should I go?"

"Sooner the better, I'd guess. Call him and make an appointment. Maybe you could do it today."

"No. I got to go to the hospital. Rachel is taking Rick in again. More tests."

"Listen, Phil," I said, "call Semmes anyway. Make an appointment and go see him. At least get that thing cleared up and off your mind."

It was one of a few half-assed rules I tried to live by— if you can't do something about the big problem, then take care of a little problem. You'll have that much more practice at taking care of problems.

"I'll call him," Garvey said.

"Good man."

After I hung up, I drove out of town to the Outrigger. Things were fairly quiet when I got there. Anyone who'd taken the day off to go fishing had left the dock hours ago. The place still smelled of oyster shells and diesel fuel.

I walked around to a large building with a tin roof where a man was working on an outboard. He had the cowling and the cylinder head off, and was looking down at the pistons and frowning. He had on grease-stained khakis, rubber sandals, and no shirt.

"Help you?" he said, like any mechanic who didn't appreciate being bothered.

"When you've got a minute," I said.

He picked up a greasy rag and wiped his hands. "Any excuse for a break," he said. "You got an engine needs looked at?"

"No," I said. "I'm trying to help a friend of mine who keeps a boat here."

"Who's that?"

"Phil Garvey."

The man smiled in a way that looked mournful under his mustache.

"Good sumbitch," he said. He had to force the words around a cheekful of tobacco.

"Yes," I said. "He's that."

"One of the few who actually knows something about boats."

"Yes."

The man turned his head and spat, then looked back at me. "Garvey got a problem?"

"I'm not sure."

The man gave me a skeptical look.

"Coast Guard boarded him a couple days ago," I said.

The man spat again, this time with disgust.

"Them no-account bastards."

"The Coast Guard?"

"Yes, shit, the fucking Coast Guard. Bunch of low-rent dictators in swabby clothes. Wouldn't piss on 'em if they was on fire."

"They do a lot of that? The boarding, I mean."

"Oh shit, yeah. It's how them dumbasses get their cookies. Playing cops and robbers. It's easier than seamanship; you can teach a kid from Detroit how to tear up somebody's boat. Comes easier to him than navigation."

"They ever find anything?"

"You mean drugs?"

I nodded.

He shrugged. "Shit, I reckon they probably do. But you know how it is. If you throw enough shit up against a wall, some of it, after a while, is going to stick. They board a whole bunch of boats, saying they are inspecting fire extinguishers, and then they go looking down in the hold and cutting into voids . . . well sooner or later they'll find some kind of illegal vegetable matter.

"Now," he said, his mouth barely moving under the mustache and his eyes looking hot as banked coals, "I want to ask you this—does it make you sleep a lot better at night knowing they're out there doing that?"

I smiled and said no.

"Way I see it, sending the Coast Guard out to board boats is just one more way the government has of fucking with people. My partner and I are trying to run a business here. Give people something they need in the way of dock space. Sell 'em some ice and beer. Little diesel fuel. Fix their engines when they burn out a bearing or blow a gasket. We don't force nobody to come here and trade with us and in five years we ain't had any real complaints. But the goddamned government treats us like we got a revolution planned, at least. OSHA, EPA, Army Corps of Engineers, EEOC, DEA, Coast Guard . . . they've all been around making life hard for us. I keep expecting somebody from the Bureau of Weights and Measures to show up and check to make sure we haven't been selling short ounces.

"And all of 'em—every last one—comes in here like they know we're guilty of something and that it's just a matter of looking hard enough to find out what it is. It's like the only reason that you're in business is because they allow it. You stand around with your hat in your fucking hand, giving them the old shit-eating grin and saying "yes sir, no sir," and then you remember that it's your taxes buying those sumbitches their groceries."

He spat angrily, looked back at me, and smiled wearily.

"Sorry," he said, "but I got a call this morning from EPA about how I dispose of the epoxies I use patching some of these boats. They're going to be sending a couple of boys around. I been wearing a red ass all morning."

"No problem."

"Too bad about Garvey getting boarded like that," he said. "You must be here to survey the boat for insurance."

"No," I said. "I'm here to see if we can't put the Coast Guard's nuts in a vise."

I thought, for a moment, that he was going to hug me to his bare, greasy chest.

"Oh man . . . my man, my *man*. If you are looking for help, then let me be the first to volunteer."

"All right," I said and smiled.

"What can I do? Just fucking name it."

"Might take a little while."

"For that, I got all the time in the world."

So we went up to his office, a tight little space that made no pretense of being anything but what it was—a place for typing, filing, and phoning. The real work got done on the docks or in the repair shed.

"Place looks like shit," the man—who had introduced himself as Pete—said. "I'd burn it up if I thought we could do without it."

I took a seat across the desk from him and got my notebook out. He asked if I'd like a Coke or something. I said no. He shrugged, opened a tin of Skoal, and loaded up. He spat out the window onto the oyster-shell parking lot, and said, "Okay. Fire away."

We talked for more than an hour. More precisely, I asked the occasional question and then he ranted for several minutes while I made notes of anything pertinent. For all the incendiary speeches, he was a gold mine of material. Like most people, he cherished his resentments. Every ugly story he'd heard about the Coast Guard, every detail of incompetence or arrogance, he remembered. And not just in the outline, either, but with something approaching precision. He was like a betrayed lover who could remember every single one of his partner's infidelities.

"There's probably more," he said when we'd finished. "Probably *lots* more. But that's what I remember. And it should be enough to get you started."

"More than enough," I said.

"Well, good luck," he said. "I'll be pulling for you."

"Thanks."

"Be like a pit bull," he said, standing up and putting a fresh load of Skoal in his mouth. "Grab a hold of their fucking neck and just don't turn loose of it until they've laid down and died."

I smiled and shook his hand. Then we left the office together. Pete went back to the busted outboard and I got in my truck and drove off to interview some of the people he said had been badly treated by the Coast Guard.

CHAPTER 12

"I've owned this boat for ten years," said the man with a lean, patrician face but a sailor's weathered skin. "And another, smaller boat for twenty years before that. I've single-handed from here to Blue Hill, Maine, been all over the Gulf, and spent half a dozen summers in the Bahamas. And I've always done things safely and properly.

"They had no cause to hail me and *certainly* no reason to board my boat. It was bad enough having to produce enough life preservers to satisfy them, then watching them test my running lights and verify that my fire extinguishers had been inspected within the proper time frame. But when they started searching my boat for contraband . . ."

He stopped talking and pressed his lips tightly together.

"Did they do any damage?" I said.

He nodded.

"A lot?"

He shook his head ruefully.

"Not in a monetary sense, no. But they did cut into a small void up forward, and I'll tell you," the man said in a pained voice, "I have never felt so . . . *impotent* in all my life. Here was this young man, with this stupid look on his face, cutting into my boat with absolute impunity. It was enough for them to say that there *might* have been drugs in there. There was nothing I could do."

"Did you talk to anyone about it?"

"Who, for instance?"

"A lawyer."

"I *am* a lawyer. Or I was, anyway, before I retired. I suppose if I wanted to spend the rest of my life and all of my assets making a case and pushing it through the courts, arguing over what constitutes 'probable cause' and 'reasonable suspicion' and so forth, until it finally got to Washington and the nine old men—well, eight old men and one old woman—then I could have seen a lawyer. But I have better things to do. Life is too short."

I nodded and asked him if he would be willing to sign a statement swearing to the events as he had described them. I'd get the statement typed up, I told him.

"For what purpose?"

"I want to embarrass the Coast Guard."

He smiled.

"Why?"

"They did the same thing to a friend of mine," I said.

"You don't think you're going to get some money out of them," he said.

I thought about that for a second or two, then said, "Maybe." Money is a motive everyone understands, and I didn't want to explain myself to the old yachtsman and lawyer.

"Well, you're a fool," he said. "You'd do better playing the lottery. But I'll sign your statement."

We'd been talking at an outside table, at the Bon Secour marina. It was a more prosperous and genteel marina than the Outrigger, the sort of place where a lawyer who decided to sail in his retirement would keep his boat. There was an air-conditioned bar not far from where we sat, and beyond that a little shop that sold designer yacht wear, cocktail glasses with signal flags hand-painted on the side, and expensive brass decorator items. The place had the feel, I thought, of one of those old, exclusive clubs where the golf course was designed by Robert Trent Jones.

I was guessing about that, though. I've never been to one of those clubs. Never been close.

"You know," the man said, when I got up to leave, "I did consider getting a lawyer. One of those people with blazing eyes and a quick mouth—the ones you always see on television talking about free speech and the right to privacy. I was that angry. I hadn't done anything wrong or even given anyone cause to believe I *might* have done something wrong. But here these men were, with the authority of government behind them, and they were tearing up my boat. *They* were the criminals and *I* felt guilty.

"But," he continued, softly, "nobody worries about the civil rights of yacht owners. In a strange way, it was a cheap education for me. Now I knew what it must be like to be poor, living with the police and the welfare people in your business all the time. Shame I wasn't younger when it happened. The experience would have made a radical out of me. I might have become one of those constitutional lawyers instead of handling estates. But then . . . I'd never have been able to afford a boat."

I thanked him, left him sitting at the table, and walked up the dock to the parking lot. I got in my truck and drove out past a rental cop, standing next to a little guardhouse in his khaki uniform and spit-shined shoes. He looked about as vigilant as you would expect for five dollars an hour.

There were other marinas Pete had told me about, where boat owners had their own stories about the heavy hand of the drug blockade. I would drive in, ask for old so-and-so, and if he happened to be around, talk to him about his experience. Inevitably, I would hear the same things I had heard from the retired trusts-and-estates lawyer. The details of the boarding might change slightly, but the feelings of violation and helpless fury in the storytellers hardly varied at all.

I had filled a couple of dozen pages of my notebook with the accounts of five separate episodes of rinky-dink totalitarianism on the high seas. It was what I'd been after and I felt ready to quit. Interviewing people can be hard work. It's not like conversation. You have to keep your distance and you have to keep thinking. For me, it's the hardest kind of work there is.

I wanted to quit and drive back to the river house. Call Jessie and see if she'd come over for supper.

But I wanted to talk to Phil Garvey again before I went home. So I left the parking lot of a small, no-frills marina and drove back into town against the afternoon traffic. I passed by a park where a couple of softball games were in progress and some kids were getting organized for T-ball. Three or four dogs were running loose through the park and there were women with babies sitting on blankets on the perimeter of each of the diamonds. It was a good time of year for that. The best. The evenings stretched out just long enough and were still cool enough that you sometimes needed a jacket. The grass was green and the flowers were blooming and people could feel the energy rising inside their bodies like sap. Instead of a drink and the unremitting gloom of TV news, you put on some sweats and went outside to run or play a little ball. It was a pleasant and hopeful time of year.

But not for Phil Garvey. The parking lot at his shop was empty. The door was locked. There was a hand-lettered sign fixed to it with duct tape. It read: CLOSED DUE TO FAMILY EMERGENCY.

I found a phone booth and called Garvey's home number. After a dozen rings, I hung up, got in the truck, and drove to the interstate spur and on to University Hospital.

A small, pale man at the front desk looked up from a computer terminal long enough to tell me that I wanted the pediatric surgical wing and give me directions. I thanked him and he nodded sympathetically.

The elevator was deep enough to handle a stretcher and the tile on the floors had been waxed until it sparkled. I felt parts of myself shutting down, the way circulation to your fingers and toes is pinched off when you are extremely cold. It was something I always experienced in a hospital. A form of natural defense.

I found Phil and Rachel in a small waiting room at the end of a little side corridor. They were the only people in the room. Rachel was sitting on a couch, with her hands folded in her lap and her eyes aimed at the wall but seeing something in the far, far distance.

Phil was standing with his arms folded across his chest like bandoliers. He was leaning, just slightly, against the wall. He didn't notice me when I came into the room. Didn't register my presence until I was standing next to him.

"Hello, Morgan," he said. His voice sounded hollow.

"Phil."

"It looks like surgery," he said. "Looks like they're going to cut my boy's head open."

What can you say? I tried, "I'm sorry, Phil."

He nodded.

"Is there anything I can do?" Short of miracle cures, I thought. Maybe bake a pie and bring it around. It had

taken me a long time to understand why people did that
when somebody got real sick, or died. Eventually it had
occurred to me that they did it because it was the only
thing they could do.

Garvey shook his head and kept his eyes on the door
across the corridor. His son had to be behind that door.
Sooner or later, a doctor would come through it and tell
him, and his wife, what was going on.

Rachel was standing next to him now, looking into my
face.

"Hello, Morgan," she said. "You're very good to
come by."

I nodded because I didn't know what to say to that. I
didn't know Rachel well. She'd been out to the house,
once, with Phil. Jessie fixed dinner and we sat around,
later, on the porch, drinking wine and talking. Jessie had
liked her and so had I. Jessie called her "solid."

"All this time, it's been a brain tumor. They want to
operate tomorrow. They're doing the blood work and the
rest of the lab run-ups now."

I nodded, trying to think of something to say. It wouldn't
be anything that would comfort them. I knew that. But
maybe I could handle part of the routine burden.

"I was wondering," I said, "about your other son? Do
you need somebody to look after him? I could take him
out to supper. Let him spend the night at my place and
then bring him into school. He could stay with
me . . . well, as long as he needs to."

There was gratitude and tolerance in Rachel's smile.

"I'm sure he'd love it," she said. "But he's already been
claimed by the parents of one of his school friends."

"Well . . ." I said.

"Of course. We'll call you. And you're very thoughtful."

"Yeah, Morgan," Phil said. "We really appreciate it."

"What about the shop, then?" I said. "You want me to look after things there?"

Garvey thought for a moment.

"You mind?" he said.

"No. Not at all."

"Just for a couple of hours. Around lunch. I've got somebody coming in to pick up some things he ordered. The paperwork is all written up on my desk and the stuff is in a box out back. If you could be there to give it to him and take his check . . ."

"Sure."

"I appreciate it, Morgan. I really do."

It seemed like such an absurdly small thing. But in that fragile atmosphere, small things seemed very large.

"Just give me a key."

I waited with them a little longer. None of us said much since there wasn't much to say. When I said my good-byes, they both thanked me. Rachel smiled and I liked her face. She was not movie-star beautiful but she had a strong, honest face and the sort of eyes that didn't deceive or conceal. I suspect that she'd been great as a nurse. You could look at her and feel like she was doing everything she could, and also telling you the truth.

"Thanks for coming," she said.

"Sure. Call if I can do anything."

"We will."

"I'll talk to you tomorrow," I said to Phil.

"Right," he said, barely taking his eyes off the door across the corridor.

I left them there, waiting for that door to open and dreading what the man who came through it would tell them.

CHAPTER 13

A SMALL, BUFF-COLORED ENVELOPE WAS wedged into the space between my screen door and the frame. I recognized the stationery, since it belonged to Jessie, and I knew with almost pure certainty what her letter would say. She'd gone somewhere on business.

I opened the envelope and read the letter. This time, it was Austin. A big conference about the ecology of the entire Gulf Coast, including Mexico. Jessie had made a lot of money in Louisiana oil and had the good sense to get out when the price was still around thirty-five a barrel and most of the other oilies were wondering how to spend the money they'd make when it got to a hundred. Now, they were in Chapter 11 or worse and she had moved on to other things. These days, she worked for a land trust, trying to keep a little of the Gulf Coast uninhabited and unspoiled. She liked to say that she was using the devil's money to do the Lord's work.

She hadn't planned on going to the conference, the letter

said, but somebody called and asked her to fill in on a
panel for someone who had canceled.

She'd miss me, she said, and in my memory she would
eat some Mexican food and scout around to find out who
was doing the best imitation Bob Wills in Texas these days.

Back in five or four days, she closed. Take care of myself.

I put the letter in my back pocket, surprised by how
disappointed and low I felt after the hospital. Company
would have been the best thing for me. But with Jessie
gone, I would have to settle for something less than that.
Something to take my mind off things. A little pick-and-
shovel work to tire the body and numb the brain. That's
what I needed.

But I didn't have any pick-and-shovel work that needed
doing at the moment. My woodpile was in pretty good
shape and my well was running clean and sweet. But I
had about a ton of cast-iron weights out in the old mule
stable that I had turned into a gym. In prison, I had lifted
weights to burn off the accumulated emotional poisons,
the backed-up rage and disappointment and the plain old
unalloyed despair that will make you do all kinds of stupid
things, everything from taking a second helping of grits
to killing a guard. I wasn't going to get fat in there, I told
myself, and I *was* going to get out. So I lifted. Sometimes
three or four hours a day.

Then, when I did get out, I kept it up. It was still the
best way in the world to cure a case of the black ass.

So I changed into a pair of shorts and walked out to the
mule barn in my bare feet. The thick centipede grass felt
like a sheet of plush carpet under my feet. The afternoon
was dying and the air had that warm orange glow. The
birds were singing, but not quite as urgently as they do
at sunrise.

The stable smelled of mule shit and mule sweat. It was sweet, not rank. I had always liked that smell, especially in a working space. I laid a towel down on a bench, tuned a radio to a local oldies station, loaded a bar, and got down to business. The first set, with light weights, seemed hard. My shoulder hurt deep in the joint. I rubbed it with Aspercreme and hit the bench again. This set went easier and the shoulder didn't pop or creak or hurt as much as before. The blood was starting to move.

I added weight and hit it again.

Now we're cooking, I said to myself. The sweat was beginning to pop.

I worked for almost two hours. Breathing hard, pushing weight, and listening to Chuck Berry and Wilson Pickett on the radio. I didn't think about Phil Garvey or Jessie Beaudreaux or Phil Garvey's poor kid. I didn't even think about not thinking about them. I just got into the steel and the smell of mules and the way my body felt as I burned up everything it contained.

It was dark when I quit and stepped outside. The birds had quit singing but some insects and frogs filled up the empty space. There was a small slice of bone-colored moon hanging over the tree line and a few early stars looking very bright and isolated in the sky around it. The night air smelled cool, damp, and very clean after the stable. I took my time walking back to the house.

After a shower, I scrambled some eggs. I drank a glass of milk with the eggs, cleaned up after I'd finished, and then made some strong tea. Most of the time, I drank a beer or two—or three—after a workout, but tonight I didn't feel like it. I liked a beer or a drink when I was feeling good, not when I was blue. And tonight was a blue night.

I took my cup out to the front steps, where I sat and

listened to the river. The moon was reflected perfectly in the river's flat, slick surface. Spokes of light radiated out from its reflection and seemed to waver like reeds in a wind. I sipped my tea and listened to the sounds of wading birds, jumping fish, and foraging raccoons. The river was a busy place on a night like this.

After a while, I finished the tea and went inside for another cup. I took this one into what I call my "drinking room," a little room downstairs that I had paneled in walnut and pecan. I put in a small fireplace and an old mahogany desk. A large, leather-covered chair. And a small butler's table that held a couple of decanters and some heavy glasses. One wall was floor-to-ceiling bookshelves. I was looking for something to read, maybe a little Mark Twain to cheer me up; when the phone rang, I felt like I had been jerked back into what the computer people call "real time."

I walked into the kitchen. I only have one phone in the house—one of those portable jobs—and that's where I keep it.

"Hello," I said, not very cordially.

"Morgan, this is Rachel Garvey."

"Hello," I said, now very much back in real time.

"Should I call back tomorrow? I know it's late—"

"No," I said. "This is fine. I was just reading."

"Well, I'm sorry to call so late. We just got back from the hospital. They finished all the tests and have scheduled the operation for nine tomorrow morning. We'll be going in early."

"Yes," I said, brilliantly holding up my end.

"Phil is out running right now. He said he just had to get some exercise."

"I can understand that." It would have been in the mule barn all night long for me, I thought.

"I just wanted to call and ask you something. It's probably not my place—"

"No," I said, "go ahead."

"Well, I wanted to ask you if there's something on Phil's mind that I ought to know about. Something besides Rick's illness and the trouble he's having with the bank. Something that would be causing him a lot of concern."

"I don't know," I said. It was a lie. But it was the best I could do.

"The reason I ask," she went on, "is that Phil seemed kind of different when he came home the other night. Sunday, I think it was. He said he'd gone by to see you and he seemed . . . oh, *distracted*. Withdrawn."

"I know he's been worried," I said.

"Yes," she sighed. "Things have been hard for him. They don't hit you one at a time. You ever notice that? It's always in combinations."

"I've noticed."

"It's especially tough on Phil. He thinks he ought to be able to do something, even when there isn't anything anyone can do. The thing with the bank is driving him crazy. He thinks he's going to lose the house or the business and that he's let us down somehow."

"I know."

"It's not *his* fault," she said bleakly. "I understand that and try to tell him. But it doesn't get through."

"Well, you want to do what's good for your family." Said like I had some experience.

"I know. He's a good man that way, and I love him for it. I just wish he'd be a little easier on himself. I feel like a preacher sometimes. I just want to tell him to do what he can and then put all the rest of it in another's hands. Leave all the worrying and try to find some peace. But he won't do that. Won't give himself any peace."

I didn't try to respond to that.

"So you don't know of something that might have happened to make him even more worried?"

"No," I said firmly. I didn't feel good saying it but I couldn't imagine giving her any other answer. But she was both brave and desperate and I wanted badly to give her some kind of solace.

"I could talk to him," I said.

She sighed again. "I doubt he'd tell you anything. He keeps his troubles inside. It's the way he is. I doubt he'll change and I don't believe I really want him to. I was just gambling that maybe you knew something and that, once I knew, maybe I could find a way to help him. But I guess not. I'm sorry to have bothered you."

"You didn't," I said. "I wish I could help."

That was the truth.

"Well . . . thank you."

Then, surprising myself, I said, "I'll be praying for you tomorrow." But that was also true. I would be; in my own poor fashion.

"Thank you. And God bless you. Good night."

"Good night," I said.

I hung up feeling like I needed to go out for another three-hour session in the mule barn. Instead, I merely turned out the lights and went to bed. I had a bad night, but nothing, I told myself, like the kind of night Phil and Rachel Garvey were having.

CHAPTER 14

I ROLLED OUT EARLY AND RAN FOUR OR five miles. Showered, dressed, and ate some dry toast for breakfast while I listened, without much interest, to the farm report. Planting season, locally, looked good. Neither too wet nor too dry, which was fine with me, since I'd been betting right along that beans would be cheap in the fall. It just didn't seem very important this morning.

Before I left the house, I filled a cooler with ice and the fish that I'd caught the other day and had planned on cooking for Jessie. I filled my traveling cup with coffee and headed out. It wasn't quite seven.

I drove straight to the sheriff's department, where I expected to leave the cooler, with a note. But Tom Pine was already in, drinking coffee and looking at the overnight sheets. He didn't look pleased.

"Bad time?" I said when I stepped into his office.

He looked up from behind his desk and shook his head just slightly, side to side, as though it took a big effort. "No, hell, come in. I could use the company."

"What's the problem?"

Tom sighed and it sounded like the death rattle of a good-sized dog.

"Drugs," he said. "Drugs is the problem. Seems like drugs is *always* the problem. We had a shooting last night out in one of the projects. Twelve-year-old kid gets lit up by one who's fourteen. And both of the stupid little bastards were flying high. Been doing a little rock together and one of 'em got pissed at the other about something. Settled it with his nine millimeter."

He stopped, put down the sheet of paper he'd been reading, and shook his head.

"What can you do?" I said.

"Nothing," Pine said. "Not a goddamned thing."

"Maybe this will make you feel better."

I held up the little hard-plastic cooler.

"What'd you do, stop by Sam Walton's store and buy me a lunch box?"

"No," I said. "The cooler is mine and I want it back. You can have what's inside it."

"What's in it?" Pine's eyebrows went up. He was interested.

"About eight nice fat bluegill. Caught two days ago. I even cleaned and scaled them."

"You must have got stood up."

"You're a good cop."

Pine stood and came around his desk. He almost had to squeeze through the space between the wall and the corner of the desk. Small office; big man. He opened the top of the cooler, looked in, and whistled with pleasure.

"Ummm. Them are pretty fish. Well, doesn't matter why you're giving them to me, they'll go good with hush puppies and slaw. Thank you, Morgan. That's real white of you."

He put the cooler next to a file cabinet and offered me a cup of coffee. I told him I'd pass. It was the sort of morning where I just wanted to get on with it and couldn't really enjoy sitting around and talking, not even with Tom Pine.

He was having the same kind of morning. He sat down behind his desk and picked up the sheet of paper he'd been reading when I came in. I slipped out and left him to it.

From the sheriff's office, I drove downtown. Parts of it looked good, with the flowers blooming in the early morning. But as you got close to the storefronts, you could see that most of them had been abandoned and that those that were still in one kind of business or another were guarded by heavy-duty burglar bars. You could even make out the shape of a dog—a pit bull, most likely—moving around behind the glass in some of the stores.

I parked half a block from the old bank building and rode up the elevator, alone, to Nat Semmes's office. I knocked at his private door and he told me to come in. He was drinking coffee and reading from the volume of Dante.

"Sorry," I said. Coming in unexpected that way felt something like breaking in on a man in the middle of his prayers. Maybe it was Semmes's choice of reading material.

He shook his head. "No need to be. I was just finishing. Listen to this: 'Men run from virtue as if from a foe / or poisonous snake. Either the land is cursed, / or long corrupted custom drives them so.' "

Semmes put the book down on his desk and smiled.

"I believe old Dante could have written that last night," he said.

"If he could put it to music," I said, "he'd have a hit."

"I think you're on to something, Morgan. Do the Divine Comedy as rap. It would sell a ton." He shook his head at the thought. Then he said, "What brings you in?"

I told him about Garvey's latest trouble. When I said that the boy would be in surgery in an hour or two, Semmes's face darkened with pain. A father's pain, I suppose. He could imagine, a lot better than I could, what Garvey was going through.

"How's he holding up?"

"All right, I suppose. Hard to know. He's carrying a pretty heavy load and it sounds to me like he's not telling his wife about all of it."

Semmes made an uncomprehending face, so I told him about the late call from Rachel Garvey.

"Unwise," he said, "but understandable. He probably thinks he's doing her a kindness. Be nice, wouldn't it, if we could get that assault thing dropped?"

"Yes," I said, "and keep him out of a civil skirmish, too."

"Right," he said, with his voice dropping into the register he used when it was time to get down to business. "So have you got anything that will help us make Mister Loftin into the Coast guard's informer so we can slow-roast his sorry pink ass?"

Semmes's eyes were hot. He hated a bad lawyer the way Tom Pine would hate a dirty cop.

I ran down what I'd learned the previous day. He listened closely, and when I finished I said, "The reason I came in, actually, is to type it up, if I can use one of the machines. Then you can study the report."

And decide on the next move, I thought.

Semmes nodded. "Sure," he said. "Use anything you want. But why don't you let somebody here type it? Are your notes that hard to read?"

Actually, they were very clean. But I liked either to do my own work or pay to have it done. Semmes's secretary didn't work for me.

"I can type," I said. "Piece of cake on a word processor. I'll be done in a couple of hours."

"All right," Semmes said. "I'm out of the office this morning. I'll read it when I get back. You want to call in, about one?"

"Okay."

"I would sure like to squash this particular snake, Morgan," Semmes said on his way out.

I nodded. I liked it when Semmes talked that way.

I sat at the computer in Semmes's law library for two hours and tapped out a report based on the notes I'd taken the day before. The report ran three pages, double spaced. I printed two copies on the office laser and made sure I saved the report on a little hard plastic disk that, for some reason, was called a "floppy." That was the "Hunt" disk, and I put it in the "Hunt" file, where I knew it would be safe.

I left Semmes a copy and headed for Garvey's shop.

There wasn't a lot to do, once I'd unlocked the door, opened a couple of windows, and turned on the lights. Garvey kept things in order.

The paperwork he'd told me about was on his desk. An order for a ScubaPro BC and regulator. The customer had made a deposit and would, according to a note in Garvey's very clean script, pay the balance when he picked up his goods.

I looked in the back and found a UPS box, sliced the tape with my pocketknife and checked the contents. One orange buoyancy compensator and a two-stage regulator. The invoice matched the paperwork I'd found on Garvey's desk.

Now all I needed was a customer with a check, and he'd probably be along during his lunch hour.

I had some time to kill, so I found a broom and swept the place out. I had to work hard to come up with a half a cup of dust. I wiped down the counters. Spaced the wet suits that were hanging on a rack so that there was exactly two fingers of separation between hangers. Then I lined up the screwdrivers and wrenches on the workbench. Oiled the fittings on the air compressor. Restacked some lead diving weights and sprayed a little silicone on some fins.

Turns out that waiting for customers is slow work. And it's probably excruciating, I thought, when you own the store. I felt bad for Garvey. From night infiltrations of hostile beaches to this.

I was looking through some manufacturer's equipment catalog—lots of photographs of cute couples in lime-green or flamingo-pink wet suits—when I heard the door open and then close. I looked up into a gaunt, yellow face that looked like it belonged to a cadaver, not a diver.

The man was wearing a short-sleeved white shirt turned a little gray by the wash, with two ballpoint pens clipped into the pocket. He had an envelope in his hand. Probably the check, I thought.

He held the envelope out and I took it. He grinned, exposing a set of stained, gapped teeth.

"Congratulations," he said, "you been served."

I should have known. Wasn't thinking. But I rallied and feigned the kind of knee-knocking shock most people feel when they come into the orbit of the law.

"Oh, Jesus," I said.

The server smiled without opening his mouth.

I turned the papers one way, then the other, then opened them and read. It was what I had expected. Garvey was being sued by Loftin, who claimed to have been threatened, beaten, injured, and so forth—one million dollars' worth.

I handed the sheet back to the man and said, "Nice try."

"You aren't . . ." He had to stop and look at the name on the papers. "Garvey."

"Afraid not."

He made a face to show that this sort of thing was always happening to him and he considered it very goddamned unfair.

He checked the address and then looked back at me.

"Well, where is he?"

I shrugged my shoulders and said, "Not my day to watch him."

"Oh, fuck."

"Hey," I said, "this is a Christian establishment. So you just watch your mouth, asshole."

He looked back at me. Bewilderment shading over into anger and then back again.

"Hit the road," I said. "Unless you want to buy a wet suit."

He started to say something but looked into my face and changed his mind. It has always struck me, for some reason, that the law in all its majesty attracts some pretty low people to do its basic, everyday donkey work. The prison guards I'd come up against were mostly ignorant sadists. Only children are surprised by stories of crooked cops. Process servers, bondsmen, and . . . well, private investigators; they aren't generally nominated for good-citizen awards. The law seems to attract not just predators but also their parasites.

The man left the shop, mumbling.

"Speak up," I said. "I'm a little deaf."

"Clean the shit out of your ears, then," he said and, probably figuring that made us even, hustled on his way. I picked up the phone and called Semmes.

CHAPTER 15

SEMMES GAVE HIS PORSCHE A WORKOUT on an old highway that meandered through the low stunted pines and palmettos on its way to the lagoon and the Coast Guard station. He ran through the gears, diving hard into the turns with the tires straining to hold the road. Then, coming out of the turns, he wound it out, pushing the redline on every gear. He was plainly concentrating and enjoying himself, so I kept quiet and let him drive. He was a good driver.

When we came out of the low ground and into an area that had been developed enough to have a few feeder streets and some roadside businesses, he went back to driving like a responsible, adult civilian.

"Ah, yes," he said. "That works every time."

"You ever get pulled over?"

"Once," he said. "And the judge purely loved it. He'd overheard me once, ranting about how judges are nothing but lawyers who are too lazy to work. 'Civil service hacks in robes,' I believe is the way I described them. This particular hack couldn't wait to fine me, take my license, and send me to driver-safety school. Most judges are also short on self-discipline. This one tried to keep from smiling while he was passing sentence, but he just couldn't help himself."

"How fast were you going?"

"Trooper said he wasn't sure, exactly, just that it was over a hundred."

"Hard to talk your way out of that, I suppose."

"Impossible," Semmes smiled. "Even though I thought I had a pretty good case. It was real early in the morning and there wasn't any traffic to speak of. Especially since the highway was closed for repairs. Judge didn't see it that way, though."

"Worth it?"

"Oh, sure. Everybody needs something that burns off all the bad gases and leaves you clean. That's worth a small fine, every time."

Like most of what Semmes said, it made sense.

He braked slightly for an approaching pickup. When it passed, he cut the wheel and accelerated. The Porsche shot down a short asphalt drive to a steel building painted red and white with the insignia of the United States Coast Guard over the door. Behind the building, jutting out into the lagoon and tied to a sturdy concrete dock, was the steel-hulled crash boat with the machine-gun mounts and the stenciled marijuana leaves outside the wheelhouse.

I followed Semmes through the front door. A yeoman standing behind a counter looked up and said, "Yes, sir. Can I help you?"

"My name is Semmes," he said affably, "and this is my associate, Mr. Hunt. We're here to see your CO."

"Commander Moss?" The idea that a civilian—*two* civilians—would simply walk into headquarters expecting to talk with the CO was almost too much for the yeoman.

"I believe that's the name," Semmes said.

"Sir . . . is he, ah, *expecting* you?"

"I hope so. We talked on the phone. And he told me to come on out. We might be a little early, but not by much."

"Yes, sir," the yeoman said. "If you'll just wait here a minute, sir"

"I'll be right here."

The yeoman turned away and walked down a hall. A second or two later, we could hear him knocking on a door.

"It is my firm impression," Semmes said, "that Commander Moss runs this outpost like Fort Apache."

I nodded, looking at the bulletin board, the fire extinguishers, and the yeoman's logbooks, which were all impeccably shipshape.

"I suppose that's necessary when you find yourself out on some lonely, harsh frontier," Semmes said, "engaging a cruel enemy."

The yeoman reappeared and said, "If you'll come with me."

We followed him down the same hall, to a door with a sign that read CDR RBT. F. MOSS USCG. The service insignia was stenciled below the name, with the gold-leaf insignia of his rank on either flank. It was a formidable-looking door.

The yeoman knocked again.

"Yes," said a voice through the door. A little high-pitched.

Semmes and I went in.

The man behind the desk wore pressed khakis with a couple of inches of bleached white T-shirt showing at his neck. A stainless-steel watch on his wrist. Metal-framed glasses on his thin, raptorlike face. He was short; his hair was gray; and his mouth was puckered in an expression of general-purpose disapproval.

"Gentlemen," he said, and gave us each a firm handshake.

"Commander," Semmes said. "We appreciate your giving us your time, and we'll try not to take too much of it."

Moss nodded, pointed to a couple of chairs, and said, "Have a seat."

I sat and looked around the room, which was functional, almost Spartan, in its furnishings. Desk, chairs, file cabinets—one with a combination lock for classified documents and codes—and a large wall chart of this portion of the Gulf Coast. The chart showed all the passes, channels, hazards to navigation, and so forth. In additon to those, there were little flags on standards made from straight pins that were stuck through the paper and into the cork backing. These, no doubt, marked the locations where his crash boat had conducted boarding operations.

"Commander," Semmes began in his most courtly Southern voice, "I have a client who runs a business that uses a boat. He keeps the boat in a marina not far from here."

The commander gave an impatient, skeptical nod and said, "Yes. Go on."

"He's a hardworking fellow, never been in trouble. In fact, he's a decorated veteran. Former Navy SEAL. A good citizen and a certified patriot."

Behind the ascetic, wire-rimmed glasses, the commander's eyes went narrow. I suspect he knew what was coming next.

"And then, the other day, some of your men, aboard that crash boat outside, boarded him for reasons he can't figure out and neither, frankly, can I," Semmes said, sounding genuinely puzzled.

"We hail a lot of boats, Mr. Semmes. And we board a number of those boats that we hail."

"How many do you search?" Semmes said. "From bridge to bilge? How often, when you board a boat, do you cut into the voids with a power saw?"

"If you want a percentage," the commander said, "I can't give it to you. But we will do that kind of search if, in our judgment, circumstances call for it."

Semmes nodded slowly, as though he were beginning to get the picture.

"Your judgment?"

"That's correct. Our professional estimate of the situation."

"Is that the same thing as probable cause? That's what we talk about in the law when we discuss what is required before you can just go invade a man's property and start busting the place up, destroying things, because you're looking for something you think he might have hidden there. Comes from the Constitution."

"We are operating under competent authority."

"Using your best judgment to estimate the situation?"

"That's correct."

"How often are you right?"

"We know what we're doing. We've been trained and we have experience." The commander didn't rattle. He had, after all, the whole government behind him.

"Then you wouldn't make many mistakes?"

"Not many, no."

"That's what I thought, at first," Semmes said. "I figured the Coast Guard knew what it was doing and that if it had made a mistake in the case of my client, well, everybody blows one now and then. But just to be sure I wasn't dealing with a rogue agency, I asked my associate, Mr. Hunt here, who is only the best investigator on the Gulf Coast . . ."

Semmes enjoyed laying it on thick that way whenever he introduced me. He did it, I'm sure, because he knew it made my skin crawl.

He finished his little digression, saying, "At any rate, Mr. Hunt conducted a typically thorough investigation and he found a number of cases where your best professional estimate of the situation wasn't worth a quart of sour piss."

When the commander turned my way, I began reading off the top page in my notebook. "March 16, off Redfish Point, early afternoon . . ."

I had to pause to turn the page over in my notebook. I started to read about another boarding but hadn't gotten far when the commander held up his hand and said, "I don't have time for this, Mr. Semmes. If you want to question the government's policies on drug interdiction, then I suggest you take it up with the people who make those policies. I'm just here to implement them."

"Oh, I'd love to talk to those folks. But what could I tell them? I'd feel like the poet Yeats when he was asked to write some verses during the Great War. You know what he said?"

The commander was so stiff he could have been starched. He didn't answer Semmes, who ignored him and went on.

"What Mr. Yeats said, in effect, was, How could a mere poet presume to speak to the giants who have given us the wonders of the Western Front? What could someone who merely comforts young women in their lonely beds possibly say to statesmen whose works include the battles of the Somme and Passchendaele?"

The commander looked at Semmes like he might be mad.

"So I think I'll skip talking to the policy makers. But brilliant as their policies are, as successful as they have been in ridding the nation of the scourge of illegal narcotics, I think they'd agree that *you* have done a piss-poor job of implementing them. Armed men boarding civilian pleasure boats, sawing through bulkheads, and rifling storage lockers . . . on a hunch. And then not finding anything. Bad enough that what you are doing is unconstitutional. But a lot of folks have learned how to live with that. What's worse—intolerable, really—is that you are incompetent. You run around behaving like a goddamned British press gang—violating the rights of American citizens—and then . . . you don't find any dope."

"You sound," the commander said, his voice as dry and gritty as sand, "like someone who's getting ready to talk to the media."

Semmes shook his head slowly. "My mama couldn't stand it if she thought I was a news source. She thinks I play the piano in a whorehouse. But I might go to Congress, where my associate could give some hungry young committee counsel all the names he has so assiduously gathered and written down in his little notebook. Then those people could come into the hearing room and tell how they were treated by the Coast Guard when they hadn't done anything except run afoul of your best estimate of the situation. I believe it would make great TV, hearings like that, I truly do."

"You do what you think best, Mr. Semmes," the commander said, his composure slipping. "But you might want to think about what's involved here. We have a coastline that is thousands of miles long. Hundreds of thousands of boats of all descriptions use these waters and some of them are carrying drugs. If you want to stop drugs from coming in—and I do, because I'm a father—then you have to be willing to take steps that would otherwise be distasteful. . . . "

Semmes held his hand up, palm out, and shook his head mournfully. "Commander, I may not know much, but I can smell shit when I'm standing in it. Why don't you save us both a lot of grief. I don't want to go to Washington and talk to people in Congress any more than you do. But I'll threaten you with it and, if I have to, I'll back up my threat. If you don't believe it, you can do a little research on the way I work."

The commander looked at Semmes with the rage of authority that has been mocked.

"You're talking blackmail."

"Horseshit, Commander."

Moss glared hard at Semmes, who smiled back, almost cordially.

"What *do* you call it?"

"I call it being an attorney and having a client who has had his constitutional rights grievously violated by the authorities. He's been subject to treatment that would make the Gestapo proud."

Moss stiffened in his chair like he'd been slapped.

"You stepped in shit, Commander," Semmes went on. "But I am not a crusader. I take clients, not causes. And I want to make my client whole. That means I have to know why you decided to board him and bust up his boat."

Moss started to speak, but Semmes interrupted him.

"And I'm not buying 'best professional estimate.' You had information—a tip—on Garvey. I want the name of your informant. Once upon a time in this country a man was entitled to face his accuser. Now his accuser just has to pick up a phone and tip some police agency to make life hell for an honest citizen. I like the old way better. I want a name so my client can face his accuser. It won't necessarily be in a court of law but"—Semmes smiled ruefully and spread his hands—"you just do the best you can."

Moss finally lost it. His face turned red and he rose at least a foot out of his chair, with his hands gripping the steel arms tight enough to turn his knuckles white.

"I can't give you that kind of information. That's official, confidential, and totally protected—" The man was pushing the words so hard they were coming out in a babble.

Semmes held up his hand. "Of course. That's the way it works. Protection for the finks and harassment for the honest citizens. You people have turned the whole thing on its head."

"We have to use informers. It's the only way."

Semmes made a face like he'd just bitten down on a piece of rotten meat.

"I don't buy that," he said. "But even if I did, I'd still have to wonder why you feel like you've got to protect an informer who gave you bad information that turned out to be damaging to an innocent taxpayer and could be real goddamned embarrassing to you."

"We have to promise confidentiality. If we didn't, nobody would come to us."

"Protecting your sources?"

"Exactly."

"Well, Commander, the sources are running you, then. If they don't have the guts to come out with their charges in the open . . . well, that's human. But if you don't have the guts to throw them to the wolves when they lie to you, that's different. You're the government. What the hell have you got to be scared of?"

Moss said nothing.

Semmes stood up and nodded in my direction. "I believe

I do need to talk to somebody in Congress," Semmes said. He mentioned a name. I didn't recognize it, but the commander obviously did. Semmes and I were on our way out of the door when he said, "Our information came from a man in town—an attorney, actually."

"Can you narrow it down a little further, Commander?" Semmes said. "Give us a name or tell us who he works for? About half the people you run into these days are lawyers. They breed like rats."

"Frank Loftin," Moss said, blurting it in a way that made it sound like an involuntary action.

Semmes nodded very slightly and somewhat deferentially, then said, "I thank you, Commander. I surely do. You just saved me a trip to Washington. And I believe I'd rather go anywhere in the world before I'd visit that sinkhole."

I followed him out and I'd swear there was a spring in his step. Like he'd just fallen in love, or hit the lottery.

CHAPTER 16

"Nice work," I said when we were back in the car.

Semmes shrugged and downshifted, then pushed the Porsche through a long, sweeping curve.

"Who is the congressman you mentioned?"

Semmes smiled broadly. "An old drunk. Been up in Washington so long he probably played poker with Truman. He's got a committee that oversees Coast Guard business."

"You know him?"

"No. But I could get a call through to him, if I had to."

"Would you have done it?" I asked. "If the commander hadn't come through with the name?"

"Maybe. Makes me pretty hot to think about them boarding people's boats."

"What's next?"

"I'm going to invite Mr. Loftin in for a little conference. First thing tomorrow morning. See if we can't settle this thing in a Christian fashion."

"Will you need me there?"

Semmes thought about it for a moment, then said, "Yes, I think so."

Sometimes Semmes liked to have me in the room with him when he was talking to somebody. He said he liked the way I read signs.

So, when he dropped me off on the sidewalk in front of his office, I told him I'd see him in the morning.

"I wouldn't say anything to Garvey just yet, but I don't think he's going to have a problem with Frank Loftin after tomorrow." Semmes shook his head mournfully. "That means he can concentrate on his business . . . and his kid."

"It'll mean a lot."

"Shame we can't do something about the other," he said, and dropped the Porsche into first, leaving me there on the sidewalk to think about it.

I drove back out to the river house, my pickup feeling distinctly sluggish after Semmes's Porsche. But I could still take him on the Baja, I thought.

It was early evening when I parked under the live oak at the end of my drive. An hour, almost two, until sunset. The big old house looked lifeless and lonely and I didn't much feel like going inside and walking from one empty room to another, with my own solitary presence echoing off the walls. Two more days, I thought, until Jessie got back. I could do two days standing on my head.

I thought about going fishing again. Maybe driving down to the beach, digging some sand fleas, and trying to pick up a pompano or two out of the surf. After dark I could go someplace for dinner. By the time I got home, I'd feel ready for bed and the old house would feel more like home and less like a museum of which I was the dried-up old curator.

So I went inside to change clothes and pick up some tackle. Before I did anything, though, I checked the phone, on the chance that Jessie had called and left a message. The little red light was blinking, so I hit the button and the machine whirred for a second, then began playing back the tape.

"Morgan," a hesitant voice said, "this is Rachel Garvey. I wonder if you could please call me, here at the hospital." There was a pause, then she recited a number. I copied it down, waited for the tape to rewind and for the three-beep signal that the machine was clear, and then reluctantly dialed the number, feeling an odd, fluttering sensation in my chest.

"Hello." She picked up on the first ring and her voice was spent.

"Rachel," I said, "this is Morgan Hunt."

"Oh, hi," she said with a little verve coming into her voice, "thanks for calling, Morgan."

"How is the boy?" I asked tentatively.

"He's going to be all right," she said, almost defiantly. "It may take a long time, but he's going to be all right. He's a tough little guy."

"If there is anything I can do . . ."

"I know," she said, "and that's why I called. There *is* something. It might sound foolish but I'm serious."

"I can handle foolish," I said.

"I want you to take Phil out and go diving. Get him out in *Second Shot* and go after some lobsters or something. Get him wet and get him tired and then, if you can, get him drunk. You don't have to screw him. Bring him home and I'll take care of that."

I laughed. When she was working as a mother, you could forget that Rachel Garvey had been a Navy nurse and was plenty salty.

"I'm serious, Morgan. He's about to go crazy and I can't blame him for it. He needs to get his mind off things for just a little while, but he won't listen to me when I tell him. There's nothing he can do here at the hospital. The other kid is with friends, so there isn't anything he can do at home. And it's after business hours, so there isn't anything he can do at the shop."

"I'll take him diving," I said. "Be happy to do it. I might have to hog-tie him first."

"You can cold-cock him and chain him to the mast if you have to," she said. "Just get him offshore and underwater for a couple of hours. That's all I ask."

"Tell me where to find him," I said, "and I'll get right on it."

An hour later, Phil Garvey and I were sitting on the bridge of *Second Shot*, making our way through Pensacola Pass. It was almost dark, just a few fading streaks of orange in the sky to the west. The lights on the channel markers blinked randomly, the last one fully a mile offshore. When we cleared it, there was no orange left in the sky.

We didn't try to talk over the sound of the diesels. It was a cool night, with a clear sky and a fair number of early stars that seemed to increase as we got offshore and further out of the electric light that clutters the sky whenever you're near civilization.

We were running a compass line, south and a little east, to the wreck of an old Navy fighter plane in eighty feet of water. We had a six-pack of cold beer and a bucket of Popeye's fried chicken for after we'd finished our diving.

The water was clear and, except for a few jellyfish, ideal. It seemed like we should have thought of it before.

About an hour after we'd passed the sea buoy, Garvey throttled back on the engines and turned on the GPS and the depth finder.

Global Positional System works off satellites; if you have a receiver, it will give you your exact position in longitude and latitude to within about ten meters. Which, as they say, is plenty good enough for government work. Garvey's unit was mounted at eye level on the console. The digital readout glowed luminescent green, and he checked the numbers against those written in ink in a small loose-leaf notebook. He looked at one set of numbers, then the other. Took out a pencil and did some quick figuring on a blank sheet he tore from the notebook.

"What's that?" I said, not quite shouting, but loud enough to be heard over the engine noise.

"Well," he said, "I don't write the real positions down in my notebook. I use a code. That way, if somebody steals the book, all they've got is a bunch of meaningless numbers. To find the real position, I've got to subtract the number in my book from my birthday, in eight digits. I false subtract, if I have to carry, just like they teach in code class. So right now, I'm trying to figure out what this number *really* means."

He held up the scratch sheet on which he'd done the figuring, keeping his hand on the wheel and his eye on the changing green numbers on the GPS.

When they matched the numbers on the scratch sheet, he turned the wheel abruptly and throttled back until there was only enough speed to keep steerage. He shifted his eyes to the screen on his depth finder, which showed the bottom, eighty feet below, as a single smooth line. After a few seconds a small blip showed on that line and, above the blip, some dark streaks that indicated fish.

"There it is," Garvey said. "You want to go up to the bow, while I go around and make another pass. I'll tell you when to drop the anchor."

"Aye-aye."

"Carry on," Garvey said and smiled. It was the first good smile I'd seen on his face in a while.

I went forward and freed the anchor from its blocks. I was holding it in one hand with the line loose in the fingers of my other hand and my feet spread for balance against the roll of the boat. It was disorienting at night. When Garvey shouted, "Okay," I dropped the anchor, which sent up sparks of phosphorescence where it hit. The line ran for a while. Then, when it went slack, I cleated it off. Garvey killed the engines, and once more I felt as though I'd gone deaf.Then I could hear again. First the lapping of the water against the side of the boat. Then the creak of the anchor line against the stainless-steel cleat. And finally, the splash of flying fish skimming across the surface of the Gulf.

"You ready to get wet?" Garvey shouted.

"Yes."

"Then let's suit up and do it. You know what, Morgan?"

"What's that?"

"This was a goddamned good idea—to come diving tonight. I sure am glad I thought of it."

I didn't see the wreck until I was almost on it. It was small and the coral growth made it hard to recognize for what it was—a Navy fighter plane, one of those sporty little World War II ships, a Hellcat or a Corsair, that had been down here on the bottom, unmarked except by the fish, for nearly fifty years.

Several large grouper and one very big ray showed in the beam of my light. I moved in closer to the wreck and grabbed an exposed strut in the frame of the wing. I held on with one hand and used my light to probe the wreck.

It was alive with small red shrimp, their eyes like large, luminous beads. Schools of small fish hugged the wreck, and above them amberjack and spadefish circled like preying birds. The big fish—the grouper and the barracuda—stayed out on the edge of things.

There is something fascinating to me in the way a single small wreck like this can become an oasis of life on the emptiness of the sea bottom. Swim for a mile in any direction, and, unless you found another wreck, the only life you'd see would be starfish and bottom worms.

Garvey was after lobsters. He was looking into the fuselage, just behind the engine cowling, probing with his light. He carried a mesh bag to hold any lobsters he caught. I noticed that the bag was still empty.

I looked down at my hand where it gripped the frame of the airplane. There was a small octopus curled up in the cavity of the wing; a single, improbably dark eye fixed on me. There was no menace in the eye; just the deepest curiosity you could imagine.

Unlikely, I thought, that Garvey would find any lobster on this wreck. The octopus would have gotten them first.

I looked around on the bottom until I'd found a fairly large clam. I picked it up in one hand and used the pommel of my knife to crush the shell. I picked the meat out of the shattered shell and, moving my hand very slowly, offered it to the octopus.

The black oval of its eye stayed on me while the rubbery plasma of its body seemed to draw in on itself. I expected it to shoot ink but, after a second or two, the octopus relaxed. I moved the clam closer, then dropped it. An arm shot out and took the clam as it drifted on some invisible current.

The octopus drew back into the wing cell, but I could see its beak devouring the clam. After a minute, the octopus moved a few inches in my direction, as though to see if I had something else for it to eat. I held out my hand. One of the long, rubbery arms came toward it, hesitantly, then withdrew. Encouraged, I moved my hand a little closer.

But I was too abrupt. The octopus drew back in alarm and released a cloud of coal-colored ink for concealment. I let go of the wing and swam on.

We stayed down for forty minutes. I still had plenty of air, but the tables say forty minutes at eighty feet or you get saturated with nitrogen and, when you come up, you have the bends, unless you stop to decompress. The tables are very conservative, but more and more in these things, so am I. Forty minutes was fine.

I climbed up the swim ladder and into the cockpit, got rid of my gear, and was toweling off just as Garvey came over the transom.

"Pretty lively," he said, "except for lobster. I didn't see a single one."

I told him about the octopus while he got out of his gear.

"Well," he said, "that'll do it every time. I don't believe even I like to eat lobster as much as an octopus does."

"Do you like to eat octopus?" I said.

"Used to. But then I got to know a few. You know, see the same one over and over on a dive site. Start feeding it and pretty soon I'd swear that the thing *recognized* me. I don't know, I just don't feel right about it anymore. And I'll eat a steak in a minute. Any kind of fish that swims. But an octopus . . ."

"I know." Another diver had told me once that an octopus only lives one year, and that he thought if they lived twenty years, or even ten, they might figure a way to communicate with humans. Because they were plainly *trying*.

"Tell you what I will eat, though," Garvey said. "And that's some Popeye's chicken. How about you?"

"And a beer?"

"What could be better?"

So we sat on the flybridge, eating cold chicken and drinking cold beer from the bottle. We threw the chicken bones over the side. The beer tasted especially good on the back of my dry throat.

We talked about the wreck and the things that were living on it. Other wrecks. Other dives. Aimless talk; the sort of talk that doesn't serve any purpose other than to fill up a silence and pass some time.

I tried hard, though, to hold up my end and to fill my share of the silences. If Garvey was talking, then maybe he wasn't thinking.

I did all right for a while. Held up my end. But then I let my eyes wander off and start picking out stars and looking for constellations, and in the lull I could almost feel Garvey's thoughts going back to his child and his other troubles. He stopped talking, too.

I tried to get it started again when I saw the sudden white slash of a fairly bright meteor flame across the horizon.

"You see it?" I said.

"Yep," he said. "Maybe it's a sign we ought to get our worthless asses back to the beach."

CHAPTER 17

Loftin was right on time.

"Mr. Loftin," Semmes said, holding out his hand, "I'm Nat Semmes. I appreciate your coming by like this. Everybody is so busy these days, I know it can't have been convenient for you."

Semmes sounded like a half-bright country boy with no special talent except, possibly, for bullshit.

Loftin shook his hand warily and looked around the room. Even though he was trying to keep his face unreadable, you could see that the office disappointed him. This was the sort of office where he would expect to find a moderately successful ambulance chaser, not a lawyer of Semmes's reputation.

Semmes introduced me as his associate and I shook Loftin's hand. He was fairly tall, with narrow shoulders and a trim waist. He wore a light gray pinstriped suit that wasn't cheap and a very good quality cotton shirt that he might even have picked up in London. The tie was a loud paisley and I suspect he had selected it with care. It was meant to make a small but unmistakable statement. Namely, that while he was a serious high-end lawyer, he also had an unconventional streak. The tie was for the women.

His hair was carefully styled in that look where every strand is carefully molded to your head, plastered there by some kind of grease. He had a thin, humorless mouth and watery, weak, calculating eyes.

"Take a chair," Semmes said. "Can I get you some coffee? I made it myself, but it's not too bad."

"Cream," Loftin said, "no sugar."

Semmes stepped over to the sideboard and filled a mug from the percolator, slowly added some milk, and then lazily stirred it. Nobody said anything. The air in the room felt the way it does when you're out on the water and a thunderstorm is about to break, with the ions so agitated that the hair on your arms stands up and you can smell the ozone.

Semmes came back across the room and handed Loftin his coffee, then took his time about getting around the desk. He sat down slowly. Put his elbows on his desk and folded his hands in front of his face, with his index fingers forming a steeple.

He looked at Loftin across the top of the steeple.

"Mr. Loftin, we've got a . . . well, a *situation.*" Semmes almost sounded apologetic. "And I thought it would be to everybody's advantage if we could sit down here and talk about it before things went any further and caused any additional distress."

"A situation?" Loftin said.

Semmes nodded and continued to look at Loftin from over the tops of his fingers as though they formed a gunsight.

"Yes," he said. "I'm afraid so. It seems you have filed a

criminal complaint against Mr. Philip Garvey. For assault."

"That's right," Loftin said.

"And you have also undertaken to serve Mr. Garvey in a civil action relating to the same episode."

"Right again."

"Well, Mr. Loftin, it looks to me like you and Mr. Garvey had a little . . . ah, disagreement. Sort of thing that happens, now and then, between men. Especially proud men who have a little temper. I believe I detect a little temper in you. Now, it seems to me that the thing to do after one of these little dust-ups is to forget about it. There's no real need to bring the courts into it. They're busy enough, God knows."

"Did you bring me in here to talk about a settlement?" Loftin said with a thin, satisfied smile.

"Well, actually, yes. That's exactly what I asked you to come in and discuss."

"You're representing that dive bum?"

"Mr. Garvey, you mean," Semmes said. "Yes, I am. Philip Garvey is my client. Now, would you be interested in discussing some form of settlement?"

"Depends." Loftin sounded confident. He believed Semmes had asked him here to make an offer. He also believed he was in a position to make some heavy demands.

"Depends on what?" Semmes said. "What sort of things would interest a man in your business?"

"You know the answer to that question already," Loftin said smugly, leaning back in his chair. "Since we're in the same business."

Semmes narrowed his eyes so that he looked more than ever like he was drawing a bead on Loftin. "No," he said. "We're not in the same business. I'd pick crabs for a living before I'd be in your business."

"Oh. What business are *you* in?"

"Well, I like to think I make my living by stomping on cockroaches—like you."

"Yeah?"

"Yeah," Semmes said, mimicking him. "I do a pretty fair job, but I can't keep up. The roaches breed faster than I can stomp. But I'm going to stomp the living shit out of you, friend."

Loftin smiled. "Make me an offer or see me in court," he said.

"All right," Semmes said, "here's my offer. If you'll drop all your charges, civil and criminal, against Phil Garvey, then I won't ruin you."

"That's it?" Loftin was almost leering.

"Right. You can keep right on doing business. Only you can't do any business on Garvey."

"That's very generous of you."

"I'm a Christian man."

"Well, that's real fine," Loftin said.

Semmes nodded.

"Just one thing, if you don't mind my asking."

"Not at all."

Loftin smiled. He was enjoying the game. Feeling good about the hand he was holding and sensing that it might be possible to beat Nathaniel P. Semmes of the gaudy reputation. "Would it be too much for me to ask *how* you're going to ruin me? I mean, does your associate here have some incriminating pictures of me with a dog or a goat I'm not married to?"

"We wouldn't stoop to anything like that," Semmes said. "Like I said, I'm a Christian man."

"So?"

"Well," Semmes said, "if you don't completely back out of Phil Garvey's face and pay him a small sum for the grief you have already caused him, then I am going to have you in court for informing on him to the Coast Guard in a malicious, false, and unlawful fashion. And I expect the federal prosecutor will charge you for making false statement to a government agency. He's a friend of mine and I think I know him pretty well."

Loftin looked stunned.

"He probably won't get anywhere," Semmes went on, "but it will be enough to get disbarment proceedings started. And you are really going to feel the heat when I come on with a civil suit in which I will charge that you attempted, by speaking slander to the Coast Guard, to ruin Mr. Garvey and his business. I will point out that Mr. Garvey is a highly decorated veteran who was forced to leave the service due to injuries sustained in combat. That he has never been charged with any kind of crime in his life. That he has a wife and two children. And that a spiteful, dishonest worm of a lawyer who has never served any cause in his entire life, except himself, spread lies about Garvey in order to satisfy his own little pissy ends."

Semmes lowered his arms and rose about halfway out of his chair. He looked down at Loftin and shook his head, almost in pity.

"You know," he said, "I've been trying cases in front of juries in these parts for a long time now. Had some success at it, too. I know how to talk to these people. I understand what gets their juices flowing. And I honestly don't believe you'd have a chance in hell against me, little man."

The color had been flushed from Loftin's face and his eyes were wide with alarm.

"That Coast Guard material is . . . confidential information."

"Is that what they told you?"

Loftin nodded mutely.

"I had reasonable suspicions."

"It'll be fun, when we get into court, to hear about them."

"I know the law . . ."

"Going to do you a hell of a lot of good, isn't it, once you've been disbarred?"

Loftin shook his head in disbelief.

"Well," Semmes said, "you've heard my offer. Why don't you take some time to think it over. I'll give you until noon. If I haven't heard from you by then, I'm going to the feds."

When Loftin tried to say something, Semmes slammed his hand down hard on the desk. Then he looked at Loftin and said, "I don't have to listen to any more of your talk, little man. Life is short and we were born to suffering. But I draw a line. You come back around at noon and sign. Otherwise . . . well, I believe I'll see *you* in court."

Loftin stood slowly and left the room, as shaky as a man who has just learned that the biopsy came back positive.

CHAPTER 18

SEMMES WAS LEANING BACK IN HIS chair with his feet on his desk. He was holding a stag-handled letter opener in one hand and nervously slapping the palm of his other hand with the flat side of the blade.

"You think he'll take the deal?" he said.

"I think he'd crawl over ground glass to take the deal," I said.

"Me too. That's a little less on Garvey's shoulders. He still has a lot to tote, but it's something."

"His wife sounded optimistic about the kid."

Semmes stopped slapping his hand with the letter opener and looked at me.

"Really?"

"That's what she told me over the phone. I didn't get the medical details."

Semmes said nothing for a moment. "Well, now . . . that is some *good* news. You want to go in with me on some flowers? Cut daisies and delphiniums and such? Get them delivered to the hospital?"

"Sure," I said. It was like Semmes to think of it.

He flipped through his Rolodex and found the number he wanted. While he was dialing, I looked out the window at the calm green water of the bay and the Gulf out beyond the barrier island. The sky was a kind of tender blue color with only a few inconsequential clouds. I thought I might drive out to the beach when I finished here. Take a swim, get some sun, run a few miles in the hard sand at the edge of the surf. The day had that kind of feel to it.

"Well," Semmes was saying, "you just do your usual beautiful work, Paula, and charge it to my account. Thirty dollars' worth, okay?"

Semmes paused, then said, "Thanks a lot, Paula. Bye."

When he hung up the phone, I reached across the large desk and handed him a ten and a five.

"I could take it out of your fee," he said.

"What fee?"

"The fee you earned going around talking to all those people who'd been boarded by the Coast Guard's press gangs. You know, Morgan, the fee that I pay you for working."

"What's your fee to Garvey?"

He shook his head and used the stag-handled letter opener to push the ten and the five back my way.

"Pro bono," he said. "That's Latin for a free lunch."

"Me too," I said, and pushed the money back across his desk. "It was my case from the jump. I ought to be paying you."

"*Excrementum equorum*," Semmes said. "That's Latin for horseshit."

We argued without much conviction for a few minutes. It was an old discussion. I didn't like to take money from Semmes, especially on jobs where I knew he didn't make any. And he didn't like for me to work for no money. After one of these discussions, he'd set up an account where all my fees went. Everything was taxed at the top rate and the forms came to me and I threw them in with all the other dismal paperwork that accumulates like barnacles on your life. Semmes even made provisions for the money in the event of my death. He was horrified to learn I had no will. The idea that my vast holdings would fall into the hands of the government offended something in him. So he made out a simple will for me and we had it executed. Now, when I cross over the river, my estate will be divided, after the government takes its bite, among Ducks Unlimited, the Nature Conservancy, and a little obscure outfit that works with Vietnamese-American kids. Your death, they say, ought to count for something, and I suppose that mine now would.

"Nat," I said, "I don't know what a good lawyer gets paid these days. Couple of hundred an hour, anyway, I'd guess. So it's costing you money to sit there arguing about fifteen bucks. Why don't you just stick it in your pocket and get back to work?"

"All right," he said, finally, and picked up the two bills, bringing that little ritual to a close. "But you are a hard-headed sonofabitch, Hunt. Worst I've ever seen."

I spent the afternoon on a strip of protected beach west of Pensacola pass. I had a long stretch of white sand all to myself and I stayed there until late afternoon. I caught a couple of pompano in the surf. Jessie would like that. Like a lot of people from New Orleans, she thinks pompano is the finest fish that swims. I think it's a little oily, but, as Jessie likes to remind me, what do I know?

I ran to the old fort at the mouth of the bay, swam a half-mile or so, and read a few pages from a book by Harry Crews, a Florida writer I have always liked. I drank two cans of beer and slept facedown on my towel for a while. When I woke up, I had a headache and a sunburn.

I walked back to my truck feeling vaguely useless and wondering how those college kids over in Panama City, Daytona, and Fort Lauderdale could do it for an entire week. Matter of desire, I suppose. Like the coaches say, you got to want it *bad.*

I drove back to the river house, parked under the live oak, and went around back to clean my fish. Then, for some reason, I decided to check the phone machine first. I suppose I was hoping that Jessie might have called.

No such luck.

But Semmes had. And he wanted me to get back to him, even if it meant calling him at home.

His wife answered in her usual cheerful, lilting voice.

"Hello, Bobbie," I said. "This is Morgan Hunt."

"Well, where have *you* been?" she said. "It's been *months.*"

"Here and there," I said. "How are you?"

"I'm fine, Morgan," she said. "Now I know you called to talk to Nat, but don't you always be a stranger, hear?"

"I won't."

She covered the phone but I could still hear her call, "Honey, it's for you. It's Morgan. Ask him for dinner sometime."

Standing there alone in my twenty-room house, I felt a touch of envy for what Nat Semmes had.

Maybe in my next life.

"Thanks for calling," Semmes said. "You catch any fish?"

"A couple of pompano," I said. "Did you run into a snag with Loftin?"

"Not exactly. He came back by the office about fifteen minutes early. He'd gathered himself up considerably so he didn't look like the guest of honor at a hanging anymore. He said he was prepared to sign my papers for-swearing forever his right to legal remedies in the matter of Philip Garvey and so on and so forth. And he was willing to go down to the sheriff's office and drop his charges against Garvey. He would even pay a little money to Garvey to compensate him for any distress." Semmes paused, sounding a little puzzled, as though it had been too easy.

"But?"

"Well, he just had one small condition. He wanted to talk to Garvey, face to face, before he did any of those other things."

"Maybe he's a masochist," I said, "overdue for an ass-whipping."

"That," Semmes said, "is one possibility that never oc-curred to me. Anyway, he called Garvey from my office and explained the situation. Asked if they could meet somewhere and talk for a few minutes. He made the ap-pointment and then he left my office. An hour later, he was back to sign the papers. He had a cashier's check for five thousand dollars made out to Garvey."

"You talk to Garvey?" I said.

"He called here to thank me. He said some . . . oh, I don't know, *touching* things about how much it meant to him and his family to be out of that trouble and how much he owed me. He wanted me to take the five thousand as my fee."

"You ask him what Loftin said?" I could guess how he'd reacted to Garvey's suggestion about the five thousand.

"I gave him an opening," Semmes said. "It wasn't my place to press it."

"What did he say?"

"That it wasn't anything. Loftin just wanted to apologize

face to face and explain that he'd been under a lot of stress."

"That's it?"

"Pretty much."

"That doesn't sound like our boy Loftin," I said.

"No," Semmes said.

"I don't suppose it makes any difference," I said. "The point is, Garvey is out of it."

"Right."

"But something about it . . ."

"Right."

"I imagine I ought to talk to Garvey," I said.

"Whatever you think best," Semmes said. "And by the way."

"Yes."

"Cook those pompano over hot coals with no butter or oil. They're oily enough already."

"Thanks."

"My pleasure," he said. "I'll talk to you in the morning."

CHAPTER 19

I DIDN'T TALK TO GARVEY LIKE I'D SAID I would. I tried. Called a couple of times and left messages, but he never called me back. I talked to Rachel, who told me that Rick was coming along. She sounded strong and hopeful. When I asked about Phil, she said that he was working hard, spending most of his time at the shop or out on the boat. She sounded more concerned about him than about Rick.

"It's been hardest on him," Rachel said. "He acts like it's his fault sometimes. You know what I mean, Morgan."

I said I did.

"I almost wish he'd go to church. But I don't ever remember him going. He needs to realize how much he has to be thankful for."

We all do, I thought.

"Anyway," she said, "thanks for calling."

"Phil will come around," I said.

"I know," she sighed. "He's just not used to situations

he can't dominate. Doesn't understand when will and strength aren't enough."

She understood her man, I thought. Phil was lucky that way.

Meanwhile, Semmes was deep in cases that didn't need my kind of talent, so there wasn't much for me to do. But Jessie had come back from her conference. She appreciated the pompano I'd caught but wouldn't let me cook them the way Semmes had recommended. She did them with white wine and shrimp sauce, and it was as good as anything I've ever put in my mouth There was nothing else for it but to catch a few more, so we spent a lot of afternoons on the beach. Now and then we would stay out after the sun went down and build a driftwood fire and lie on a blanket watching the flames pop blue and green from all the minerals that had soaked into the wood. We even spent one night on the beach, wrapped up in the blanket and watching the stars until we went to sleep. We woke up as the sun climbed out of the Gulf, all wet and gold, like something forged by gods.

They were good days, and I hardly even missed the action. I probably would have gotten bored if it had gone on forever; but then, I was in no big hurry for it to end.

I still hadn't heard anything from Garvey and was beginning to suspect it might be a long time. If ever. I would remind him that he'd needed help once, and that wouldn't sit easy with him. I'd need to find another diving partner, I thought, but I'd live. Garvey was a buddy and, in this life, they come and they go.

Then, late one afternoon, while I was reframing a door in one of the upstairs bedrooms, I heard somebody coming up the drive, crushing oyster shells.

I was expecting Jessie but it was still a little early. That didn't necessarily hold her back, though, so I put down the tools and went down to the porch, wiping off the sweat and sawdust.

Phil Garvey's truck was parked next to mine, under the live oak. He was standing at the foot of the steps, looking out at the river. He heard me step out on the porch, turned, and smiled with more animation than I'd ever seen in his face.

"Morgan," he said. "How are you doing, man?"

"Good, Phil. How about you?"

"Never better," he said. "Never better. The sun has finally decided to shine on this old dog's ass."

"That's great, Phil," I said, and I meant it.

"Rick is off all the tubes and even moving around a little. He's going to be all right."

"That's the best news of all," I said.

"If you'll give me a cold beer," he said, "I'll tell you all about it. There's something I want to show you."

So I went inside and fished two bottles from the refrigerator. He took his, raised it ceremonially, and said, "Luck. If that's what it takes, then I'll take it every time."

We both drank a swallow. It tasted good after the work I'd been doing.

We walked around to the side of the house and sat on a step that overlooked the river. It was low and hardly seemed to be moving.

Garvey took off his glasses and looked out at the river. There was something a little different about his eyes. The change was not radical or shocking, but it was there and I noticed it. Mingled with the seriousness that had always been there was something new. Something a little secretive and calculating.

"Morgan, I've got a lot of faults, but ingratitude is not one of them."

"If you say so."

"I do," he said, "and I'm here to prove it."

He reached in his back pocket and pulled out a plain white envelope, folded neatly in half.

"Here," he said.

I took the envelope and, even knowing what was in it, I was surprised by the amount. A cashier's check for five thousand dollars.

"Phil . . ."

He held up his hand and said, "I know what you're going to say before you say it. So you listen to me first."

"All right."

"You bailed me out, Morgan, and now I can pay you back. It would mean a lot to me if you would just cash that check and not give me a lot of grief about it."

I thought about it for a moment. I knew what he meant. I'd been through the same drill with Semmes.

"Can you tell me anything about it, Phil? You hit the lottery or something?"

"What you want to know," he said, "is . . . am I doing something dirty, right? Like maybe I really am the kind of guy the Coast Guard should be boarding and searching."

I nodded.

"No drugs, Morgan. Not ever. I might do that, if I had to, for my son. But if it was drugs, I wouldn't be able to come out here and give you the money. You understand that?"

"Sure," I said. "Absolutely."

"It's legal," he said and drained his beer. "My part of it is, anyway. And that's all I'm worried about. It's a lot more legal and legitimate and a lot cleaner than the way that man was running his bank when I went to him for money and he loaned it to me and then almost ruined me."

"All right," I said.

"If you'll get me another brew, Morgan, I'll show you something and tell you all about it."

"Okay."

"Put that check someplace safe and get yourself another one, too. This will take some telling."

I went inside while Garvey walked to his truck. When I got back and handed him his beer, he was sitting on the step, holding a small purple velvet bag, the kind people use to protect their valuable jewels. Going by the way he held it, whatever was inside the bag was very heavy.

"Thanks," he said when I handed him the beer. He held out the little purple bag and said, "Take a look at this."

It was even heavier than I had expected. Heavy enough that the shapeless thing inside could have been lead.

I loosened the little gold-colored drawstring at the top and shook out the contents into the palm of my hand.

It looked like a biscuit, shaped from a lumpy dough and ready for the oven. Maybe three inches across and an inch thick, more oblong than circular. It was a dull, metallic color and the edges had been rounded in a rough fashion, the way a kid might use his thumbs to smooth out something he had molded from clay. I let it rest in the palm of my hand, where it felt ponderous and strangely dead.

"What is it?"

"Silver," Garvey said, almost reverently. "Pure silver."

"You need to hit it with a Blitz cloth," I said. "It's a little tarnished."

"That," Garvey smiled, "is because it has been at the bottom of the sea for about four hundred years now."

*　　*　　*

I didn't say anything for a moment while I let my mind work on that. Then, I said, "Sunken treasure?" It sounded a little melodramatic, even though I didn't mean for it to.

"That's what it is," Garvey said in the same tone. "Sunken treasure."

I turned the heavy biscuit over in my hand. There was small figure cut into one side, near the edge. A cross and something that could have been the letter C or the crescent shape of a new moon. Very faint. Worn down by all that time in seawater.

"Where did it come from?" I said. When you have a lot of questions, best to start with the most basic. I already knew what it was. Now I would find out where it came from. Sooner or later, I would find out how Garvey had gotten involved.

"Probably came from some Indian mine down in Mexico or Costa Rica. The Spanish stole it and were carrying it back to the mother country when they hit a patch of bad weather."

"And you found it?" There were people all up and down the Gulf Coast who knew about the wrecks of treasure ships and dreamed of finding them. Some of them worked very hard at it, with all the latest technology. Now and then, somebody actually found something to justify all the expense. They all dreamed of hitting the big score, the way Mel Fisher had, down in Key West, after nearly twenty years of looking, which cost his investors millions, and Fisher's son his life. Fisher claimed the remains of a Spanish treasure ship called the *Atocha*. Gold, silver, emeralds, and relics worth, according to the news accounts, more than a hundred million dollars. Fisher had said it was worth all that he'd gone through and lots of people believed him.

I would never have figured Garvey for one of those people. He didn't even seem like the type to buy a lottery ticket with the grocery change.

"Yes," he said decisively. "I found it."

I wrapped my fingers around the silver biscuit.

"Well, I'll be goddamned," I said.

Garvey smiled and took the silver slab from my hand. "Me too," he said.

"I probably shouldn't ask where you found it."

"You might be the one person I *would* tell, Morgan. But you don't want to know. It would just bring the hounds down on you."

"How's that?"

"Who do you think that slab of silver belongs to?"

"If it doesn't belong to the Indians," I said, "then I suppose it has to belong to you . . . or whoever finds it."

"You might think so," Garvey said. "But you'd be wrong. Doesn't belong to the Indians. Doesn't belong to the Spaniards. Doesn't belong to me. Even though we've got the only hands that have touched that chunk of silver in the last four hundred years. No sir, that thing, and anything else that I find—or anyone else finds—on that wreck site is the property of the state of Florida, Department of Antiquities. The attorney general would put my ass in the jail if he knew I had that thing."

"Come on."

"Fact."

I made a face that showed I didn't understand that one.

"I didn't actually find the wreck," he said. "I wish I had, but I didn't."

"Who did?"

He shook his head and said, "People who didn't feel like turning the location and everything on it over to the state of Florida. And who weren't sure how to get the stuff up without people figuring out what they were doing. They needed a diver. Someone who could work at night, swim to the site from a long way off and use a rebreather so there wouldn't be any bubble trail."

"Dangerous?"

"Nah. Strictly routine. Real garbage work, though. Shallow water. Pretty poor visibility. Strong tides. And I'm working at night, without any help. But," he smiled, "the pay is real good."

"Have to be," I said. "So what happens if you get caught?"

"Never happen. There isn't anyone working for the state of Florida who can stay with me . . . especially not underwater, at night."

It was true. I smiled and said, "Be fun to see someone try."

"Yeah boy."

"How about the people you're working for? Would they dump you if they got caught?"

He shrugged. "Maybe. But they're the big fish. I'm just the hired help, doing the heavy lifting. There is a risk in it, but there's a risk in everything. I thought it over and decided to take the risk."

He shook his head and stood up, stretching as though to work out a deep stiffness in his bones.

"I've got all the excuses and I could run them up the pole for the judge if I did get caught," he said. "My boy needs doctors and they don't work for free. Hospitals, CAT scans, chemo—all that stuff costs money. I could look at the judge with big, wet eyes and say that I'm just a poor veteran trying to make it by and I wouldn't never have done nothing illegal, your honor, except for my kid, who needs doctors and medicine."

He raised his arms over his head, clasped his hands and

then lowered his arms, slowly, behind his back. Something in his shoulder made a popping noise.

"That's horseshit, though, top to bottom," he said. "The truth is, I'd have probably done this whether my boy was sick or not. I like the pump. It ain't as good as some things I've done, but it's a whole lot better than most of what I've been doing lately. You know what I mean?"

"Yes," I said. "Believe I do."

He grinned and, as he raised his joined arms back over his head so his shoulder popped again, he said, "That's right. You would."

"I was about to ask you if you needed any help. I've trained on a rebreather and I can swim a compass course at night."

"You serious?"

I shook my head. "I don't have any good stories for the judge. And he probably wouldn't like my resume."

"Too bad."

"You're probably better off working alone," I said. "The more people, the better the odds on a screwup."

He nodded and picked up the little velvet bag that held the heavy silver biscuit.

"Well, I'd like it if I could have you for a partner. I wouldn't worry about screwups then. Otherwise . . . yeah, I believe I'd rather work alone. But let me ask you something, Morgan."

"Sure."

"Am I thinking wrong? I mean, there are some things I wouldn't do just for money. I'd do 'em if it meant saving my boy's life, but not just for money. And, if it got right down to it, there probably isn't anything I wouldn't do if it meant saving my boy's life. You with me?"

"Yes."

"But this thing—I don't know. I'd do it if it was strictly

legal and probably say I was just doing it for the money. I mean, it ain't exactly challenging diving."

"Right."

"But it being illegal, you know, that just makes me want to do it even *more*. I'd probably be willing to do it for less money this way, against the law, than I would if it was legal. You follow what I'm saying?"

"Yes."

"Well, what about it? Does that make sense to you?"

"Absolutely," I said. "That's what treasure is about."

CHAPTER 20

I PUT GARVEY'S CHECK IN A SAFE place—a lead-lined box that weighed about four hundred pounds and was buried under the floor of a shed, where the old captain had used it to keep a summer supply of crystal-blue blocks of ice, each of them weighing one hundred pounds and coated with sawdust for insulation. Since I had electricity, I used the icebox to hide things like my passport, insurance papers, my will, and the odd cashier's check for five thousand dollars.

I didn't feel right about that check. But it meant something to Garvey, so I owed it to him, in a fashion, to go ahead and cash the thing. If I didn't want to spend the money, then I could just give it away. Which wasn't really a bad idea. One of Jessie's land trusts would know what to do with it. Or maybe I could give it to one of the outfits named in my will.

But as a way of putting off doing anything at all about that check, I decided to look into the source of Garvey's new wealth.

I started with the one thing I knew tangibly, the slab of silver. It existed—I knew that much—but was it what Garvey claimed, or had been told, it was? It could have been made last week, from the melted-down remains of some family's wedding silver. It was tarnished, but that didn't mean it had been submerged in salt water for four centuries. It might have been soaked overnight, like a set of false teeth.

There is a university a couple of hours from the river house. Actually, it would be hard to find a place anywhere in Florida that isn't within an hour of some university. Anyone who finds himself in such a remote location can be sure that he's within commuting distance of a junior college, anyway. Florida's vast system of higher education was created back when people still believed that more colleges would inevitably produce a more civilized and cultured population. This was back when people also anticipated a boom in leisure time, an ever-rising standard of living, and an end to communicable disease.

I drove out to the university, which sits, at some 150 feet above sea level, on some of the highest ground in the state. The red-brick buildings are scattered tastefully across a plateau that rises above the Escambia River delta. Stately, hundred-year-old pines grow in the spaces between the buildings. Kids in jams and sandals walk on the thick centipede grass that grows in the shade of the pines. Though it does not appear at all ancient or venerable, you could look at the university and imagine that real learning goes on there and, no doubt, some does. But other things go on there, too. The Florida university system has lately become a killing ground. Coeds, if they're still called that, are in special danger. The monsters who drift up and down the Florida coasts seem drawn to the campuses. Something about those women, their youth and their confidence—

which a twisted mind would see as arrogance and a challenge—excites the juices in those creeps. Ted Bundy, the most celebrated serial killer in United States history, did some of his most gruesome work in a sorority house at Florida State University.

West Florida had been spared anything that lurid. There had been only one unsolved killing on campus in the last year. A fairly straightforward rape and stabbing. Still, the uniformed guard gave me a cold, skeptical look when I stopped and asked for directions.

"Are you a visitor here?"

"Yes."

"What's the nature of your business?"

I suppose I could have told him that I was a taxpayer, out checking on how my money was being spent. The Florida university system does not deny itself many comforts. But I wasn't up to it. Anyway, the guard paid taxes, too, and had as much reason to resent the lush campus as I did . . . maybe more.

"I'm here to see Professor Horan," I said. "I have an appointment, if you want to check."

"That's all right," he said. "I'll trust you. Just don't steal any paintings." There had been stories in the papers about the expensive artwork the university was buying to decorate the offices of presidents, deans, provosts, and such.

"I promise," I said, and parked in a lot outside the building that housed the small archaeology department. I found my way to Horan's office, at the end of a corridor of glass display cases filled with what looked like Indian relics.

"Yes," said the voice that answered my knock.

I opened the door and said, "It's Morgan Hunt, professor. I called for an appointment."

"Sure. Come on in."

Horan sat behind a moderately cluttered desk in a high-backed swivel chair covered with something designed to suggest leather. He was a thin man with an alert face, half of which was hidden behind a beard. A lot of the rest was hidden behind the thick lenses of a pair of steel-rimmed glasses. He was wearing a faded khaki work shirt and old jeans. He looked edgy and impatient. Also friendly. I imagined him as one of those vaguely evangelical teachers, the kind all the students like and the rest of the faculty resents, then punishes for not publishing a sufficient number of unreadable journal articles.

"Sit down," he offered. "I don't have anything to drink here in the office, but there are some machines down the hall."

"Nothing for me, thanks," I said.

"Then what can I do for you, Mr. Hunt? I thought I recognized the name when you called. But just saying that you were an investigator didn't tell me much, you know."

I nodded.

"So I went to the library and looked you up. You've been in the papers a lot. And the man you work for . . . Semmes?"

"That's right."

"He's all over the papers. The Clarence Darrow of the Panhandle, I'd say."

"Not exactly," I said.

"Oh?"

"Semmes would never have taken Leopold and Loeb," I said.

Horan smiled at that. "No, from the stories I read—there was even one in the *American Lawyer*—he likes *poor* losers."

I nodded again.

"Do they have to be innocent?" Horan said.

"Not necessarily. But it helps."

"What is the rule, then?"

I had thought about that a lot since I first got to know Semmes, back when I was one of his clients. I surely wasn't innocent. I had been convicted of murder and I had killed a man, no question about it. My victim was one of those who'd been born rich and never had occasion to learn that some things were not permitted to you, even if you were a Coca-Cola heir and could ski, play tennis, shoot, and get your picture into magazines that breathed wet and heavy over people with trust funds and no other visible means of support.

"Semmes is a lawyer," I said, carefully, "who believes that the law is not perfect. And that it is getting more imperfect every day. He does what he can to help people who are victims of that trend."

"Going by what I read, he's been very successful at it."

"He works hard," I said. Which was true, but only a small part of the story.

Horan nodded. "And you work for him."

"Yes."

"Are you working for him now?"

"Not exactly."

"Are you working for someone else?"

"No. I'm doing something that involves a friend."

"Well, I'm sorry to hear that."

"Why?"

"I'd been sort of hoping that this would be a break for me," he smiled. "Get me into something exciting. At least a gig as an expert witness. Excuse the terrible pun, but after a while, relics can start to seem a little old."

I smiled. Tolerantly.

"Ever since you called, I've been fantasizing about working for the great Nathaniel Semmes on one of his cases. Compared to going out on another dig, that seems like real action. You know what I mean?"

I nodded. I understood about the action.

"Ah well," Horan said. "Maybe another time."

"We'll be sure to call you," I said, "first time we need an archaeologist."

He enjoyed that and smiled.

"I'll hold you to it," he said. "In the meantime, how can I help you?"

"It's about a piece of silver," I said. "A large piece of silver. It appears to be pretty old."

I described the slab of tarnished metal that I'd held and examined. Horan looked straight at me and nodded. When I came to the part about the marking, he took a notebook off his desk and sketched something on a blank page. He had a good hand and with a few quick strokes had drawn the cross and crescent very accurately.

"Like that?" he said, holding up the notebook.

"Exactly."

"Obviously you don't have the silver billet with you."

"No."

"But you saw it?"

"And held it."

"Heavy?"

"Like lead."

"The person who was showing you this piece of silver, did he have some kind of proposition?"

"Not exactly."

"That's good."

I asked him what he meant by that and he nodded again, tossed the notebook back on the desk, then put his hands behind his head and locked them there while he talked.

"The markings you described—they were very accurate. You'd make a good detective."

I smiled politely and he went on.

"That's a mint mark. When the Spaniards were energetically plundering the continent, they established crude mints where gold and especially silver could be melted down to form rough billets like the one you saw. Each mint had its own mark pressed into every billet. The Spanish were real bastards as occupiers—cruel tyrants and absolute shits—but they were compulsive administrators. They kept very good, elaborate records on the loot they were sending back to Spain. They knew how much was produced by a mint between the sailings of treasure fleets. They knew how much each fleet carried. They knew how much made it across the Atlantic. They didn't know how much contraband was smuggled aboard their ships, but they had a very accurate count of the legal cargo.

"This mark comes from a mint in Panama where they worked a lot of the silver they stole from the Indians in what is now Honduras and Costa Rica. A very large shipment from that mint left on a fleet under the command of a man named De Luna, in the early sixteenth century— 1546, I believe it was. I'll have to check.

"De Luna sailed up the Gulf along the Yucatán, around Texas, and then on to this coast. He was stopping here and there along the way, taking on more cargo. He got here in the early summer and stopped to do a little maintenance on his vessels before he went on down to Cuba and then made the hard crossing. This was a good port, one of the best on the Gulf Coast, and there were lots of big tall trees that were full of pitch. Good materials for his shipwrights to do their work. Also, there were Indians here during the summer and he could trade with them, even though they never really had much worth trading for.

"De Luna must have had the old *mañana* disease, though, because he hung around for most of the summer. Wonder most of his men didn't get the fever. Anyway, they made it through and were just about to sail. But they had forgotten one thing—or, more accurately, they had never really known it."

"What's that?" I said when he paused and looked at me, probably to see if I was still paying attention. Teacher's trick.

"They forgot about hurricane season. Or, like I say, maybe they didn't know there was a season for those storms. Probably they thought they just brewed up according to God's will or His whim or something. They had God instead of meteorology back then. Just about everything came down to God. I believe it was for His glory that they ripped off the Aztecs and Incas.

"So, when the hurricane hit here, they weren't prepared. Part of the fleet had already started out for Cuba and made it through pretty much all right. The ships that had stayed behind and were going to catch up later just disappeared. Nobody knows if they had left the harbor and were on their way south or if they were still inside and got caught at anchor. There were only half a dozen ships, but one of them was loaded to the gunwales with treasure—hundreds of billets of silver like the one you saw. All gone."

He stopped again, unlocked his hands from behind his neck, and gave me the look to see if I was still paying attention.

"And," I said, "people have been looking for that wreck ever since, right?"

"Exactly. The Spanish came up here from Cuba and drowned God knows how many Indians sending them down in the bay to look for the wreck. After a couple of hundred dead Indians, they decided that the ships must have made it to deep water before they sank. They didn't have any deep-diving Indians so they gave up.

"But that wasn't the end of it. People have been looking

for that ship for almost four hundred years now. Nobody has a real good idea of where to look, so it isn't easy. Every now and then you'll hear about somebody who claims to have come across the diary of a survivor who went to live with the Indians. According to the stories—and there are a lot of variations—the diary marks the spot, with land bearings, where the ships were riding at anchor when the storm came up. You start looking and widen the search until you find a half billion dollars' worth of gold, silver, precious stones, and relics."

"But," I said, "it hasn't happened so far."

"No. And a few years ago a couple of swashbucklers who called themselves treasure salvers came in here saying they were going to put an end to the suspense once and for all. They had a diary that they claimed had been certified as authentic. I don't know how and they weren't saying. But they were pretty confident. Unbearably so, as a matter of fact.

"They had side-scan sonar and magnetometers, and some kind of super dredging apparatus that would just vacuum the bottom. They ran into a problem, though. There's so much old iron and various scrap on the bottom of the bay that a thirty-by-ten-foot cache of silver could hide among the old car bodies and scuttled timber barges. They made so many hits with the mag, they couldn't check them all out. They ran out of money before they even got to try out that sexy dredge."

"So the ship—and the treasure—is still down there?"

"Maybe," Horan said. "Or maybe it's in three or four hundred fathoms out in the De Soto Canyon, a hundred miles offshore. Nobody has ever found anything to prove that ship is even in the bay. Those diaries are probably phonies."

"How about the silver with the mint mark?" I said.

"What would it prove if you found one of those billets?"

He smiled like a debater who had just cinched an argument. "Nothing."

I gave him a look.

"Did you find it?" he asked.

"No."

"Was there more than one?"

I thought about my conversation with Garvey. It had been long on sensation and short on content.

"I don't know," I said.

"Finding one—that might not mean anything at all. The Spaniards traded some of those things to the Indians. And the Indians probably stole some. There were a fair number in circulation before that ship disappeared. If you found just one—or even a half dozen—on the bottom of the bay, they could have sunk there when an Indian canoe rolled over. There are a lot of possibilities."

"And they could have sunk there when the ship went down."

"That," he said, "is one of the possibilities."

"What do you think the odds are?" I said.

He shrugged. "That ship is *somewhere*. We know that. There is a lot of water it can be hiding under, just in that bay, if that's where it is. And it might be somewhere else. You say the person who found that billet is a friend of yours?"

"Yes.

"Well," Horan said, leaning forward and smiling with the satisfaction that comes to a teacher at the conclusion of a successful lecture, "if I were you, I'd tell him to hang on to his day job."

CHAPTER 21

I DROVE FROM THE CAMPUS OUT TO GAR-vey's shop, but it was locked up tight, and there was no note on the door. When he left for charters, he usually had someone come in to run the cash register and take in tanks that needed to be filled. I wondered if he'd just given up on his business now that he'd found treasure. Most people would. But for some reason it disappointed me to see it happen to Garvey.

I drove from his shop to the Outrigger, thinking that maybe I'd catch him working on the boat. But *Second Shot* wasn't there and neither was he. I imagined him out somewhere at anchor, loading bars of silver onto the boat, bringing up as much as he could carry on every dive. But he'd told me he had to work at night.

Maybe he had a charter, I thought. Or just an urge to get out on the water.

It seemed strange, though, that if he was out all night working a wreck site, by himself, he would decide to spend his afternoons on the boat. Be more like him to spend the time at home with Rachel and the kids.

He hadn't seemed entirely like himself the afternoon he came by the river house to show me his bar of silver and give me the cashier's check, but then I couldn't be sure that I'd act like myself if all of a sudden I dove into the middle of one of the richest treasure wrecks in the world. Like everybody, I like to believe that I could handle it. Stay cool, not change anything essential, just dress up a few of the surfaces of my life. Take Jessie to Paris on the Concorde, stop off in London and get fitted for a Purdy shotgun, pick up a mint Cobra to drive on those occasions when a pickup truck wouldn't be quite right . . . a few things like that, but nothing *extravagant*. And, like everybody, I believed that no one else was capable of handling it. I was troubled, in some vague way, about Garvey.

It was nothing I could put my finger on, so I did what I usually do when I'm spinning my wheels. I called Jessie.

"Hello." She had an almost musical way of answering the phone that always gave me a little thrill.

"Say, lady," I said, "would you buy a serviceman a beer?"

"No, young man," she said, "but I will pray for you."

"Forget it," I said. "I've been prayed for already."

"Then I guess I'll have to buy you a beer."

We met at a place not far from the Outrigger. It was called The Reef and overlooked the lagoon. There was a deck where we sat and watched the herons stalking the flats while we drank our beer.

I asked her what sort of day she'd had.

"Hard . . . no, *frustrating*. I believe the whole government is designed to do nothing but make the average, well-meaning citizen feel like going out and kicking a dog."

"Bad?"

"Oh, Morgan, you don't know."

I'd had a little experience with the government, but I didn't want to break in and remind her. I liked listening to her when she was like this. So I sipped the thin beer while she went though the frustrations of her day, trying to get a piece of coastline transferred from the Air Force to her land trust.

"First, we had some four-eyed cold warrior in the Pentagon who thought the property might have future strategic value. He must have believed that the Costa Rican army is going to invade or something. Somebody finally convinced him that the country was probably safe and the government needed our money more than it needed a few hundred acres of sand and saw grass."

She drank deeply from the long-necked bottle and wiped her mouth with the back of her hand, managing somehow to make the gesture feminine and even seductive.

"Then, we got into it with this congressman from over there. One of those old peckerwoods who can't see past the next campaign contribution. He wanted to know why the land should be tied up in trusts instead of sold to local 'bidnessmen' for development.

"You can imagine just who those 'bidnessmen' would be, can't you? Every one of them would have a picture of the congressman on his office wall and would have given as much as the law allows, and maybe more, to his last campaign. Jesus, Morgan, where do we find these people? And how come we keep on electing them?"

"Ask me an easy one," I said.

"Right," she said. "Well, we finally made it clear to the pigheaded congressman that most of the land wasn't suitable for development anyway. And we educated him on the desirability of keeping a portion of the coastal lands undeveloped and relatively inaccessible. And then one of our big contributors told him that if he didn't just drift away, he'd go out and find some hungry young lawyer to run against him next time and raise of couple of million for his war chest."

"So the congressman went away?" I said while she drained her beer.

"Almost instantly," she said and exhaled deeply. "You want another?"

We went inside for two more, and when we got back to our table, one of the wading herons had come up on the beach, not more than thirty feet from the deck.

"One silly-looking bird, isn't it?" Jessie said. "Always made me smile to watch them in the bayou, back home."

She shook her head and drank a little from the fresh bottle.

"Anyway," she said, "we've been talking about my troubles too long. What about you?"

I told her about Garvey and my conversation with the professor.

"You don't think what he found is what he thinks it is— the big load of silver and stuff? Is that what's troubling you, Morgan?" she said when I finished.

I thought for a moment. "That's where it starts," I said. "It just seems too wonderful to me that right when he needs it most, when his child is sick and running up astronomical hospital bills and his business is about to go under, right at that moment Garvey happens to find a sunken treasure ship."

Jessie shook her head, not to disagree but in a way that showed she was skeptical, too.

"That's why I went to see the professor," I said. "I was

hoping he would tell me that the whole thing was impossible and that somebody had salted the bottom with that silver biscuit."

"Why would somebody do that?"

"So Garvey would find it."

"And then what?"

"Then he'd have Phil on a string."

"Why would somebody want that?"

"So he could pull it, I suppose. Get Garvey to do something he wanted done."

"What?"

"Damned if I know."

She nodded and rocked her empty beer bottle back and forth pensively.

"The professor wasn't much help, though," I said. "According to him, it could be that Garvey is on the actual site of a sunken Spanish treasure ship. Or it could be that he's not; that there's an innocent explanation to account for that billet."

Jessie smiled and said, "You were hoping some expert could settle it for you, Morgan. Save you having to do something you don't want to do."

"What's that?"

"You don't want to ask Garvey himself what's going on. Men are funny that way. When they've got a friend who's in trouble, they won't say anything about it unless the friend brings it up first. If his friend said he needed a spare arm, a man would just cut it right off and hand it over. But he would die before he'd ask his friend what's causing him pain. How come that is, Morgan?"

"Like everybody says, men are dumb."

She shook her head. "No, come on. Why? I really admire how men are loyal that way. I think most women do, even if they won't admit it. Women aren't that way. Maybe they save that part of themselves for their children. But I can't figure the other part of it—why a man won't say anything to his friend when he knows he's hurting."

I thought for a second. Thought about another beer or a way to change the subject. Then I said, "I can't speak for all men, but I suppose I don't say anything to Phil because I figure he might tell me to mind my own goddamned business and then never tell me what I want to know. If I wait, he'll tell me when he's ready."

"You respect his pride, then?"

"Yes. I guess that's it."

"You think Garvey would tell you to mind your own business if you said something to him?"

"I don't know," I said. "But if I wanted to ask him, I'd have to find him first.

"He's missing?"

"He's not home and he's not at his shop. His boat is out and I imagine he's on it."

"Working?" she said. "Bringing up some of that treasure?"

"No. He does that at night."

"Then what?"

"I don't know. But it seems like the Garvey I know would be home with his kid, who just had major surgery, and his wife, who could probably use his company . . . even though she's probably tougher than he is."

"I see."

"It's just not like him" I said.

"And you're worried," Jessie said tenderly.

I sighed. "Yes. I suppose I am."

CHAPTER 22

I SPENT THE NIGHT AT JESSIE'S, AND when I got back to the river house the next morning, the little red light on the answering machine was blinking. I looked at it and felt, for some reason, like I was being nagged. So I changed into some shorts and went out to run without playing the tape. It would wait and, anyway, I didn't know anyone who would appreciate a return phone call at five in the morning.

When I got back, I showered outside. Shaved, dressed, and made coffee. It was almost seven when I ran the tape back and the message played.

"Morgan, this is Rachel Garvey. . . . Morgan, have you seen Phil? Or talked to him? Call me please as soon as you get this message. It's midnight and I'm sorry to be calling so late."

That was the only message on the tape. It was followed by a shrill beeping sound, then the hissing of the tape as it rewound.

I picked up the receiver and called Rachel, worried that

she might have already left for work. But she answered, almost desperately, on the second ring.

"This is Morgan," I said.

"Oh, God. Morgan . . . thanks for calling. Have you heard from Phil? Have you seen him? Do you know where he is?"

"No," I said. "I haven't. Not for a few days."

She didn't answer right away and, when she finally did, her voice had a hollow quality. "Morgan, something is wrong. Something is *bad* wrong. He's never done this before. *Never.*"

What I heard in her voice was a sense that she knew she had better brace herself for the worst.

"When do you go to work?" I said.

"I'm taking care of Ricky today."

"I'd like to come by and talk to you," I said.

"All right. Do you think there's anything you can do?"

"We'll see."

It took me about an hour to get to her house. It was a small, undistinguished brick place not too far from the water but not too close, either. The Garveys couldn't afford waterfront, at least not before Phil had discovered treasure.

But the house was as neat and orderly as you would expect the home of two Navy people to be. Everything was in place. Even the magazines on the coffee table were lined up perfectly.

Rachel was pale and her face was drawn tight, puckered around her mouth and eyes. She offered me a cup of coffee, said she had some made, and when she brought it in from the kitchen, the cup quivered, just slightly, in her fingers.

When we were both sitting, I asked her, "How long since you've seen him?"

"Three days," she said. "Four tonight."

"Did he tell you where he was going?"

She hesitated, then said, "He was doing a job for some-one. Salvage diving."

"Did he tell you anything about the job?" I said, trying to make it sound like a routine question. "Any details."

She looked at me. Her face was grim and her eyes were calculating.

"How much did he tell *you?*" she said.

"He told me a lot," I said. "I don't know if it was all of it, but he told me a lot."

"Spanish treasure?"

I nodded. "He even showed me a sample."

"Then you buy it?"

"I don't know. The sample looked real enough. And the expert I described it to said that it could have come from a ship that disappeared in these parts more than four hundred years ago. What about you?" I said. "Do you buy it?"

"I don't know." She shook her head. "I sure wanted to buy it. If that silver had been waiting four hundred years for someone to find it, then it couldn't have picked anyone who needed it more. I spend every minute worried sick. Either I'm worried about whether or not Ricky is going to make it or I'm worried about how we're going to pay for everything he'll need before it's all over.

"I also worry about Phil's business because I know he's having trouble and the bank is after him. I worry about the mortgage. I worry about whether I'll be able to keep working and taking care of Ricky, because even if nurses don't get paid much, we need the money.

"So I guess I sure wanted to buy it when Phil told me about the job and showed me that slab he carried around

in the little velvet jewelry bag. Probably I wanted to buy
it so bad that I did, even though I knew better."

"Why do you say that?"

She shook her head wearily. "Because I knew miracles
don't happen. They don't happen in hospitals and they
don't happen in real life."

I took the last swallow of my coffee, which was now cold
and bitter.

"Did he ever tell you who he was working for?"

"No. He said he couldn't. We screamed a little about
that. That's something we never did . . . never *do*," she
caught herself quickly and firmly. "But the pressure has
been getting to us. Phil said he couldn't tell me because
he'd made a promise to the man he was working for. It
had to be secret because of the state laws. Did he tell you
about that?"

"Yes."

"So I don't know who he was working for or where he
was working."

"He told me it was shallow water."

"Well, that certainly narrows it down, doesn't it?"

I nodded.

"Morgan, you offered to help me. To keep Ben while
Ricky is in the hospital."

"It's still an offer."

She shook her head. "No. But there is something,
Morgan."

I looked at her and waited.

"Would you look for him?"

"Sure."

"I don't know if I'll be able to pay you . . ."

I shook my head, thinking of the check that Phil had
given me. "Not important," I said. "But let me know if

you hear anything. I'll see if I can find out who Phil was working for."

I stood up to let myself out, but she walked with me to the door.

"I'll stay in touch," I said.

"Thanks, Morgan. Thanks very much."

I didn't have any good ideas about where to start, so I drove to the Outrigger on the chance that someone had seen Garvey leave in *Second Shot* and, just possibly, remembered seeing him talking to someone who might be the man I was looking for. It was a reach, but I couldn't think of anything much better.

Things were slow around the marina. It was the middle of the day in the middle of the week. A few of the boat slips were empty, including the one where *Second Shot* was usually berthed. Looking at the empty slip, I felt the way I had coming back from an operation where we'd lost somebody and I had to go through his duffel bag. The man's shaving gear and clothes seemed to hold some last thin remnant of him and you could destroy it by boxing those few items up and sending them to his next of kin.

I felt sure, for some reason, that Phil Garvey was dead. He would be erased when a replacement moved into *Second Shot*'s slip.

I prowled around the Outrigger until I found the man named Pete I had talked to earlier, when I was looking into Coast Guard boardings. He was working on a big outboard with a pair of needle-nosed pliers and a small socket wrench.

His face was a tight knot of rage.

"Rotten sum*bitch*," he was saying when I came into the little shed where he was working.

"Sorry."

"Not you," he said. "I was talking to this goddamned Japanese outboard."

"Poor engine?" I said.

"Nah, hell, it's a *great* engine. Them Ornamentals really know how to build them. But they build 'em so good they think nobody is ever gone to have to work on them. Plus they all got little-bitty hands. There just ain't no way I can get to the sumbitchen fuel filter without skinning my knuckles."

He put down his tools and wiped his hands with an oily rag. There was blood on the knuckles of one hand. He wiped oil into the broken skin.

"So what can I do for you?" he said.

"Answer some more questions," I said. "If you don't mind."

He gave me a long look. The light was bad and his focus had been close and detailed. It took him a while to recognize me.

"Hell, you're the one wanting to know about the Coast Guard boarding people and busting up their boats, ain't you?"

"That's me."

"How'd you do with those bastards? Run any of them into the jail?"

"I did all right," I said. "Not quite that good. But they knew they'd been in a fight."

"Well, good for you, man. You still working on it?"

"No. I'm working on something else now."

As he listened, Pete reached in the back pocket of his oil-stained khakis and pulled out a tin of Skoal. He held it out toward me and said, "Chew?"

"No. Thanks."

"Nasty habit. I've tried 'em all and it's probably the nastiest." He loaded his mouth, then stuck the tin back in his pocket.

"So, how can I he'p you?" he said, working the words around the chew.

"I'm looking for Phil Garvey."

Pete nodded and thought for a moment. Turned his head and spat onto the dirt-and-shell floor of the toolshed.

"He left out of here three or four days ago. I thought maybe he'd gone somewhere to get some work done. Found him another mechanic. Hurt my feelings a little to think that."

"I don't think that's it," I said.

"No?"

I shook my head. "Right now, he's missing."

Pete's mouth turned down at the corners and his whole face seemed suddenly grave.

"No shit."

I nodded.

"Well," Pete said, "whatever it is, it ain't Garvey's fault."

I asked him what he meant.

"You see 'em, all up and down this coast, who shouldn't be allowed anywhere around a boat. They couldn't tell you port from starboard if you gave them three guesses. Dangerous, you know. Dumb and don't have the sense to know it. But Garvey, he knew everything there was to know about that boat and the water where he took it. He's one squared-away dude. If he got in trouble, then it was either some real freak thing—goddamned sea monster or something—or somebody did him in. And it would take some kind of righteous stud to do that because Garvey's nobody to fuck around with. He's been in the SEALs, you know."

"I know."

"He can take care of himself," Pete said.

"He can do that," I agreed.

"So what do you think happened to him?"

"I don't know," I said. "I thought I'd see if you remembered him talking to anybody who wasn't familiar around here. Someone who looked kind of out of place, maybe."

Pete's face had become pensive now. He turned his head again, to spit, then looked back at me, his mouth working slightly around the chew, his eyes gone away a little in thought.

"There was one," he said, after a minute or so. "A real civilian. Wore suspenders, you know, to keep his fucking pants up. Three-hundred-dollar sunglasses. He came out here . . . I can't remember, must have been the same day that Garvey left and didn't come back. Maybe the day before."

"Anything special about him, other than the suspenders?"

Pete spat and said, "Well, I didn't get close enough to see if he had a mole on his right ear or anything like that. All I can tell you is that he was a kind of a skinny shit, like they all want to be these days. Expensive clothes that looked about two sizes too big for him. And the sunglasses and suspenders."

"What kind of car was he driving?"

"Oh, yeah," Pete said. "I should've thought of that. It was one of those goddamned limey wagons for people who wouldn't be seen in a Bronco or a Blazer or an ordinary fucking pickup truck. You know, what do they call them things?"

"Range Rover?"

"Yeah, that's it. A Range Rover. It's for people who want to spend forty or fifty grand on a four-wheel-drive vehicle that won't ever see anything under its tires but pavement."

"Color?"

"Red."

"License?"

"Come on . . ."

"Right," I said. "Anyway, the color is a help."

"But there's probably more than one red Range Rover around," Pete said, "just like there's more than just one rich asshole in the world."

Couldn't argue with that, I thought. But it wasn't exactly a productive line of discussion, so I asked Pete a few more questions. He tried hard but he couldn't remember anything that might help me. He was getting impatient to get back to work on the tight-fitting outboard and I didn't have any reason to keep him from it. I thanked him for his time and was turning away to leave when three men wearing suits came through the door in that way that lets you know they're with the authorities.

"He'p you fellows?" Pete said.

"State Attorney's Office," the lead man said, "Department of Investigations." He reached inside his jacket pocket and produced a leather wallet holding his credentials. He flashed them, but at that range, and in that light, there was no way of knowing what the ID said or who had issued the badge. I suppose the professionalism of the gesture was supposed to convince us he was the article.

It didn't make a big impression on Pete.

"Well, no shit. You boys run an engine too hot? Need me to replace some bearings?"

The three men had come closer, now, and I could make out their very official faces in the gloom of the little shed. One of the men was black, but skin pigment meant less with these three than the inner conviction of authority and toughness that glowed right through the skin.

"We want to talk to you about one of your customers,"

the one in the lead said. Evidently, he was the spokesman. One of his partners was looking me up and down. I looked back at him. He looked away.

"Why? Somebody break the law? You got so many of the goddamned things, it's hard to take a step without breaking one law or another."

The spokesman ignored Pete for a moment, turned in my direction, and said, "Who are you?"

"An American citizen," I said. "Minding my own business."

He glared at me and I imagine I was supposed to melt in a puddle of hot wax. When I stayed upright, he said, "Like I said, I'm a special agent with the State Attorney's Office."

"I'll bet your mama's proud."

The cords in his neck went tight.

"You ever notice," Pete said, spitting a load that just missed the spokesman's shoes, "how goddamned many cops there are these days? Just coming through this one little rinky-dink marina, you've got Coast Guard, the Florida Marine Patrol, Customs, DEA, FBI, and the U.S. Marshals. Those are the boar hogs. We also get sheriff's deputies and special undercover agents. Local cops. Highway patrol boys. And Wackenhut's checking out insurance claims. None of them has ever busted anyone here, or found any evidence to help 'em bust anybody anywhere else, far as I know. But, *hail*, I'm just a civilian, so what do I know. But it sure seems like with all the law hassling all the honest citizens, we still have a lot of goddamned crime."

Nobody said anything for a long, tense moment. Pete spat another load into the dirt, a little further this time from the special agent's feet.

"We'd appreciate some cooperation," the spokesman said, finally. He sounded like a kid being forced to apologize.

One of the other agents shook his head in disgust.

"We don't want to take you away from important business," the spokesman went on, forcing the words through his teeth. "But if you can take a few moments, we'd like to ask you some questions. It might help us in an important investigation."

"*Hail*," Pete said, "then why didn't you say so?"

CHAPTER 23

THE SPOKESMAN, WHOSE NAME WAS
Horton, told us that they were looking for a man named
Garvey who was "known to keep a boat at this marina."

Pete said he pretty much knew that himself. And that
he hadn't seen Garvey for nearly a week.

"What's the problem?" Pete said, spitting out his old
wad and going to the Skoal tin for a fresh load. "He wanted
for something?"

"Yes," Horton said. Grimly.

"Is it all right to ask what for?" Pete said. "Might help
me answer your questions."

"If our information is correct," Horton said, "then Philip
Garvey is in violation of the Florida Antiquities Preser-
vation Act."

"What the fuck is that?" Pete said.

"It's a law to protect archaeological assets and relics from
treasure hunters."

"You mean," Pete said, "that you brought three men out

here to bust somebody for bringing up old anchors and cannonballs out of the bay—*sheeeit.*"

Horton bristled. "We're not interested in cannonballs and ship anchors. Our information is that Garvey has found an ancient wreck site and is plundering it. The site is invaluable from an antiquities standpoint and the treasure that is on it is worth millions."

"Garvey found *that?*"

"According to our information."

"And nobody else could find it."

"That's correct."

"Not even the great state of Florida."

Horton said nothing.

"So it sent you three dickheads out here to steal it away from the man who found it. I'd say that's average for these days."

"Just tell us when you last saw Garvey."

"Four days ago. Maybe five," Pete said happily. "He was leaving in his boat."

"Did you speak to him?"

"Just to say hello."

"He give you any sense of where he was going?"

"Nope."

"Have you ever seen Mr. Garvey return to your marina with relics or artifacts?"

"Seen him bring in a few cannonballs."

"That's all?"

"That's what I said, ain't it?" Pete replied, and spat.

"And you don't have any idea where Garvey is?"

"Nope."

"Well," Horton said, taking a card from his wallet and handing it to Pete, "if you hear from him or he brings his boat back to this marina, we'd appreciate a call."

"Absolutely," Pete said, shoving the card in the pocket where he kept the Skoal.

Horton turned in my direction.

"And you," he said. "Do you know anything about any of this?"

"No," I said. If a friend of mine is in trouble, I will lie to protect him. Every single time.

"You keep a boat here?"

"Not yet," I said. "I just came by to look the place over."

Horton looked at me with the skeptical eye of authority, then turned away and said to Pete, "Where did Garvey keep his boat."

"Slip twenty-six."

"Okay," Horton said to his partners, "let's go take a look."

Pete and I watched them walk out of the shed and into the daylight.

"And we pay the salaries of them sumbitches," Pete said. "That burns my ass like a three-foot flame."

I asked Pete if there was a phone I could use. He said to help myself to the one in the office, so I left him to the clogged-up outboard and his other furies. When I walked across the parking lot, I could see the three agents in their sport coats, all of them with their hands on their hips, standing in a rough semicircle and looking at an empty boat slip as though they were expecting a miracle at any moment.

I dialed Rachel Garvey's number on Pete's office phone. She picked up on the first ring.

"Hello." There was real urgency in her voice.

"It's Morgan. Did some special agent types come by to see you?"

"Yes," she said. "Morgan, what's going *on?*"

"I'm not sure. Not entirely, anyway. But this may not be such a bad thing."

"Morgan," she said, "they've got a warrant for his arrest."

"I know," I said. It meant that the law would be trying hard to find him. An arrest warrant meant a lot more to them than a routine missing-persons complaint from an apprehensive husband or wife. It was the difference between looking for a lost kitten and hunting for a trophy deer.

I tried to explain this to Rachel. Delicately.

"That's the main thing, right now," I said, "to find him."

"But if he's in trouble . . ."

"We'll get him a lawyer. I know a good one. The best in these parts."

"The same one who took care of you?"

"That's right."

"Well," she said, "Phil will be in good hands, that's for certain."

"I'll go talk to him now," I said. I gave her Semmes's number in case she needed to call.

"Thank you, Morgan."

I told her I'd get back to her. Then I hung up and called Semmes at the office. He was in court, his secretary said, but she expected him back at the office during the lunch recess. I said I'd be there and she said she would tell Semmes to expect me.

Turned out I beat him there by ten minutes.

"Well, well," he said when he saw me in the little waiting room outside his office, "business or pleasure?"

"Business," I said.

"Then let's go out and eat one of those business lunches and write off eighty percent of it."

I said that would be fine.

"Give me a couple of minutes."

He checked his messages and made one quick return call, then we rode down the elevator to the street and walked six blocks to Nick's Oyster Bar, where we always went for a business lunch.

We took a table near the back, away from the chaos of the counter, where two oyster openers, three or four waiters, a bartender, and the kitchen help were all shouting at one another like they were on the brink of murder.

The table was dark, heavy oak, so old that the corners had been worn smooth by the pressure of thousands and thousands of elbows.

We both ordered our usual business lunch. A bowl of gumbo and a Dixie beer.

Semmes took a sip off the top of his beer and sighed. "That surely tastes good," he said. "I don't believe there is any thirstier work in the world than persuading a skeptical jury."

I said I'd take his word for it.

"Morgan," he said, "you look like a man with no time for small talk. Maybe you'd better tell me why we're having this lunch."

I started with the evening when Garvey had come by the house to show me his silver treasure. I had made it to the call from Rachel Garvey and my visit with her that morning when the gumbo arrived and we took a break.

Nick's gumbo was thick, dark, and rich. He made it with a roux, the part most restaurants skipped, which Jessie said should be a hanging crime. Nick was generous with the oysters, shrimp, and crabmeat. He also put in some sausage that he made himself. And his gumbo had plenty of green peppers and onions along with the okra. It simmered so long that the flavors were entirely mingled and you could just about eat the stuff with a fork. He also added plenty of pepper—black and red—because, he said, "You don't want your tongue to get bored."

Semmes finished a spoonful or two ahead of me.

"You couldn't get a meal that good at the Four Seasons," he said, "even if you carried a gun."

He asked the waiter for coffee. I ordered another beer.

"So you went back to the marina," Semmes said while we were waiting. "What then?"

I finished the story and Semmes listened with an expression of intense but clinical interest that I knew as well as my own image in the mirror.

He thought for a minute when I had finished, drumming his fingers idly on the table. Then he said, "What's your guess, Morgan?"

"If you were coming in cold, just looking at the physical evidence," I said, "then you'd have to believe that Garvey is on the run."

"Why's that?"

"Mainly his truck, I think."

"What about it?"

"It's not at the marina. It's not at his house. Rachel said he left in the truck five days ago."

"Right."

"The boat is not at the marina. Neither is the truck."

"Has anybody seen the truck at the marina in the last five days?"

I shook my head. I had asked Pete that, and he said he couldn't remember coming in to work in the morning and seeing Garvey's truck in the lot. Not for a couple of weeks, anyway. Garvey had been going out at night, mostly, and coming in before dawn, he guessed.

"The way it looks," I said, "is that Garvey stashed the

truck somewhere and then took off in the boat. If he'd gone to the marina and gone out in the boat expecting to come back, he'd have left his truck parked in the lot."

"You don't believe he's on the run, do you?" Semmes said.

"It just isn't like him," I said.

Semmes spoke carefully. "He could be hiding, Morgan, even if it doesn't seem like the kind of thing he would do. Think about the pressure he'd been under. If he *was* bringing up silver and he had a lot of it, why not run? He gets to keep the silver—or sell it."

I nodded. I'd considered that.

"Maybe he found something even better than the silver. When Mel Fisher found the *Atocha*, down in the Keys, one of his divers brought up a jar full of emeralds. Worth probably a couple of million. If Garvey found something like that . . . well, it would be an irresistible temptation to take off. He wouldn't have to share it with anyone—not his partner, whoever that is, not the Infernal Revenue, and not the investigators you saw this morning. He could just leave the business that was causing him so much grief. Let the bank have it. That would look awfully good to someone with Garvey's problems."

I'd considered that, too.

"What about his wife?" I said. "And his sick kid?"

Semmes spread his hands and said, "Maybe they know. Maybe he told her already, and she's playing a part. Think how much better it would be if people *did* believe he had some kind of accident. That maybe his boat caught fire and then sank when he was out at this secret location at night. Or maybe he had an accident while he was diving. Maybe he got trapped in some debris and drowned."

I'd considered that, too.

"Then what about the truck, Nat? If he wanted people to believe that he'd died in some kind of accident, then he would have left the truck."

Semmes finished his coffee and thought for a moment. "All right," he said. "I'll buy that. Maybe he is running, but he didn't tell his wife. Not yet, anyway. And maybe he needed the truck more than he needed to leave behind a perfect scenario. Or thought he did, anyway. Or maybe he just wasn't thinking too clearly. Maybe he was desperate and just doing whatever it seemed like he had to do next."

That didn't sound like Garvey, I said. Not any of it.

"No," Semmes said. "I don't suppose it does. But people will fool you, Morgan. When I was prosecuting, you'd hear it all the time. 'He couldn't have done that, sir. He just couldn't have. I *know* the boy, and there just isn't any way he could of done that.'

"He'd done it, all right," Semmes said, "whoever he was, but there wasn't any way you could convince the people close to him. Because they *knew* him and they knew he wasn't that way.

"You might be wrong about Phil Garvey, Morgan. He might have changed. Pressure might have gotten to him. If it looks like he ran, then that's probably what he did."

CHAPTER 24

WE FLIPPED FOR THE CHECK AND I GOT it. Semmes went back to court and I went up to his office to work the phones.

It took me about three calls to locate someone in Miami who handled relics and the kind of stuff that might turn up on a beach or that a diver might find—doubloons and such. There's a market for everything, and somebody making a living by making the market. This man sounded old and clever and slightly amused by it all.

"You're the second one today," he said, and snickered.

"Who was the first?"

"He showed me some identification that came from the state of Florida."

"I see."

"Somebody found something. That's what the authorities believe. But they aren't always right, even if they think so. Who are you with, Mr. Hunt?"

I explained that I was working for Semmes. That we had a client and thought he might be involved with something that could cause him trouble. We were trying to help him.

"Before he gets in too deep, as it were," the man said, and snickered again.

"Yes."

"So he found those things the authorities are looking for?"

"They think so."

"Do *you* think so, Mr. Hunt?"

"I don't know. I suppose I would if certain things were suddenly for sale."

"I see."

"Can you tell me what you told the authorities?" I said.

"I believe so. It's still a free country. Not as free as it used to be, when you could keep what you found, but still free enough that I don't need permission to answer a business inquiry. Normally I charge for consultations, Mr. Hunt. It is how I make my living."

I told him to send a bill, and then asked how much it would be. It was the wrong order but Mr. Ramierez—that was his name—turned out to be a fair man.

"It's a simple consultation. No appraisal and it doesn't take much of my time. But I'm a businessman, Mr. Hunt. One hundred dollars will be my fee."

I asked him how much he'd charged the state.

He snickered again and said, "Mr. Hunt, the authorities take what they want, you know that."

He was right. I did know that.

"What did you tell them, Mr. Ramierez?"

"That none of the materials they were looking for have turned up here—or any other place that does legitimate business. If somebody has found these things, they haven't gone to the market with them. They could be waiting or they could have found a private arrangement. But I don't think so."

"Why not?"

"Because people who have found such a thing cannot keep quiet about it. People don't climb Everest and keep it a secret. The accomplishment is worth as much as the treasure. I think the state has bad information. It would not be the first time."

"Thank you, Mr. Ramierez. Please send us your bill."

"My pleasure, Mr. Hunt. And I hope your client's situation is satisfactorily resolved." He snickered again and hung up.

I called a few marinas to see if Garvey had brought *Second Shot* in, maybe to be hauled. It would be a kind of safekeeping for a boat. But the law was ahead of me there, too. The people at the marinas had told the state boys the same thing they told me—no sign of Garvey or his boat.

So I called Tom Pine.

"Morgan," he said, his voice rumbling through the phone line like an underground blast, "where you been keeping your sorry ass?"

"Here and there," I said.

"Well, this time of year, we ought to get out on the water. Couple of hours, anyway. Drink some beer and tell some lies."

"I'd like that, Tom."

"Let's do it, then. I fried up those brim you brought me. I'd like another mess."

"Let me know when you're off."

"I'll do it, Morgan. Now I know you need something. But I'm the cheapest cop that ever went on the pad. I'll sell my soul for a mess a fish. You wondering about your friend . . . Garvey, right?"

"Right."

"We're supposed to be looking for him, Morgan."

"Supposed to be?"

"We had two killings over the weekend. Normal ration of assaults, burglaries, drug deals, and GTAs. Not to mention domestic disturbances and a half-marathon to raise money for crippled children that kept two deputies busy directing traffic for most of Saturday morning. We're handling this Garvey thing on a when-you-get-around-to-it basis."

"I see."

"No votes in it, you know. And it is an election year. Sheriff isn't going to get reelected because he kept the county safe from treasure divers."

"No. I can see where that wouldn't make much of a platform."

"There's a truck, I believe. And we're keeping an eye out for it."

"Could you let me know if it turns up?"

There was a pause. "He's your buddy, right?"

"And client."

"You wouldn't be trying to help him stay ahead of the hounds, would you, Morgan?"

I could have gone off like I'd been insulted, but the truth was, it was exactly the right question. And under certain circumstances I would have happily helped Garvey stay a step or two ahead of the law, especially if it meant he could keep his treasure. But I didn't think there was any treasure. I wanted Garvey found and didn't much care by whom. Semmes could sort out his problems later.

"Tom," I said. "I want the man found. If I learn anything that will help, I'll pass it on to you."

"Okay, Morgan," Pine said. "I'll buy that. We don't have nothing, but when we do, you're my first call. How about Saturday for some fishing? I don't have to work and Phyllis is gone to see her mama."

"I'll see you Saturday morning," I said.

*   *   *

Before I left Semmes's office, I made two last calls. The first was to Rachel Garvey. I told her that she would be getting a letter from Semmes saying he'd been retained. I also told her that I hadn't made any progress but that didn't mean anything, one way or the other.

The second call was to Jessie. I told her I couldn't make dinner that night.

"You don't sound like you'd be much good company, anyway, Morgan. What is it?"

I told her what I'd been doing.

"It doesn't sound good, Morgan. Doesn't sound a bit good."

"No. It doesn't."

"I'm sorry, baby," she said, softly. "Real sorry. Anything I can do, you know to call."

"I know. Thanks."

"I want you to do me two favors, Morgan."

"I know what the first one is," I said. "You want me to be careful."

"That's right. You sometimes don't have good sense when you get like this."

She was right.

"Okay," I said. "I'll be careful. What's the second thing?"

"You'll call me up and talk to me. Let me know how you're doing. Maybe I can make you feel better."

I said I'd do that, too.

"Okay, Morgan. Good luck."

Lacking anything better to do, and going strictly on intuition, I looked up the address of Frank Loftin's law firm and drove out for a look. There was nothing much to see. Just another brick building with wrought-iron balconies to make it look old and distinguished. Half the attorneys in town worked in buildings that looked like that. They must sell the plans at a discount in all the state law schools.

But a red Range Rover was in the back parking lot in one of the spaces marked PRIVATE. So I parked down the street next to a car wash and watched the building. To kill a little time, I washed my truck, dried it with a chamois, and wiped all the inside surfaces down with a little ArmorAll.

Half an hour after I finished, Loftin came out of the back door of the one-size-fits-all office building and unlocked the door to the Range Rover. I waited until he was in traffic and then I followed.

He drove out to one of the new developments that are carved out of the pine and scrub oak and about as common as the building where he worked. This one was called Camden Gardens for reasons that probably no one on earth could explain. Loftin took four or five turns and pulled into the driveway of a house that was made of brick and pine stained to look like weathered cedar. It was the house of a modestly successful, young, small-town lawyer. Loftin walked to the front door, carrying his attaché case, and let himself in.

If I'd stayed parked on the street, watching the house, somebody doing his duty for the neighborhood watch would have called me in and I would have had to explain myself to one of the deputies who worked for Tom Pine. So I drove back out the way I came in. But there was only one entrance to Camden Gardens, so I drove down the highway, pulled off on the shoulder far enough away that I could watch it, and cut the engine. If anyone reported me, I would tell the deputy that I was waiting on a friend who had a bass boat. The old boy was supposed to meet me right here, officer, I'd say. But he's running late. Must have got into the beer.

I wouldn't have minded a beer myself. Or a cup of coffee.

I settled for a toothpick, which I chewed to splinters in the four hours I waited and watched the entrance to Camden Gardens. No sign of Loftin or the Range Rover. No doubt he had eaten dinner, done a little paperwork, watched Murphy Brown, and gone to bed.

Sometimes I found myself wishing for nights like that, but I knew that after a string of them I would start thinking about blowing my brains out. I started the truck and pulled out on the highway.

I stopped for a chicken leg on the way home. It was late and the house was dark when I got there. As soon as I had a light or two turned on, I went to check the answering machine, hoping that there would be a message from Garvey. I didn't believe, in the rational corridor of my mind, that it would happen, but the other part of me imagined him calling and saying in a whisper that he'd found a jar of emeralds and had made it to someplace safe where he would live out his days without benefit of bankers. He'd be calling for Rachel and the kids soon. Wanted me to tell them he was safe. Wanted me to know, too.

I'd tell him I appreciated the call and hoped to see him again someday.

He'd say . . . Sure, Morgan. Someday.

There was one message. From the lumberyard. My order of cherry logs would be going on the saw in the morning.

Well, he could call anytime. Maybe the phone would ring after I'd gone to sleep.

Could happen.

CHAPTER 25

GARVEY DIDN'T CALL. FOR THREE DAYS there was no sign of him. Nobody heard anything. Nobody saw his truck or his boat. His wife was sinking quietly into desperation bordering on grief. She could have been acting, but I didn't think so. She said that she didn't believe Phil would do this to her or to his kids; that if he hadn't gotten in touch with them by now, something was terribly wrong. Which meant that most likely he was dead.

I thought so, too, but, like her, I couldn't quit on Garvey without some kind of conclusive news. I needed something firm. A witness . . . or a body.

I couldn't sit around the house, or Semmes's office, waiting for a call. So I drove around and talked to charter skippers I knew, asking if they'd seen Garvey's boat. Some of them had already been talked to, by the law, and none of them could help. I talked to shrimpers, with the same results. I went down to one of the fish houses and talked to some of the Vietnamese fishermen who docked there. They worked inshore, mostly, and at night. Garvey had been doing his treasure diving at night, he said. And it was in shallow water, so it could have been inshore.

The smell of *nuoc mam* and the atonal sound of those voices carried me back. I didn't have any kind of violent flashback and start reaching for my knife, but I did feel vaguely transported back to flat, tender green paddies and dark, airless jungles. I didn't like it any more than I like the sound of steel on steel.

I didn't remember much Vietnamese, but that didn't make any difference since everyone I talked to knew plenty of English. More than enough to tell me that they hadn't seen Garvey's boat in the last couple of weeks.

As a last throw of the dice, I called a man named Hawthorne who ran a little flying service out in the soybean fields across the Alabama line. He made his money doing odd flying jobs. Crop dusting, hauling sky divers, and giving lessons. He'd been a FAC in Vietnam and was happiest in little planes at low altitudes.

I hired him for a day and we went out over the Gulf, looking for Garvey's boat. I felt foolish and impotent, like a man looking for a runaway daughter by walking the streets around Times Square. But, like that desperate father, I couldn't come up with anything better.

Hawthorne was wearing khaki shorts, shower shoes, a very faded old locker-room T-shirt, and an LSU baseball cap. His eyes were tired and he plainly didn't feel like making a lot of conversation. He wore headphones whenever he was in the cockpit. It was fine with me. I didn't feel like talking, either.

So we flew out over the Gulf in his Cessna 172, which was the closest he could get to the O-1 that he'd flown in Vietnam. He watched the water as it passed under the left wing. I did the same on the right. He had worked out a search pattern and figured we could fly for five hours. He'd added considerably to the plane's fuel capacity. We didn't say anything for the first few hours, merely watched the water as it passed beneath us.

You can forget how big the open sea is. When you travel the coast and see all the boats tied up at all the marinas, you start to think the sea must be an awfully crowded place, but, actually, from four or five thousand feet, we could look a long way in any direction and often see nothing but water.

The boats we did see looked like small, insubstantial insects leaving tiny white trails on the green surface of the Gulf. We could tell from the profile of most of those boats that they weren't worth checking out closely. A shrimp boat didn't look much like a sportfisherman.

When we couldn't be sure, Hawthorne would stand the plane on one wing and take us down until we were close enough to confirm that the boat was not a Bertram like the one we were looking for. When we came close enough, the people on the boat would look up and wave. We would turn away and continue our monotonous search.

Five hours into it, I saw a boat out on the edge of my visibility. It didn't seem to be making any wake, which didn't necessarily mean anything. The boat could be anchored—it was about twenty miles offshore, in a little less than fifty fathoms of water—or it could be drifting down the edge of a weedline so the fishermen could cast.

I nudged Hawthorne above the elbow and pointed to the boat. He stared for a moment along the line I made with my finger, then nodded and dropped a wing so the little Cessna made a deep turn. At the lower altitude, he increased the richness of the mixture and gave the ship a little more throttle. The boat must have been ten or fifteen miles away. It took a while to cover the distance. As we got closer, my pulse seemed to rise like the pitch of the Cessna's engine.

From a mile away I could see plainly that the boat was a Bertram. If it wasn't Garvey's, then it was a boat just like it.

We flew directly over the boat, bow to stern at a hundred feet, and I was sure. There was a swim platform with two ladders mounted on the stern. I had helped Garvey build it from jury-rigged parts. There wouldn't be another like it anywhere on the Gulf coast.

I nudged Hawthorne and nodded. He nodded back and made a motion with his hand to ask if I wanted him to go around again. I nodded. He put the plane over on its wing and we made another pass. This time, I was looking for signs of life.

There was no one above decks. Nor was there any debris or wreckage in the cockpit. No sign of a struggle, as the police would say. The boat looked as neat and orderly as it did when it was tied to the dock back at the Outrigger.

I made a circling motion with my finger to indicate one more pass. Hawthorne nodded and put the wing over.

I wasn't sure exactly what I was looking for on this pass. Maybe I was hoping that Garvey was belowdecks, sick perhaps, and that he'd find some way to signal us. But I knew that if he were alive and needed help, he would have gotten it long before now by using the radio. Garvey ran a radio check before he left the dock. Every single time. And he carried backup radios with backup batteries.

Still, I looked down at the empty boat and hoped for some kind of sign.

What I saw, instead of a sign, was a length of line running off a cleat on the bow. It might have been an anchor line, but it slanted off into the water at an odd angle, not quite shallow enough to be simply a loose line but not drastic enough to have been attached to an anchor, either.

The line was attached to a sea anchor, I realized. A section of fabric—nylon, probably—stretched around a frame so that it took the shape of a bucket or a funnel. It wouldn't hold the boat stationary but it would slow its drift considerably. Garvey occasionally used a sea anchor when he was diving over a place he wanted to keep secret. The slight drift kept anyone from taking an accurate fix on the boat's location. But it would not drift so far that it would be out of sight when he came up. He would swim to the boat on the surface, a couple of miles being nothing to Garvey.

My best guess was that he'd been diving somewhere and left the boat with the sea anchor out. When he came up, either he couldn't find the boat or couldn't get to it for some reason. Or . . . he never came up.

I tapped Hawthorne on the arm and pointed to my ear. He lifted the headphones and leaned slightly in my direction.

"G . . . P . . . S," I shouted.

He nodded and pointed to the small flight bag pushed up under the seat between my legs. I reached into it and found, among the charts and manuals, a small hand-held set about the size of a kid's cassette player. I found the power switch and turned it on. Adjusted the gain and then read the numbers off the digital display and wrote them in my notebook.

Hawthorne had been watching me, and when I looked up into his face I nodded and pointed north, toward land.

He nodded back, banked the little plane steeply, and we headed for home.

I thought about my next move on the way back to the little strip in the bean fields. The safest move was obvious enough. Get to a phone just as soon as we landed and call the law. Tom Pine would do. He could make the next calls and I would be able to explain how I'd found the boat and things would be clean and in the open. For me, anyway.

But I didn't want the Coast Guard and those red-hot agents from the State Attorney's Office to be first on that boat.

It wasn't just sentiment. I didn't think they knew what to look for. And if they didn't know what to look for, they wouldn't find Garvey, which, probably, they didn't care about anyway.

I wondered if I could be charged with obstruction or something if I did what I had it in mind to do. I could call Semmes and find out. But I didn't want to be told either that it would be obstruction and I shouldn't do it or that it would not be obstruction and I shouldn't do it. I wanted to do it and didn't much care if it was obstruction or not.

I did care about not getting caught, though. I explained that very carefully to Hawthorne.

"You're a crazy fuck," he said. "But then, all you Sneaky Petes were."

He wanted more money. I paid him what he asked for, along with a bonus. He didn't ask what that was for. He didn't have to.

Half an hour later, we were flying south-southeast at five thousand feet. The sun was off the right wing. And I was wearing a parachute.

Now and then, Hawthorne would look across the cockpit at me and shake his head.

Garvey's boat had drifted less than half a mile. When he saw it, Hawthorne took one last look at me as though to ask if I was absolutely sure I wanted to go through with this thing. I gave him a thumbs-up and maneuvered my way behind the seat into the little cargo space. I opened the door as Hawthorne was throttling back. In a second or two, the plane was straight and level.

I looked down at the water, across the arch of my bare foot. There was no wind, or next to none, since the surface of the Gulf was completely smooth. Not a single ragged whitecap. I was wearing a pair of old swimming trunks and a T-shirt. And my watch. I had no altimeter strapped to my chest, as one usually would in skydiving. But I didn't need one since I wasn't going to be doing any free-falling. I planned to kick out, get stable, and open. With the modern canopy, shaped like a sail, I could cover nearly a mile of ground from five thousand feet of altitude. When I'd learned to jump—so long ago that it sometimes seemed like something that had happened to an ancestor—the chutes were shaped like umbrellas and there was so little steerage in them that it was all you could do to miss a single tree. Now you could pick your own blade of grass and land right on top of it.

As I watched the water, I felt a familiar increase, slight but unmistakable, in the pace of my heart. We used to say, back when we were jumping three and four times a day and another time or two at night, sometimes from thirty thousand feet or more, that if you ever stopped feeling that last-second case of nerves, then you should quit.

Then I had the boat in the vee sight I formed with my feet. I pushed hard against the skin of the plane and I was falling.

I spread my legs and arms, arched my back, and in a second or so I was stable. My eyes were blurred by the speed of the fall so that all I could see beneath me was a vast green sheet. When I began to feel that sensation—a wonderful tightening that seems to draw your stomach and your balls together and makes you want to keep falling forever—I reached in my pocket and pulled out the pilot chute and threw it into the wind. It deployed instantly and I could feel and hear the suspension lines and the canopy uncoiling above me. Then I swung in the harness and I was no longer falling but hanging in the air, like some kind of large raptor, riding a thermal.

I found the boat and toggled the chute to get a line on it. I was close enough to corkscrew off a couple of thousand feet of altitude. After that it was a simple run. When I was about a hundred feet over the water—just a guess, since slick water makes those kinds of judgments awfully hard—I put my thumbs and fingers on the releases. When my feet touched water, I cut away. I hit so softly, I barely made a splash.

CHAPTER 26

THE WATER WAS WARM AND SALTY AND
had the clean blue color that you see way offshore where
there's no silt or mud. I had landed less than twenty yards
from the boat, on the line of its drift. I swam to it easily
and climbed aboard, using the ladders and swim platform
that Garvey and I had built. I had a moment going over
the transom; the feeling you get when you walk into a
room that is supposed to be empty but may not be.

I dropped onto the teak deck, in a crouch, feeling naked
and pitifully vulnerable. The deck was hot from the sun.
There was no movement anywhere aboard. Just the soft
side-to-side motion of the boat itself. There was no smell,
either, which was a relief. There were no dead bodies on
this boat . . . nor any live ones, so far as I could tell. I
worked my way forward and looked below, just to be sure.
No one. Nothing. The boat was empty. And in the same
kind of precise order that you would have found it in tied
up back at the Outrigger. It was almost as though it had
slipped its lines and drifted out to sea.

I retrieved the parachute with a boat hook, then climbed the ladder to the flybridge. The electronics were still working, but I imagined that they had pulled a lot off the batteries in the last few days. I cranked the engines to get them recharged. The diesels turned over right away and settled into a purring idle.

Garvey's black loose-leaf book full of waterproofed paper was lying next to the radio. I picked it up and flipped the pages. There were lines of numbers, all of them in eight digits, running down each page. Maybe a dozen numbers to a page. Each set of numbers represented a dive site. Each one had been coded according to the key that Garvey used. If you knew his birthday, you could break the code. I remembered that he had told me he'd been born on Veteran's Day. Eleventh day of the eleventh month, 1959. The key, then, was 11111959.

I flipped the pages of the notebook. The entries stopped about fifteen pages from the end. After that, all the sheets were blank, waiting for Garvey to discover new dive sites and enter their locations, in code. The last entry on the last page was 29997701.

I picked up a pencil from the dash next to the radio. The wood was hot in my fingers. Using one of the blank sheets at the back of the notebook, I did the false subtraction, taking the key from the eight digits of the last entry in the book. The answer was 30018650—thirty degrees one minute latitude, and eighty-six degrees fifty minutes longitude. I picked up the chart that was mounted under Plexiglas on a lapboard and stowed under the controls. I read down and right until I found the location that matched up with the eight digits and I made a pencil mark over it. Then I looked at the digital readout on the GPS mounted next to the radio. I found that position on the chart.

Garvey's navigation tools were stored in a drawer under

the controls. I opened it and took out a pair of dividers. I connected my two dots along one edge and ran the other out until it intersected the compass rose. My course was 070. East-northeast. Looked to be about five or six thousand yards. According to the chart, the depth at that point was about forty fathoms. Deep, but not too deep for Garvey.

I slipped the engines into gear and turned the wheel until the compass lined up on 070. The sun was at my back. If Garvey had left any kind of buoy, I ought to be able to see it. But polarized glasses would help. I opened another drawer and found a pair. Garvey thought of everything.

I put the glasses on and they cut the glare considerably. If there was a marker, I'd see it for sure.

Turned out, it wasn't easy. Not even with the glasses. The buoy was small, about the size of a volleyball, and painted black, which didn't exactly stand out against the blue surface of the water. Whatever Garvey was marking, he sure didn't want anyone to find it. I throttled back and turned on the depth finder. It showed 240 feet. A very gentle slope to the bottom. Nothing, at first, that looked like bottom structure, either natural or man-made. The man-made kind can be either intentional—fisherman will sink old cars or boats to make a reef and the government has scuttled old Liberty ships for the purpose—or it can be accidental. Ships will sink and airplanes will crash, and when all the tragedies have been largely forgotten, a good fishing reef still remains. Two hundred and forty feet was awfully deep for an intentional reef. If anything was down there—and I felt sure something was—then it was either a natural formation or the remains of some kind of misfortune.

It showed up on the third pass around the buoy. Just a very small blip with only a few fish schooled above it, which was odd. Out here, where the bottom was barren, any structure at all should have been covered up with fish.

Unless it was very new and hadn't had time to attract much life.

The little blip on the depth recorder wasn't telling me anything. Neither was the small black buoy riding the insignificant swells. All I knew was that there was something down there—that much was certain—and that Garvey had been interested in it—near certain—and most likely interested enough to go down and look for himself. Which was the only way I was going to find out what was down there and . . . if Garvey was still down there with it.

The depth was a lot for me. Deeper by forty or fifty feet than I'd ever been. More than a hundred feet deeper than all the experts said was safe and prudent. But then I'd never tested high on safe and prudent. If there had been a couple of tanks and a weight belt aboard, I'd have gone right over and followed that buoy line on down to the bottom. But there were no spare tanks. The only diving equipment amounted to a couple of masks, some gloves, and a wrist compass. If I wanted to make this dive, I would have to go back to shore and tool up first.

If I went back, it would be in a boat that every law enforcement agency and half the civilian boating population of the Gulf Coast had been alerted to look for. That thought recalled, for some reason, those people who are on the run, trying to live invisibly, and then find themselves lit up on national television on one of those most-wanted programs. Everybody in prison believes that he's there because of bad luck, and that's just about the worst kind of bad luck there is. Getting *Second Shot* to shore, loaded up, and back out here would be testing the odds. And if I was seen, and picked up . . . well, that would raise some interesting legal questions that I would have to hope Semmes could sort out. If, that is, he were willing.

I did the little exercise with the chart and the dividers again and found a course for the beach. Three-fifty north-northwest. I gave the engines enough throttle to bring the hull up on a plane. I didn't want to get to shore too early; after dark would be the safe and prudent time.

It was about an hour after dark when I eased past the sea buoy at the south end of the Pensacola ship channel. Off to the west I could see the single flashing light that marked the rusting hulk of the old *Massachusetts*, a battle-ship that had been sunk in a test of shore-battery fire back around the turn of the century. During daylight you could still see one turret rising barely above the waterline at low tide. In another few hundred years, the old ship would be completely rusted away, which is the way the sea goes about turning swords to plowshares and probably the best we can hope for in this life.

I turned up into the bay and ran down the channel. At one point, I was less than half a mile from the Coast Guard station where Semmes and I had gone to brace the skipper. I felt sure he would have liked to take personal command of the crash boat with its machine-gun mounts and come out into the channel, standing at the bridge, with its mar-ijuana-leaf decals, to order me to heave to for boarding. But he had gone home to the family and his men were probably drinking coffee and telling war stories while they watched *Major Dad* on television. I put their little outpost behind me and turned up into the bay.

I ran about five miles at an unobtrusively safe speed,

then turned toward a dark patch of shoreline. I throttled way back, until I had just enough speed to keep positive steering, and searched the bank for the profile of a dock. The depth finder showed twelve feet.

After a few nervous minutes, I found the dock. A small Whaler was tied up on one side. The other was empty and I put *Second Shot* up snug against it, brushing a piling with the rub rail and thinking that Garvey would have never done that. It was something I deeply wished I would be able to apologize for, but I didn't think it could happen.

I put a line around the piling and cut the engines. When the boat was snug, I started up the dock to Vince Hawthorne's house.

He was home. Alone. He came to the door with a nickel-plated Ruger pistol in his hand.

"Jesus, Morgan, you just about scared me out of my skin. Lucky I didn't shoot you."

"I appreciate it, Vince. Truly."

"You must have come mighty quiet. I always hear people drive up."

"I came by boat. I'm tied up at your dock."

"Same boat."

"That's right."

"Anybody on it?"

"No."

He nodded. Ran a hand over his head and said, "Are you all right?"

"I'm fine, Vince. But I need some help."

"Are you legal?"

"Probably not. But I'll pay you and I won't rat on you."

He smiled and, for a second or two, he looked like a man who felt like he'd just gotten another chance in his life.

"Okay," he said, "I can handle that. Come on in."

*   *   *

What I needed from Hawthorne was his dock and a ride back to his landing strip, where I'd left my truck. And, I suppose, his willingness to lie if anyone came around asking if he'd seen me.

He was game.

"Long as it isn't drugs," he said. "I got a thing about that."

"No drugs," I said, "but I don't want to tell you any more than that."

"Need to know," he said. "I can handle that, too. I been there."

I picked up my truck at the airstrip and told him it would be a couple of hours, at least, before I made it back to his house and the dock.

"I'll be there," he said.

From the airstrip I drove into town and eased past Garvey's shop three times before I felt confident it was not being watched. I still had the key he'd given me and I used it to unlock the back door. I loaded four tanks and some other gear that I thought I might need into the bed of the truck. It was almost midnight when I pulled out of the lot and back onto the highway. At that time of night it was nearly empty, and I felt something like a small animal on open ground. I wanted to get back to the boat but I had one more errand.

I had been asked, after I'd volunteered to do some cleanup after a hurricane, if I would join the county emergency rescue squad. I'm not a very good joiner but I'd said yes. I'd helped find a kid who had wandered away at a family picnic and gotten lost in the woods. And I'd helped drag the river for a bass fisherman who'd fallen in and drowned. Easy work.

Like everyone on the team, I had my own key to the shed where we kept our supplies. I drove by the shed, saw the lights were out, and pulled off the road, into the trees, a couple of hundred yards away. I walked back, let myself in, and without using a light was able to find what I'd come for. It was a familiar piece of equipment made out of ordinary material, but it was the sort of thing most people would have a hard time just touching. But if my guess about Garvey was right, I'd need a body bag. So I took it.

I put the bag in the bed of the truck along with the tanks and the other dive gear and drove back to Hawthorne's place. He was still up and he'd made some coffee. I drank a cup while we talked.

"Just a couple of things more," I said. "Then I'm gone."

"It could be a couple of dozen," he said. He was into it and for a moment I thought about asking him to come with me on the boat. But I decided against it. More people makes more problems.

"First," I said, "take this money. I'll get more later."

I gave him all I had. Not quite a thousand in cash. He looked at it on the table and nodded to indicate he'd take it. But he didn't reach for it to count it or to put it away someplace safe. The money was important to him. As earnest as much as for itself.

"Okay," I said. "Now, if you don't hear from me in twenty-four hours, get in touch with Nat Semmes."

"The lawyer," he interrupted.

"Right," I said. "He's in the book, and if you want to give him your name, you can trust him until Gabriel blows reveille. But if you don't want to give him your name, that's fine. Just give him this position"—I wrote the numbers out on a sheet of paper—"and tell him that there will be a buoy there and probably the boat, too, if it hasn't drifted off. Tell him it will be a job for divers."

Hawthorne studied the numbers. "That's pretty far off-shore," he said. "How deep is it, Morgan?"

"A little more than two hundred feet," I said.

"And you're going to dive it?"

"Yes," I said. I started to explain about Garvey but stopped myself.

Hawthorne nodded and said, "Morgan, I'm going to ask you the same thing a chopper pilot asked me one time, when my plane was all shot up and on fire and I was trying to land it in a little clear spot in the jungle about as long as a football field."

"What's that?"

"Can I have your truck?"

CHAPTER 27

It was still very dark when I went back out through Pensacola pass. Except for the sunken battleship, mine was the only vessel in sight.

I sat on the flybridge, drinking milk and eating a peanut-butter sandwich. Hawthorne had given me the food before I left. Said he lived off peanut butter and it was easy to believe. He was a textbook case. Of all the things that had once worked, only flying still did. A woman would have been the thing to hope for, not that long ago. But it seems like men and women don't do that much for each other these days. Too many other considerations.

I watched the horizon, the stars, and the smooth white wake for the two hours it took to run back to the position where I'd found that small black buoy. It was still dark when I got there. I was eager to get into the water and find out what was resting there on the bottom, marked by that buoy. But I wasn't going to do it in the dark. I cut the engines, threw out a sea anchor, and went below, where

I lay down on the vee berth and got a couple of hours of something that passed for sleep.

The sun was up when I woke, but not high enough yet to turn the day hot. My eyes felt dry and grainy and I was stiff enough to have spent the night on cold ground. I went topside and stood in the cockpit, getting my eyes adjusted to the light and letting the sun warm my skin and burn off the deep stiffness in my back and legs. I stretched and yawned, startling a gull that had landed on the flybridge. The gull squawked rudely and flew off.

I thought about coffee. Decided I didn't need it. Went up to the bow and brought in the sea anchor. Then climbed up into the flybridge, where I started the engines, checked my position on the GPS, and steered for the location of that small black buoy. As much as I wanted to go down that buoy line and find out what was down there, I was full of a kind of heavy reluctance. It was, I suppose, the way you'd feel when you had to open a grave.

I found the buoy in fifteen or twenty minutes. Killed the engines and dropped the sea anchor. Then went back into the cockpit to suit up.

First, I mounted a regulator on one of the tanks and, using a spare anchor for weight, lowered it off the stern until it was about twenty feet deep. I'd need to make a decompression stop on my way up. There was a long hose between the first and second stages of the regulator. Thirty feet or so. I could ascend to ten feet and make another stop. According to the Navy dive tables, I could stay down at 240 for fifteen minutes if I made a four-minute stop at thirty, a six-minute stop at twenty, and another twenty-one-minute stop at ten.

I had that covered.

I got into a wet suit. It would be cold at 240 feet. Then

I rigged another regulator on another tank and mounted it on a vest. Then I strapped a big chrome-plated knife in a hard plastic sheath around my ankle and calf. Buckled on a weight belt with a couple of two-pound chunks of lead.

I slipped into the vest and tested the purge on the regulator. Dry air came blasting through the mouthpiece. I put on my flippers, seated my mask, put the regulator in my mouth, and rolled over the gunwale into the warm, indigo-colored water. I exhaled and began to sink like something inert dropped overboard as trash.

I checked my watch. Five minutes after the hour. I'd need to be back up at the spare tank no later than twenty after. The ascent would take three minutes or so.

I dropped past the tank with its regulator and extra-long hose. It stood out in perfect relief. The water was very clear. Visibility was about as good as it gets in the Gulf. Eighty or a hundred feet.

I kicked, and the motion of my flippers pushed me through the water to the line that ran from the black buoy to the bottom. I rolled and pointed my head toward the bottom and began a long descent down the line, which disappeared into the blue like the contrail of a high, vanishing jet.

I felt the pressure in my ears and my mask. Cleared. Kicked hard and went deeper. I began to feel as though I could sense the weight of all that water above me now, as I passed a hundred feet. Tons and tons of water. How deep before the pressure would crush you? Already my lungs were compressed to a fourth of their normal size. I cleared and sipped air through the regulator, trying hard to conserve.

I looked down at my trunks and saw that I had gone

deep enough to lose the reds from the color spectrum. The bezel on my watch was still blue. But at the end of this dive, that color would also vanish.

Through 150 and the water turned noticeably colder.

I began to look for the bottom, straining the way you do when you scan a horizon for a distant ship or airplane. At 180, I could make out an indistinct mottled gray sheet. The air seemed to have real weight and density as it came through the regulator. It felt almost liquid as it rolled down my throat into my lungs.

At two hundred feet, I made out the shape of the thing that was marked by the single black buoy.

It was a twin-engine plane just big enough to carry a dozen passengers. The sort that the airlines use for short commuter hops and that corporations use to move their executives around the empire. The fuselage was intact. Both props were bent from the impact when the plane hit the water. The tip of one wing was fractured. But the sheet metal was clean. The organisms that would attach themselves opportunistically, even at this depth, had not yet begun to appear, so the crash had to have been fairly recent.

I dropped down the anchor line until I was ten or fifteen feet above the plane. I had never been this deep before and I was tempted to look back up the anchor line at all that water piled up on top of me. It was the same impulse that would make you look down when you were standing at the edge of a mountain, an urge to physically assess the threat that you had so far evaluated only with your mind. I fought the urge and kept my eyes on the plane as I dropped down onto its nose. There was a groaning sound in my ears, deep and almost mournful. My depth gauge read 230.

The cockpit glass was still intact. I looked inside, expecting to see the bodies of the pilot and co-pilot, but both seats were empty. I swam around to the left side of the plane, where the small door was open and swinging slightly as though it were moved by a breeze. I pushed it open far enough to put my head and my shoulders reluctantly inside, all of my old claustrophobic terrors rising inside me like bile.

I took the flashlight out of my pocket and aimed the feeble beam down the length of the small cabin, where it picked up the shape of two bodies.

The one in the front seat was pretty far gone. Bone, mostly, after what the fish and the small crabs and the other scavengers had done to it. There was still a lot of hair on what remained of the scalp, waving like sea grass in the slight currents that drifted through the plane. The hair, the soaked remnants of a skirt, and a pitiful pair of high-heeled shoes made it pretty clear that the body had belonged to a woman.

The other body was held together by a neoprene wet suit. The hands had been gnawed down to bone, as had the face except where it was protected by a mask. There was a tank strapped to the body and a regulator dangling uselessly from the tank. Without being able to recognize him, I knew that it was Garvey.

One of the many things you worry about when you're first learning to dive is what will happen if you vomit into your regulator. The answer is—you don't. If you feel it coming, you take the regulator out of your mouth and try hard not to suck in a lot of water once you've thrown up. Then you put the regulator back in your mouth and clear it.

I didn't want to take the regulator out of my mouth at 230 feet. So it was fortunate that, in spite of a nearly total sense of panic and horror, I didn't gag. I'd seen worse, by whatever measure applies to these things. Maybe that had something to do with it. Or maybe it was because I was expecting what I'd found. Or maybe I just have a strong stomach.

The sight of the body in the thin beam of my light froze me for a few moments. Maybe as long as fifteen seconds. Then, when I could think, my first instinct was to back quickly out of the plane and climb the anchor line, through the tons of water, up into the air.

I pushed out of the plane, my arms working almost involuntarily. Then I stopped. I told myself to breathe slowly, to get control, that I couldn't afford to hyperventilate.

In a minute or so, I had my breathing regulated again. I wasn't sipping the air, like Garvey had taught me to, but I wasn't gulping every molecule, either. I was still half wild with some need I couldn't pinpoint, but I wasn't gripped by panic. I was back in control. I pushed into the plane and kicked down the aisle toward Garvey.

I felt like I was swimming through some new medium, thicker than water. Like I was pushing my way through mud or wet cement. It took an age to travel fifteen feet until I could reach out and touch him. I hooked my hand through his weight belt, and what was left of him, under the neoprene, gave in a soft, sickening way.

I pulled and there was something surprising in the unyielding way the body came toward me. No resistance. Which was something I would never have associated with Garvey, or even with this bundle that had once been Garvey and that, for a moment, I was almost embracing.

I began to work my way out of the airplane, dragging my burden, trying to keep my breathing under control, trying not to look at my watch. How long had I been down?

My foot hit something. I looked down at the floor of the plane and saw a small metal case. There was a line running from the handle of the case to Garvey's weight belt. When the line came taut, Garvey's body no longer followed me so willingly. I picked up the case with my free hand.

I had another moment at the little door of the plane. It didn't seem possible to squeeze myself and the body and the case through the hatch, and I was seized by this overwhelming, irrational sense that I was trapped like some miner deep underground, still able to see a small beam of light. But that passed, too, and I pushed the body through ahead of me and then followed, carrying the case in my hand.

It was awkward going up the anchor line and it felt impossibly slow, even though I was rising almost as fast as my bubbles. The body rose with me, yielding easily.

I looked away from Garvey and up toward the surface, where I could make out the spare tank and its long regulator hose. I swam to it, changed regulators, and checked my watch. I had been down for a full fifteen minutes, which meant that I needed to spend thirty-one decompressing. Half an hour, still, underwater, holding on to the body.

I'd been at twenty feet for about five minutes when a couple of remoras appeared from somewhere and began circling Garvey's body like vultures. The same black bodies, the same cold, uncaring eyes. I kicked at them and they swam away, startled. But in a few seconds they were back. I wondered if there were sharks somewhere that the remoras had been following, and tried to think about what I would do if the sharks approached to feed on what was left of Garvey. I scattered the remoras again.

I had the knife. Would Garvey expect me to stay with him and use it if sharks did come? I could release him and let his weight belt carry him back to the bottom. He'd never know. There hadn't been any real need even to bring him up, merely to take him back to land and bury him again, this time under dirt. He might have been buried in the proper place to begin with, deep under water. With the sharks.

The remoras returned, but there was no sign of anything larger. I kept them away from the body until it was time to go up to ten feet. They followed but stayed off a few feet, circling, unwilling to leave but afraid to come closer. Waiting.

I breathed compressed air and my body bled nitrogen. I couldn't feel it any more than Garvey could feel anything at all. I needed to stay down a little longer, to avoid the bends. Garvey could stay here forever.

I watched the remoras. Checked my watch. And held on to my two bundles. At ten feet, I was so close to the air that I could almost feel it. I hung there, breathing, for the full twenty-one minutes and then slowly rose the rest of the way to the surface. A part of me regretted that no sharks had appeared. I wanted to use the knife.

CHAPTER 28

I SWAM TO *SECOND SHOT* AND GRABBED one of the ladders Garvey and I had rigged to its stern. Breathing real air felt something like being resurrected. I cut the line between Garvey and the metal case, then threw it over the transom into the boat. Garvey would have hated what that did to his teak.

Getting his body aboard wasn't so easy. If there was anything to be grateful for under the circumstances, it was the neoprene wet suit that held him together, more or less.

It took a while, but I finally had him aboard. I followed and quickly shucked my regulator and, just as quickly, laid out the body bag and rolled Garvey into it. I zipped it up and moved it up close to the side of the boat, where the gunwale provided some shade.

A lot would depend, I realized, on whose plane that was and the identity of the woman whose body was still inside it. And I might learn that by looking inside the case that had been tethered to Garvey.

It was one of those aluminum cases photographers use

to ship their cameras. Long on durability and short on elegance. Many of them also have an O-ring around the opening, so that even if they are submerged—which isn't beyond some airline baggage handlers—the contents will stay dry.

It wasn't chain-locked and didn't have a combination. Just the sort of spring-loaded latches you see on an attaché case. I suppose I could have found a small probe and jimmied the lock. But I was in a hurry, so I used the knife and the heel of my hand. The locks gave like a paper-shell pecan.

The case was packed tight and neat. A few stacks of currency. Large—very large—bills. Documents that to my ignorant eyes looked like bearer bonds. A notebook with a list of accounts in what had to be offshore banks. Two small bags filled with uncut stones. The family jewels.

It looked to me like someone's getaway kit.

But I couldn't find anything to tell me who owned the plane or identify the woman still inside it.

I closed the case and took it below.

I filled a large mug with fresh water and then climbed up to the flybridge, where I sat sipping and thinking. The compressed air had dried me out inside and the tepid water in my mug tasted like it could have come straight from the spring behind the river house. My thinking was less conclusive.

Right away I wished that I'd had the sense and the composure to look at the numbers on the airplane's wing and memorize them. I could have gone back to shore with Garvey's body and some kind of story for the law and done my own search of those numbers. Whoever owned the plane would miss the things in the aluminum case, if not the woman.

There was some reason for doubt on that point—the

chief reasons being that the pilot was not with the plane, and that whoever owned it hadn't reported it to anyone official but had somehow arranged for Garvey to dive the wreckage and bring up the case and its contents. There was no way of knowing whether or not that person had paid Garvey to find the plane or had already known where it was but couldn't make a 240-foot dive himself. Most people can't.

It was possible that the plane had been intentionally ditched and its passenger murdered. Perhaps by its owner, who had also been its pilot. Or the pilot could have been a hired hand and dealt with later. Or the pilot—owner or otherwise—could have gotten out of the plane and then died in the water. I hadn't seen a plan yet that without any effort at all couldn't be screwed up.

All manner of things were possible, and there wasn't any good way of checking them out without knowing who owned the airplane. Which made me feel especially stupid for not getting those numbers.

I could, I thought as I finished the water and wished for more . . . I could fire the engines and head for the beach and turn it all over to people who were smarter than I was, or had the authority to deal with it, or—in some cases, perhaps—both. I could tell my story. I didn't think I'd broken any laws—Garvey's boat was derelict and I had salvaged it. And I had gone diving on a buoy that could have marked anything. If I had broken laws, they were small ones that Nat Semmes could handle as easily as swatting gnats.

I *could* do that—with or without handing over the case and its contents. The law could send its own divers out to bring up the other body and get the numbers off the plane. That would be easy enough; but it might be very hard to prove that the owner, or anyone else, had hired Garvey to go down there and bring up that case. And, once the law was in, I would be out.

I wanted to be in. Which meant I needed those numbers.

According to the tables, it would take twelve hours for me to fully decompress. I didn't think I had that much time. After eight hours I would be able to go back down to 240 and stay for fifteen minutes before having to come up and go through the stops again. This time I would stay four minutes at forty, seven at thirty, seventeen at twenty, and twenty-seven at ten.

There wasn't much to do during the eight hours I had to wait while the nitrogen bubbles slowly shrank and dispersed inside me. I rigged for the next dive. Checked the blade on the dive knife. Like all of Garvey's tools, it was well maintained. The cutting blade could peel a sliver off the top of my thumbnail and the saw edge on the top of the knife could easily cut through a piece of aluminum railing.

I moved a mile or so off from the buoy and put the sea anchor out. I found a bag of oranges in a cooler down below and ate three or four of them. I checked the tables again to make sure of my figures. I slept a little.

Finally, late in the afternoon, with a little chop coming up on the surface and the sky clouding over from a thunderstorm, I was ready to go back down the 240 feet to the bottom.

It seemed like I made it to the bottom more quickly this time. Maybe it was because I knew what I would find there.

But the water seemed colder this trip and slightly turbid. Large particles drifted through my field of vision like soot in city air. I was nearly two hundred feet down before I could make out the shape of the plane in detail.

I checked my watch as I drifted down slowly onto its fuselage. Half past. I needed to be on the way up at twenty till. I set the bezel on my watch and went to work.

The left wing was fractured near the middle and bent at an odd angle. There was a small gap between the underside of the wing and the sea bottom. Just enough space for me to slither under the wing, facing up, with my tank digging a trench in the sand. It was a small, closed space, and I felt the way I always do when I find myself in a small, closed space. Trapped.

I reached down to my calf and took the knife from its hard plastic sheath and pushed the point into the skin of the wing. The aluminum parted easily.

I used the back of the blade and began sawing, letting the teeth do the work, trying hard to control my urge to use sheer force and physical strength. The teeth would cut as long as I kept to a smooth rhythm. If I worked too hard I would use too much air, and I didn't have a lot to spare.

The knife did its work and the aluminum skin gave. Three inches, then six, then twelve. I needed to cut a rectangle about a foot by a foot and a half. The numbers on the underside of this wing were written small. And I wanted them from the underside in case somebody—a Coast Guard diver, for instance—came down to look the plane over. I doubted the diver would work his way under the wing and discover what I'd done, and I didn't want anyone else to know that I had the numbers or what I planned to do with them.

I dropped the knife. *Goddamn.*

I could barely turn my head. Not far enough to see the knife. I felt around for it with my hand. Hastily, at first, then more deliberately. I wasted a full minute finding it.

Keep your mind on your work, I told myself, and jammed the point of the knife back into the thin skin of the wing.

I sawed. The aluminum gave. I made myself take shallow, almost dainty sips of air, when what I wanted to do was fill my lungs to bursting again and again.

I had three more sides to go. Checked my watch. Almost seven minutes gone. Another five minutes of work, at least. Too long. But I couldn't go up and come down again. I looked at my pressure gauge. Fifteen hundred psi. I probably wouldn't make it.

I kept my arm moving, trying to groove the stroke like a piston. The metal gave, but seemed to do so slowly, almost reluctantly.

Come on.

I sawed and I watched the metal part ahead of the knife's teeth.

There you go.

Another side. Check the watch and the pressure gauge. Ten minutes. Less than seven hundred psi. And another long side of the rectangle to go.

I jabbed the blade into the aluminum skin one more time. Began a series of short cutting strokes, pulling at the flap of aluminum with my free hand as though I might be able to tear it like worn fabric. It parted slowly ahead of the blade. I made myself stay with the rhythm.

A couple of inches from the end of the last cut and I began to strain at the regulator, sucking hard for the last air in the tank. Each breath was harder. Another stroke with the saw. Then another. A glance at the pressure gauge. The needle was on zero, a thin black line at the bottom of the red zone. One more pull on the knife. Then a hard pull on the regulator. Nothing. My entire body seemed to vibrate now, demanding air. Instinctively I sucked at the regulator again. There was no air.

I pulled once more with the knife and more forcefully with my free hand. The last corner of aluminum gave. The jagged panel was in my hand. I rolled out from under the wing and kicked wildly for the surface, holding my breath for the first twenty or thirty feet.

Then I tried for more air. A breath came through the regulator like a miracle and the screaming in my body stopped.

It wasn't a miracle. Mere physics. The pressure decreased as I ascended, allowing the last of the air in my tank to expand and make it through the regulator. I exhaled for ten or fifteen feet and took another shallow breath, like a man in the desert parceling water from his last canteen. At 150 feet I knew I would make it. Garvey had taught me to make a free ascent from this deep.

When I reached the spare tank, I put the regulator in my mouth and breathed lavishly. My ears were pounding, the sound of my heart furiously pumping blood through my oxygen-starved body. I'd never enjoyed breathing so much.

After a few minutes I had settled down enough to take inventory. I looked at my watch. I had been on the bottom a full fifteen minutes. While I hadn't drowned, there was still the bends to think about.

I inventoried my body for strange sensations. Pain or tingling in my joints. I'd been told by a doctor once that when he went through medical school and was learning symptoms of various exotic diseases, he thought he recognized every one in himself. Likewise, I suddenly felt like I had arthritis. My bad shoulder with its torn rotator cuff that I'd never had fixed suddenly felt like it was in a vise. My knees ached.

I told myself I was imagining things.

I checked my watch. Breathed. Examined the piece of scrap metal in my left hand. Now I felt fine. Or thought I did. But maybe I was fooling myself. Probably I wouldn't know until I was on the boat.

A remora circled me, watching out of one eye, probably trying to decide if I was the sort of creature he could attach himself to for a free ride and maybe a meal.

After a few minutes it swam off. I was sorry to see it go. The fish had given me something to think about.

The hour passed. Slowly. One minute my shoulder and knees felt fine. The next minute they burned.

Did I have the goddamned bends or not?

I looked at my watch. I couldn't make the face out and thought, for a second, that I was losing my vision. Was that a symptom? Was I blacking out?

Then I realized the sun had gone down. The watch had a luminous dial. I had another fifteen minutes at ten feet. When I came up at last into the air, it would be night. I remembered, with a new surge of panic, that the boat was on a sea anchor and would have drifted a good ways while I had been down. I wondered if I'd be able to find it or if I would spend the night floating around the Gulf, supported by the vest, crippled by the bends.

If it wasn't one goddamned thing, I thought, then it was another.

CHAPTER 29

I CAME TO THE SURFACE AND LOOKED around for the boat. It had been drifting for more than an hour now, and I didn't have a moon to work with. I tried the small light I carried but couldn't find the boat in its thin beam, and after five minutes I gave up trying.

I blew some air into the vest, ditched my tank and weight belt, and wondered about the effects of spending all night floating in the Gulf. I probably wouldn't die of exposure—or hypothermia, as they called it now—and I almost certainly wouldn't get attacked by sharks, which was the first thing most people would worry about. Garvey had told me that he knew of only one serious shark attack on this coast over the last twenty years. People died of hypothermia all the time, but I had the wet suit.

I decided I would probably make it through the night, and began wondering about the odds of being found once the sun came up. I remembered flying with Hawthorne over those long stretches of empty water. The same water where I'd be floating. Boat traffic was sparse out here and

I didn't have any signaling equipment. No flares, no radio. Just my flashlight and a little whistle attached to the inflator on the vest.

The only thing for it, I thought, was to swim downcurrent and hope to spot the boat, maybe when the sun came up. That, or be spotted myself by another boat.

I checked my drift, and when I was sure that I had the correct compass line I began swimming, trying to keep the needle from dancing more than a few points left or right. It wasn't easy.

But it must have been my night. I hadn't gone a hundred yards when I saw the small, bright flash of a single strobe. I stopped swimming and watched along that bearing. Some time passed and for a moment I thought I had imagined the strobe, that it was just a random neural impulse fired off at the back of my eye.

Then I saw it again. A small, quick pop of very intense light.

I swam toward the strobe, taking my time and listening for voices. But I didn't hear any. Just the flying fish.

Finally I could make out the profile of the boat, the dim white silhouette of a sportfisherman. The boat was showing no lights. Only the strobe. Nobody was moving topside. The boat could have been derelict. In my imagination, already feverish, I constructed a scenario in which the people on the boat had been washed overboard or had killed one another in a fight or some kind of suicide pact. There were all sorts of possibilities, and I was still running through them and trying to get closer to the boat when it came to me—I was looking at *Second Shot*.

Garvey had rigged the strobe to a tremble circuit. When the boat rolled far enough, there was contact and the light fired. You could disengage the whole system with a simple toggle switch on the console marked EMRG LGHT on a strip of plastic tape. Garvey had probably put it there for just those times when he was diving at night, alone. It was the kind of backup system that was typical of him. He used to say that you stayed alive by paying attention to the details. It hadn't worked for him, I thought, looking over at the black rubber bag on the side of the cockpit. But his attention to the details had sure bailed me out.

I ran a couple of hours before I saw the lights at the pass. I was cold and tired, losing the edge of my anger and feeling all sorts of uncertainties and fears, some specific and some that were mere nameless dreads. I tried to think, but chiefly I wanted to sleep.

It was still another three or four hours until dawn when I eased the boat through the pass and turned up the barge channel, ran past the Coast Guard station, then went on up into the bay. Except for a tug pushing a string of barges loaded with coal and a single shrimp boat headed for the pass, I was the only boat on the water.

I found the lights to a bridge that crossed the bay a couple of miles inland. There was an all-night gas station at one end of the bridge. I anchored near that end, in twenty feet of water, and swam ashore. There was a sleepy kid at the gas station, in the bulletproof booth where the cash register stayed. He woke up when he saw me walk in, dripping wet. Plainly, I hadn't come for gas.

He watched me walk across the parking lot to the telephone booth, probably thinking that he ought to call the sheriff. Actually, I was saving him the trouble. I dialed Tom Pine's number at home and then the number of my credit card.

"Pine," he said before it rang a second time.

"It's Hunt, Tom." I didn't bother apologizing or explaining that it was important. He'd know that.

"What's the problem, Morgan?"

"I need your help with something," I said. "I found Phil Garvey."

"Dead, right?"

"Yes."

"You with the body?"

"Yes."

"Tell me where. We can talk when I get there."

Twenty minutes later, Pine pulled into the lot. The kid in the booth had kept his eye on me all the time, and when he saw a very large black man dressed in jeans, running shoes, and a sweatshirt step out of a truck and speak to me, he must have thought I had been casing the place and then waiting for my partner.

"Show that kid your badge, will you," I said, "before he melts into a puddle."

Pine pulled his wallet out of his back pocket and flipped it open so the kid could see his badge. The kid nodded and gave Pine the okay sign.

"Wonder who he thinks you are," Pine said.

"No telling. But he'll have a story for his buddies."

"What about me, Morgan? You got a story for me?"

"Let's sit in the truck."

"Go ahead. I'm going to get some coffee. You want a cup?"

"Black."

Pine sipped his coffee almost daintily while he listened to what I had to say. He said nothing until I had finished, then he spoke in the soft tones he sometimes uses and that always surprise whoever is listening, no matter how well he knows Tom.

"Garvey was a good man. Straight as a string. I'm sorry, Morgan."

I nodded.

"You all right? Didn't get you a case of the bends, going back to saw on that wing?"

"No. I don't think so," I said. I had told Tom everything, including the part about the airplane numbers. I couldn't ask him for favors if I was holding back.

"I don't see how you can do that," Pine said. "Go diving down that deep. I wouldn't be able to think about nothing but coming back up and breathing real American air."

I nodded again.

"What do you suppose killed Garvey?" he said.

"I don't know. An embolism, maybe. Something that snuck up on him. That happens, even to good divers. He'd been in the water a lot."

"Well, the ghoul will probably find out when he does the autopsy. I'll make sure that takes a long time, the way you want."

"Thanks, Tom."

"You sure his wife didn't file no missing persons report, now?"

"Pretty sure." She hadn't the last time I talked to her, I thought. But that had been a couple of days ago.

"Because if we get a report and we get a body we can't identify, then we got to notify the person who made the report."

"I understand. I'd just like to keep it quiet about Garvey's body being found. Keep it out of the papers, if that doesn't make problems for you."

"I got no problem lying to the papers," Pine said. "None at all. I've been reading lies in the papers all my life."

"You won't get yourself in a box?"

Pine sighed and shook his head, "I might. But it won't be nothing I can't get out of. Bodies come in for identification all the time. If some reporter could identify the body, then good for him. But that don't happen. They wait around for the ghoul to make a positive ID. Then they go with it."

"But you can identify this body."

"How do you know?" he said. "I haven't seen it yet."

"You're taking a chance, Tom."

"They ain't going to fire me, not for lying about knowing who Garvey was. Not for jerking the reporters around."

"You sure?"

He shook his head very slightly. Like a lot of big men, Pine could stay so still for so long that eventually the least movement seemed dramatic.

"Nah, Morgan," he said, softly. "In the second place, I'm their tame nigger. I do great things for the minority-hiring statistics, not just in this county but all across the state. Lose one black sheriff's lieutenant and the numbers go south. You got the FEPC, lawsuits, all kinds of things tearing at your ass. And then, in the first place, I got a good reason for doing what I'm going to do."

"What's that?"

"Doesn't seem to be any other way to find out what's going on. We got a plane crash that, far as I know, ain't been reported. Not to mention a body on the plane. Along with that case full of goodies. And Garvey dead. I'd like to know how to account for all that, and I don't believe I'd learn if we went at it in a strictly official way. Between the truth and proper procedure—it's not a hard choice."

"Okay, Tom," I said. "I'll keep you informed."

"I'm counting on it," he said. "Now we'd better get to work. I need to find a body and you need to hide a boat."

CHAPTER 30

RACHEL GARVEY'S FIVE-YEAR-OLD JEEP Cherokee had a kiddie seat and a hairline crack that had migrated halfway across the windshield. A few dings and rust spots on the side panels. An antidrug bumper sticker. You could look at the car and know a lot about the owner and her struggles.

I was tired. It had been a long night and then a longer morning. First, getting *Second Shot* into a covered boathouse that belonged to a man I'd done small favors for. Then I'd had to call Hawthorne and get him to bring me my truck. After I took him home, I went back to the river house, cleaned up, and put on some clothes. I wanted to lie down and sleep about twelve hours, but I had to talk to Rachel, so I called and found out when her shift ended, then drove to the hospital. Now I was sitting in my truck, in the nurses' parking lot, sipping bitter coffee and checking my watch. It was just about time.

The side doors marked EMPLOYEES came open and people wearing starched white uniforms began drifting out singly and in pairs. Mostly women, but some men. They peeled off to different parked cars and started the engines. It was quitting time, and none of them seemed inclined to linger.

Rachel was among the last to come through the doors. When I saw her, I stepped out of my truck. She noticed me and stopped dead still for a moment. She knew. If it had been good news, I would have called her and interrupted whatever she was doing. Left a message, anyway. This approach meant that everything I had to tell her had to be said in person. That the news couldn't have been worse.

"Goddamn," she said. "Goddamn."

I reached out to touch her by the arm, the way you might offer to support someone who was about to faint. She closed her eyes and put her head on my shoulder. But she didn't lean hard, the way she would have if she'd needed support. And she didn't bury her head in my shoulder and weep. She just rested her forehead there, on my shoulder, like someone who was very tired.

She didn't say anything for a minute or two, then spoke softly. "It was stupid, wasn't it? He was trying to solve all his problems with one big risk?"

I didn't say anything. Her head stayed on my shoulder.

"How did it happen, Morgan?"

"Diving," I said.

She raised her head and looked at me with an expression of disbelief but not hysterical denial. Anyone who'd known Garvey would have a hard time believing he would ever be a diving fatality. It went against the grain of his being. He was too good, too careful.

"It wasn't a dumb accident," I said.

"Sure it was," she said. "Phil used to say there wasn't any other kind. They were all dumb."

I shook my head a little. I didn't want to argue with her.
But I did want her to calm down and listen.

She sighed and swallowed hard and looked away. "You'd
better tell me all about it, Morgan. And don't leave a single
goddamned thing out."

It took about ten or fifteen minutes, standing there in
the parking lot in front of the hospital, with people coming
and going, some of them in wheelchairs or on crutches. I
gave the parts about my second dive and not being able
to find the boat the light treatment, and I didn't go into
detail about the way Garvey looked. In her line of work,
she would know.

Her face barely moved while she listened. A slight
compression around her mouth when I came to the part
about finding Garvey. A narrowing of her eyes when I
described the steel box and its contents.

"So what was he up to, Morgan?" she said when I had
finished. "I thought he'd hooked up with some crackpot
who was looking for Spanish gold."

"So did I."

"Then what's this about?"

"That's what I want to find out."

"Then leave it to the law. Don't be like Phil, playing kids'
games. Grow up and leave it to the law."

"I've talked to the law," I said.

"And . . ."

"The sheriff's lieutenant I talked to—he's a friend of
mine—he thinks I've got a better shot than he does."

She waited for me to go on.

"I need some help from you."

"Me? What could I do, assuming I wanted to do
anything?"

"We don't want anyone to know that Phil's body has been found."

She thought about that, then said, "Yes. I can see why not."

"The coroner has the body. As far as he knows, it's just another unidentified male. Nobody has come to the law with a missing-persons report that fits. My friend at the sheriff's department doesn't think anyone will notice."

"Or care," she said bitterly.

She had a point. Unidentified and unattached males washed up and down this coast more or less constantly, like trash on a tide. Tom Pine could make what remained of Phil Garvey fit the profile.

"It means that you won't be able to have a proper funeral for a while," I said.

"I don't care about that," she said. Then she thought a moment and asked, "You're sure that it is Phil, aren't you?"

I nodded.

"That's good enough for me, for now. Later on we can do a real funeral. With a flag and somebody playing taps. The kids are young, but they'll remember that." Like just about everyone in her generation, Rachel remembered the Kennedy funeral in Arlington and the young son holding a salute as the bugler's notes hung on the air. That's what she wanted for Phil; and why not? He was entitled.

"If anyone calls you," I said, "asking about Phil . . ."

"Yes."

"Stall. Say that he's been out on the boat and you're not sure exactly when he's getting back. Don't act worried. Try to find out who it is and get in touch with me. Or Tom Pine at the sheriff's office."

"All right," she said. "I can handle that."

"Is there anything . . ."

"No," she said. "There isn't."

She turned away and walked to the Cherokee. Got in and started it up. When the engine caught, a small cloud of thick, greasy smoke rose from the exhaust. She was burning oil. Phil would have wanted her to have a new car for sure. One that burned clean and didn't use even a tablespoon of oil between changes.

But she didn't have any patience with that just now. And probably wouldn't ever again.

From the hospital, I drove across the bay bridge and then across the sound to the beach. It was still a little early in the year. The tourists hadn't yet arrived to fill up the rental houses, motels, bars, and restaurants. The places that silk-screened T-shirts or rented sailboards were still closed. The streets had the slightly melancholy feel of a beach town out of season, half-deserted and scratching to get by.

There was a year-round population of people who liked the beach either for the parties or the privacy. For Ron Hawkins it was clearly the privacy.

He is a very smart man who has made a lot of money on a few big plays against the experts. Typically, Hawkins had IBM puts all over the place when the company finally admitted that it had been cut in too many places to ever stop bleeding. He'd run hedge funds for a while but, predictably, he quit. He didn't like having clients.

So Hawkins now managed his own accounts out of his beach house and tried to find other things to keep himself occupied. I wouldn't have known him except that he looked me up after my name was mentioned in a newspaper story about Semmes. I'm still not sure why he called. We talked about markets—steers and oats and hog bellies. He was way ahead of me and I told him so. But he wasn't impressed with his own vast abilities, probably because it all seemed so easy to him.

He started calling fairly regularly, and then we started meeting for lunch—beer and oysters—every couple of months. We talked about markets and other things. At one of those lunches I mentioned some trouble I was having on a job for Semmes. Hawkins offered to see what he could do, using his computer. An hour later, he'd found what I'd been looking for. Since then, I'd called him on several things and he was always eager to help. He struck me as profoundly lonely, and I wouldn't be surprised to pick up the paper some morning and read that he has killed himself.

We were the only two people in the oyster bar where we always ate. There was something stale and forlorn about the air, even though outside it was spring and things were blooming.

"Morgan," Hawkins said, holding out his hand. "You're looking good. But then you always are."

He cuffed me on the shoulder and it recalled my suspicion that Hawkins might be one of those old-fashioned Southern men who just can't get their minds around their own homosexuality. Not even in this age.

None of my business.

"You look good yourself, Ron," I said. Actually he was a little sallow, probably from spending too much time inside. He was tall and a little stooped, with a kind of olive-colored skin and thick dark hair that looked vaguely out of control. His eyes were both melancholy and very alert.

"Don't try to bullshit me, Morgan," he said. "Can't be done."

"Okay, Ron," I said. "The actual fact is that you look like somebody left you in the basement and forgot about you. Why don't you get out in the sun?"

"Better," he said. "How about a beer? I'm buying."

"Fine."

He brought two frosted mugs to the table near the back, where we always sat. When he put the mugs on the table, they made small puddles.

"I ordered us a couple of dozen. All right?"

"Fine. They'll probably be the last of the season."

We raised the mugs and touched them firmly enough to make the glass ring.

Hawkins put the mug down and said, "Ahhh." He had taken half of it down in that one swallow.

"Now," he said, "tell me how I can help you."

He listened while I told him about it. Then he made me go through it again while he took notes in a little book he kept in the back pocket of his khakis. He read off the numbers from the plane's wing twice to make sure he had copied them correctly.

"It won't be any trouble finding out who owns the airplane," he said.

The man behind the counter shouted to us that our oysters were ready. There was no table service.

"You get the trays," Hawkins said. "I'll get us a couple of mugs."

When we were back at the table we ground a little fresh pepper and squeezed some lemon juice on the oysters. They were small, the way they get late in the season. I put one in my mouth. Out of season they can be bland and muddy, but these still had the metallic, salty taste that seems to concentrate the sea.

"Not bad," Hawkins said. "Not bad at all."

We ate three or four each. Drank a little beer. Then I said, "I'm going to need to know a lot about whoever it is who owns that plane. There were no reports about a missing plane, according to Tom Pine. Nobody called up hysterical because somebody was overdue. So the pilot didn't file a flight plan. And whoever the pilot was, he wasn't in the plane. Maybe he got out all right."

"And didn't report the crash?"

"Right."

"So maybe the crash was intentional?" Hawkins said.

I nodded. "The plane looked in pretty good shape to me."

"And the pilot just swam twenty miles to shore?"

I shrugged and ate another oyster.

"Leaving the box full of bearer bonds and jewels down there with the body of that woman?"

I shrugged again. Hawkins ate a couple of oysters and thought for a while.

"I can see what you're up against," he said.

I nodded and we said nothing while we finished the oysters and sipped at the beer. If I'd been with Jessie, I might have ordered another dozen and another mug. Hawkins and I always stopped after the first dozen and the second beer.

Hawkins looked away at the wall, his expression more pensive than usual, almost grave. I had no idea what he was thinking about. Seldom did.

"Amazing how hard some of these people will work, and the risks they'll take," he finally said, "just to make some money that isn't legitimate. You've got to believe that the scheme is the thing, you know what I mean?"

Sure, I thought. Anyone who's been in jail knows that.

"That's missing in me. I'm just not made that way. But I almost admire it. Anyone who finds life . . . oh, a little *dull* would have to."

"Try skydiving," I said, "if you need some kicks. Or bungee jumping."

He shook his head. "No. You don't understand people

like me, Morgan. I get a little taste when I do these computer things for you. Even that makes my fingers tremble."

"You've made plays that would paralyze most people."

He shook his head. "Not the same."

"It might be."

He shook his head and gave me a little rueful smile. "It's
kind of you to say so, Morgan. Now I'll go on back home
and break a few computer codes. My version of life on the
edge. Remember that great line from Milton—'They also
serve who only stand and wait'?"

I nodded.

"My version is, 'They also serve who only sit and hack.'
This shouldn't take long. I'll call you in three or four
hours."

CHAPTER 31

I SAT IN THE KITCHEN, DRINKING COFFEE to stay awake, and called Jessie to tell her I was still alive and hadn't fled to Panama.

"Oh, man," she said, "are you all right? Are you sure?"

"I'm fine. I'm sorry I've been out of touch."

"Can you tell me about it?"

"Sure."

"Why don't I come over?"

"I'd like that."

Jessie and I have our bad moments. Like everybody else, I suppose. Times when the air between us seems a little foul and we both want to get away and breathe. That seems to happen when things are going well for both of us, in our own little lives. You resent the other person doing well without you, I guess. Part of the pissy side of human nature.

But when things go bad for one or the other of us, we draw together. I don't know if it's love or loyalty. But either way . . .

She was at the river house in ten minutes. Wearing a kind of loose cotton print dress with her hair tied back. She said she'd been in the garden.

"You look great," I said.

"And you look tired."

"Can't imagine why."

"Let's take a walk," she said, "while you tell me about it."

So we walked around the backyard and then down the path to the slough, where I turned the canoe over and launched it through the lily pads. She sat in the front seat and listened while I went on with my story. She paddled, too. Wouldn't have it any other way.

We had cleared the mouth of the creek and were in the main river before I'd finished my story.

"Well," she said, "so much for the romance of sunken treasure. What you have instead of Spanish dubloons is bearer bonds, numbered accounts, and uncut jewels. Same old tired stuff. Do you think it's drugs?"

"I don't know. If it is, Garvey didn't know about it."

"Do you think he knew it was just criminal loot, not treasure?"

"He believed it was treasure, that night when he came to see me."

"And after that?"

"Well, they had to tell him there was *something* down there, in 240 feet of water, before he'd go down looking for it. I suspect they baited him with the treasure. Got him thinking about the big money, and when the boys from the State Attorney's Office started coming around, they could say they had to let that one rest for a while, but there was another little job he could do to earn some money. Seems like that's one way it could have happened, anyway."

She made a few strokes with the paddle while she thought about that. There was something essentially peaceful and languid about the river. It felt wrong, somehow, to be talking about murder and such.

"Now you've got the case—and its contents—so you can make them come to you?" Jessie said.

"Right."

"Will Tom Pine back you up?"

"All the way."

"And be there if you need another body or some extra firepower?"

"Yes."

"You'd better get some sleep then, Morgan. Let's turn this barge around and get you back to the house."

The phone woke me. I came up so fast that for a moment I didn't know where I was or why I had suddenly broken into consciousness. I was looking for something to put in my hand and saw the telephone handset.

"Yeah," I said.

"Morgan?"

"This is Morgan Hunt."

"Is everything all right?" Hawkins said.

"Yes," I said. "Fine." I looked at my watch. I had been asleep three hours.

"You sound—"

"I'm okay, Ron. Just fell asleep. You find something?"

"Quite a bit, actually," he said. "Probably more than you bargained for."

"Well . . ."

"There's a lot of it, Morgan, and I don't like talking on the phone. I know it's a long way back out here, but maybe I could meet you somewhere. Split the distance."

We settled on a place and I told him I'd see him in an hour.

He said to make it an hour and a half. That gave me time to sit on the step in front of the river house and watch the last of the sunset while I sipped some coffee to get all the systems running.

I left the house and eased the truck along the blacktop, with the high beams full of insects and the radio on an oldies station. Half the songs were about young love, and they never seemed more banal. After ten or fifteen miles I switched the radio off and listened to the monotonous hum of the radials on the road.

Hawkins and I met at a little place on the bay where a couple of old freight docks and warehouses had been renovated. They were now full of trendy boutiques and restaurants. I sat in a wrought-iron chair at a small round table and studied the menu. It was all ice cream and brownies. And coffee. What I needed was more coffee.

I wondered what Tom Pine would make of the place. Especially the price of a cup of fresh-brewed Kenyan coffee, which is what I sipped while waiting for Hawkins. It wasn't bad, but I wasn't sure it was two dollars a cup worth of not bad.

"Been waiting long?" Hawkins said when he sat down across from me.

"Nope. Just half a cup."

"We could go somewhere else, Morgan," he said. "A bar, maybe. This is the only place I know in town. I generally stick to the beach."

"It's fine, Ron."

"What kind of coffee did you get?"

"The Kenyan."

"Good choice," he said. "But next time try the Sumatran. It's really special."

"Okay," I said. That sort of distinction was important to Hawkins.

He pulled several sheets of paper from his jacket pocket when he sat back down. They looked like they had come off one of those tractor-feed printers. He took a sip of coffee and said, "I started where you wanted me to start—with the airplane. One thing led to another, and I just kept following the data. Airplane registrations. Court documents. Newspaper stories. RTC records. Nothing to it. You just follow the data."

"Should we start with the plane?" I said.

"Sure. The plane you found on the bottom of the Gulf belonged—still belongs, I suppose—to Vernon Culp."

"The banker?"

"I suppose you could have called him that, once upon a time," Hawkins said. "These days it would be more accurate to call him a defendant."

"Is the plane still his?" I said.

"It is. Although the IRS and the bankruptcy courts have all been doing their best to pry it away from him. Culp fights them on everything."

It was Culp's bank, once it had been taken over by a much tougher outfit, that had been leaning on Phil Garvey. Too much of a coincidence, I thought, that he should have drowned salvaging Culp's airplane.

"Was Culp a pilot?" I asked.

"He may have known how to fly," Hawkins said. "He was one of the original high fliers, in another sense of the word, but he was no pilot, at least not according to the FAA records I scanned."

"Then he probably hadn't been flying the plane himself when it crashed. If that had been an intentional ditching, it would have taken a good pilot with some nerve. People like Culp hire that kind of talent."

"Sounds right," Hawkins said.

"And he never reported the plane as missing?"

"Yes he did," Hawkins said, with a trace of smugness.

"Tom Pine told me nothing had been reported," I said.

"Maybe not around here," Hawkins said. "But that plane was reporting missing a long way from Pine's jurisdiction."

"Where?"

"In the Bahamas, east of Andros, on the way to Nassau. It was big in the *Miami Herald*. Our local journal of record ran it very small. They must have had a kid's golf tournament that day." He paused for a moment. "Anyway, according to the story in the *Herald*," Hawkins went on, "Culp's wife had taken the plane to Miami. He knew about the trip and the pilot had filed a flight plan. She'd gone down there to visit her sister."

"Seems like I read that Culp's wife had left him and moved to Colorado," I said.

"He claims they were trying for a reconciliation," Hawkins said. "Maybe they had a love so strong that even bank auditors and federal prosecutors couldn't rend it asunder."

"What was the plane doing in the Bahamas?"

"Culp said he didn't know."

"Then how did he know that it had crashed . . . where did you say it was, off Andros?"

"Correct. Where, as it happens, the water is about six thousand feet deep and you don't go looking for sunken airplanes unless you have a submarine."

"So how did he know, Ron?"

"The pilot survived the crash. He's the one who reported it. He was picked up by a fishing boat. No injuries. Just a little sunburn."

We'd finished the coffee. Hawkins was pushing a spoon around the table idly, waiting for me to say something.

"That's a twin-engine airplane," I said.

"Right."

"They don't just stop flying. I could buy it if he was in a single-engine ship and he lost oil pressure or something all of a sudden."

"The pilot said he was a little surprised himself. His guess was some kind of fuel contamination."

"That long after takeoff?"

"He'd stopped at Andros and topped off."

"Why did he stop there?"

"He was having a little radio trouble. He fixed it himself. Bad fuse."

"I see."

"It's all right here," Hawkins said, tapping the printouts.

"And all bullshit," I said.

"Beg pardon?"

"Well, no matter what those reports say, the plane with those numbers is not down in the Tongue of the Ocean off Andros. It's about ten miles northeast of the nipple, off Navarre, Florida. I've been there."

"Absolutely. The reports are just an official version . . ."

"So, could be there's another airplane down in the Bahamas. Maybe with another body. But I don't think so."

"Why?"

"It's a complicated plan, to begin with. Why make it any harder, bringing in doubles? Especially if you have to kill them. The extra plane would be tough enough."

"So you think the body you saw in Culp's plane is his wife's?"

"Yes. And I imagine it could be proved with dental records. Nothing else would work."

"No," Hawkins said, "I suppose not."

"Can I take these pages?" I said.

"Of course," he said. "That's why I brought them. And Morgan?"

"Yes."

"If you'd like, I could look at the contents of that case and give you a better sense of just what you've got your hands on. Might help."

"It would. Thanks. I'll call you in the next day or two. Thanks for this, too," I said, holding up the pages.

"Glad I could help," he said. "Call any time."

CHAPTER 32

It was about eleven that night when I parked my truck under the broad branch of the live oak in my front yard. I hadn't been sleeping much, but I was a long way from feeling tired. The air was warm and fragrant with the scent of wisteria.

I went inside and made coffee. Those people in the medical schools doing research on the effects of coffee could lay off their white rats and study me. Maybe I could hire out.

I filled a cup and took it into my drinking room, where I sat at the desk and went through the sheets of printer paper that Hawkins had given me, reading and making an occasional note.

It was a lot of reading. Hawkins had copied pages of stuff off the retrieval services, like Nexis, most of it background on Culp. I scanned it and didn't see anything to make me like him any better. He and his wife had gone on a hundred-thousand-dollar eating tour of Europe just a few months before he flamed out. There was a story about how his wife had flown to New York one day on a private jet to buy a dress, then flown the dress back the next day because she had changed her mind about the color.

I skimmed that stuff. The story in the *Miami Herald* about the pilot who reported ditching Culp's plane was more my meat. It had a name, for one thing—the name of the pilot who was slopping at Culp's trough. His name was Jerry Jenkins.

At the end of that sheet of paper was a note in Ron Hawkins's hand. Jenkins had a local address and phone number. I dialed it.

"Hello." He sounded bored. Or drunk.

"Mr. Jenkins," I said, half whispering.

"Yeah, who's calling?"

"Are you the Jenkins who does some flying for Vernon Culp?"

"Used to," he said, more bored now, "but I'm retired now. You need a pilot, try the Yellow Pages."

"I don't need a pilot, but *you* are going to need some help. You're running out of altitude, airspeed, and ideas at the same time. You know what I mean?"

"No," he said, not bored anymore. "I don't. Who is this and what do you want?"

"I expect that it's a question of what *you* want," I said. "I mean, how much of the rest of your life do you want to spend in jail for that stunt down in the Bahamas?"

He said nothing, and the silence lasted long enough that I thought he might have disconnected.

"Who is this?" he said finally. He was close to pleading. One phone call and his comfortable retirement had been blown away like smoke in a high wind.

"I'll meet you in one hour at the barricade to the beach road on Perdido Key. You know where that is?"

"Yes."

"One hour."

I was there twenty minutes early, dressed in dark clothes and crouched in a small patch of palmettos, watching to see if anyone came early. Anyone the frightened pilot might have called for help. Anyone with an ambush in mind. One car pulled up to the barricade, its high beams on, and stopped. A couple looking for some private beach. But they didn't want to walk. The car made a clumsy turn, rear tires almost getting stuck in the soft sand just off the shoulder, then headed off the way it had come.

I scanned the dunes. Nothing moved, and I felt certain that nothing larger or more dangerous than a raccoon or an armadillo lurked out there in the clumps of pine, jack oak, and sea oats. I wasn't absolutely confident about many things, but my night vision was one of them.

I flattened a mosquito on my throat and checked my watch. Five minutes. If he didn't show . . . what? I wasn't as good at contingency planning as I was at seeing in the dark—or *through* the dark, to be more precise. I was not as impulsive as I'd once been, but I still needed to work on my long-range planning.

So what would I do if the pilot didn't show?

I was thinking about it, considering the merits of going right to the source, to Culp himself, when another car turned onto the beach road and eased toward the barricade, using just the parking lights. It had to be my boy.

The car was certainly right for a pilot who had just landed in the chips. A Lexus coupe that looked new. The sound system alone in one of those things costs more than Mozart made in a lifetime of writing music.

The car stopped at the barricade and the parking lights went out. I couldn't tell if the driver cut the engine because . . . well, that's the point of the car. It's engineered to be quiet. Me, I like a certain amount of motor noise.

The inside lights of the Lexus came on when the driver opened the door and stepped out. He closed the door behind him and stood, looking across the I-beam barricade and down the beach road. He was waiting, with his hands in the pockets of his windbreaker, for someone to appear on the other side of the barricade when I came up on him from behind. It was easy.

"Evening, brother," I said. "Don't turn around."

He jumped a foot.

"God," he said.

"No," I said. "He left on other business. Told me to take care of things for him. Your bad luck."

"What—"

"Before we talk," I interrupted him, "maybe you'd better get down on your knees and lock your hands behind your neck. Let me check and make sure you aren't armed or wired."

"I want—"

"Just do it." I was carrying a handgun. I prefer something that goes up against your shoulder. I've never been much with pistols, but at this range I'd be competent enough. I worked the slide. The gun was loaded—be kind of silly to carry it any other way under these circumstances—but I wanted him to hear the sound. He was on his knees before the ejected round hit the ground.

"Good. Now just be still. Very still."

I patted him down. It felt oddly and distastefully intimate. He was clean.

When I finished, I hit him just below the ear with my cupped hand. Not hard enough to hurt him, but with enough force that he'd be stunned and pay attention. He rolled on his side with his face in the sand.

"Stand up."

He got to his feet, gagging and spitting.

"Let's walk on down to the left, here, toward that little clump of pine trees. You take the lead. Keep the hands locked behind your neck."

He walked unsteadily, his Guccis sinking into the soft sand, until I told him to stop.

"Kneel down, just like before."

He did, and I slipped an old flour sack over his head. Then I wrapped his ankles in a couple of feet of wire. Even if he tried to run, he wouldn't get very far.

"Okay. You can roll over and sit, just like a dog. Get comfortable and put your hands on your knees where I can see them."

He did that, too. He was very well behaved.

"Now," I said, "why don't you tell me why the airplane you claimed sank off Andros, and the body of the woman who went down with it, is sitting on the bottom of the Gulf about thirty miles straight-line distance from here? Take your time and don't leave anything out."

He couldn't tell it fast enough.

CHAPTER 33

I LEFT HIM COUNTING TO A THOUSAND and walked back to the spot in the pines where I had parked my truck. I'd told him that if I stopped hearing him I'd come back. When I reached my truck, I could still hear him loud and strong.

His story hadn't been quite what I expected. You never allow enough for ineptitude, screwups, and ordinary bad luck. I'd been looking for a smooth, intricate operation. Instead, I was finding a true Chinese fire and boat drill.

The only thing that had gone according to plan was that the woman, Diane Culp, was dead.

He'd flown her down to Miami, Jenkins told me. Culp had known she had the bearer bonds, the stones, and the documents she needed to close out a numbered account in a Nassau bank. That account was fat with money that Culp had skimmed from his own failing bank, but hadn't gotten around to spending yet. He wanted his tormentors to think that she had gotten it all.

He'd flown her to Nassau, where she had cleaned out

the account, and they had been heading home when Jenkins actually did have a problem with his radio. He landed, replaced a fuse, and took off again, on a straight-line course for Pensacola, flying low. His passenger had gotten into the rum in Nassau and she went to sleep an hour out. With the plane on automatic pilot, he walked back into the passenger section and shot her in the head. Twice, according to the current doctrine. They call it a "double tap."

He was supposed to rendezvous with a boat far enough offshore that there wouldn't be any other boats straying into the area to witness what came next. It would be well after dark when he reached the rendezvous. He and the boat both had GPS and radios so they wouldn't have any trouble finding each other.

But the best plans supported by the best equipment have a way of going froggy. That is one of those laws of the universe that nobody can quite understand or explain, like quantum mechanics and entropy. I believe they call it "Chaos Theory."

When Jenkins thought he was where he should be, he looked around and saw nothing but empty black water. He tried the radio and discovered that it was dead. The fuse again. He was getting stray voltage from somewhere and, as it turned out, that had also partially fried his GPS. He was getting a bad reading. He thought about turning north and making a landfall, then looking for a strip where he could put the plane down. But there was the problem of the body and the steel case. He couldn't think of any good way to explain them. Also, he wasn't sure he had enough fuel to make it to the beach.

At that point he did the only sensible thing. He panicked.

One thought took over. He had to get away from the airplane, the body, and that steel case. They represented the electric chair. If he ditched and let the plane sink with all the evidence, then at least he had a chance.

The ditching went smoothly. He was floating on the Gulf, in a small survival raft, before the plane had even sunk. He did a quick inventory of his survival gear and found both a radio and a handheld loran unit, the next best thing to a GPS. He got his position and then tried the radio. On the first call he made contact with his pickup boat, which was waiting right where it was supposed to be, about twenty miles away, in much shallower water.

In fourteen hours he was back in the water, this time off Andros, with a story for whoever picked him up. Culp and his people had those loran numbers, so they knew where the plane was, with the steel case still inside. But it was in water three times as deep as the plan called for.

Which was why they needed a diver like Garvey. But Jenkins hadn't known that part. I figured it out for myself.

I slept deeply, but was up and outside before the light began to accumulate between the trees. I stood on the riverbank, just breathing and watching. Gradually, there was enough light that things began assuming specific shapes. Nothing moved and nothing made a sound. No birds sang. It was as though they were waiting to make sure that the dawn was genuine. This was the Indians' sacred time. It lasted only a few minutes.

An owl broke the silence. Then some crows. When I heard them, I started up the shell drive toward the black-top, running. It felt good to move.

I was sitting in my truck, parked in Loftin's private space behind his office building, when he pulled up in the Range Rover at nine.

"That's my space," he said.

"I think you'll want to talk to me," I said.

"I can't imagine why," he said. "Now get out of my space."

I stepped out of the truck and walked back to the tailgate. I was looking at him through the driver's window of the Range Rover.

"Stay away from me. I mean it."

He might have a gun, I thought. Lots of people did. Scared people with nice things they were afraid of losing and didn't know how to defend with anything less than a 9mm automatic. But I wasn't going to give him an excuse to shoot me.

I leaned against the tailgate and said, "I found something that might interest you. It isn't Spanish gold, but it's close."

"I don't know what you're talking about. Now move it or I'll call the cops." He held up his car phone for me to see. It seemed like a strange thing to be threatening someone with.

I reached into the bed of the truck and lifted out the jagged sheet of aluminum skin I had cut out of the airplane wing. I held it up so he could read the numbers.

"Look familiar?"

"No. And you're wasting my time." But he didn't start punching numbers on the phone.

"Okay," I said. "In that case I'll take my story some other place. Sorry for the inconvenience. Maybe I'll see you around."

I started back toward the cab of my truck.

"I can't do it right now," he said, behind me.

I turned back around.

"Something more important to do?" I said. He belonged

to the busy and important set. Always close to the phone. Always scheduled tighter than skin on a sausage.

"I . . . ah."

"Speak up," I said. "Don't be bashful. Just us girls."

"Where will you be in . . ."—he looked at his watch—"two hours?"

"Anywhere you want me to be," I said. He didn't realize yet that he could miss all his appointments from now on.

"Back here?"

"That would be fine."

I got in my truck, cranked the engine, and pulled out of his space. That was another thing he could forget about. The private parking space and the little cheap thrill of status he got when he saw his name on the cement parking block. He could forget about the Range Rover while he was at it. Damned shame is what it was.

I drove from Loftin's office to Rachel Garvey's. She answered a second or two after I knocked.

"Morgan," she said. "Hello. Come in. Pour you some coffee?"

She looked tired. Pale, except around the eyes, where the skin looked almost bruised. But she wasn't giving in and letting herself go. She had makeup on and her hair was fixed and she gave me a smile and a sisterly hug as I stepped into the room.

It had been turned into a kind of recovery room for Rick, with one of those hospital beds that cranks up at each end, a stainless-steel table with bedpans, instruments, and medicines, and a walker so the boy could get out of bed now and then to relearn what he had just recently learned how to do the first time. He was lying in the bed, his head wrapped in what must have been three yards of bandages.

His end of the bed was cranked up and he was watching television.

"Rick, honey, you remember Mr. Hunt."

"Hi," he said weakly.

"Hi," I said. "You coming along?"

"Yes, sir. Coming along good."

Rachel led the way past his bed and into the kitchen. "Have a seat, Morgan," she said and poured coffee. She handed me a cup and sat across the table from me.

"It won't be too long, now," I said. "Maybe as early as tonight. No more than a couple of days."

She shrugged. "I know you're doing your best. Just make sure you get them, Morgan. Don't let the bastards get away."

"I won't," I said. Then I took a folded envelope from my shirt pocket.

"What's that?" she said, turning wary. She was as suspicious of charity as Phil had been.

"It's something that Phil gave me. Seems like it belongs to you now."

She opened the envelope and examined the five-thousand-dollar check.

"It's made out to you, Morgan. That makes it yours."

"And it's dated almost a month ago," I said. "I could have cashed it, but I had a deal with Phil."

"What deal?"

"That I wouldn't cash it until he had that salvage-diving project wrapped up. He agreed."

"I see."

"I don't see how anyone could call it 'wrapped up.' So I think the check ought to go to you."

She looked at the check, brushed her eye with a knuckle, and said, "He sounded like a kid at Christmas, the night he told me about it. The hard times were over. We could buy a new house. We wouldn't have to worry about Rick's doctors. I'd be driving a new car. . . . He'd been so worried about money for so long that there was this great . . . oh, I don't know, this *release*. He was laughing and babbling like he was a little drunk. I said it seemed too good to be true. Turned out it was."

"Take the check, will you?" I said. "We had a deal. I wouldn't feel right and I don't need it."

She took a deep breath.

"Okay," she said. "But you aren't fooling me with that bullshit about a deal."

The Range Rover was securely in the slot marked PRIVATE FRANK P. LOFTIN. I wondered what the "P" stood for and took one of the slots marked VISITOR.

The room where you waited until your attorney was free was done in Chippendale with deep, muted Persian carpets on the floor and somber framed prints on the paneled walls. All meant, I suppose, to suggest the gravity of the work that went on in these offices. And to suggest, also, that it didn't come cheap.

"May I help you, sir?" the receptionist said in a way that suggested she didn't think so.

"Mr. Loftin is expecting me."

"Yes, sir. Would you like to take a seat while I see if he's free?"

"No. I'll stand."

She buzzed Loftin's secretary, who then buzzed him. The receptionist seemed surprised that he was willing to see me at all, much less right away.

Loftin's office was more of the same. He sat behind a small desk, looking down at the floor, and didn't look up until he'd heard the secretary pull the door shut behind me.

His expression told me he hadn't had any brilliant ideas in the two hours since we'd last talked. There was no color to his skin and his mouth was puckered with worry.

"Maybe you should explain what you're doing with that . . . ah, *thing*," he said.

"Nah," I said. "Why don't you see if you can explain why I found it about a thousand nautical miles from where it's supposed to be? I expect you know."

He shook his head. It was a gesture of denial, not remorse.

"I didn't know what they planned for Diana . . . Mrs. Culp. I wasn't in on that. They knew I wouldn't go along."

"Were you the one who sucked Phil Garvey in?"

A nod.

"Was that little tantrum part of the plan?"

He shook his head. "No. I went to him before that and said I had an offer. He wanted to know what kind of offer. And I said the kind that could make him rich. But he wanted to know more. Said something about could he tell his wife about the job? I said, 'That depends on if your wife has a sense of humor.' Then he said, 'Well, could I tell the sheriff about the job?' I told him that would be unwise, and he told me to find another boy."

"So you decided to learn how to dive yourself?" I said. "Why didn't you just go hire one of those rig divers over in Morgan City? They're all out of work."

"Culp didn't want anyone who would come back for more. We knew Garvey was straight. But he was also in trouble with the bank. We thought maybe we could get him to go for one big payoff. After that, he'd never want to see us again. I took the diving course from him just to stay close. I never wanted to dive. The jellyfish thing cinched it."

"Then?"

"Then I found out about the sick kid. After I talked to Semmes, I figured it was worth one more try with Garvey. Culp came up with the idea of telling him it was treasure. Said that Garvey wouldn't mind that kind of illegal diving. Once we had him, we could get to the other thing."

"And you were salting that supposed wreck site, weren't you? Dropping a few little baubles for him to find. You didn't have any idea where that Spanish ship went down."

He shook his head miserably. "That was one of the things Culp had been spinning money into—treasure salvage. He'd been in one of those early limited partnerships with Mel Fisher, but he never made anything, so he quit investing the year before they made the big find. That bothered him a lot, so he went out looking for another operation to invest in. There were a couple of boat bums up here, two or three years ago, who called themselves treasure salvers. They had a lot of expensive equipment and claimed to have some historical research that located a Spanish treasure ship. Culp fell for it and started putting money into it."

"His depositors' money?" I said.

"Yes."

"What happened?"

"They couldn't keep going. Too expensive."

"Culp couldn't steal it as fast as they could spend it, huh?"

"They were stealing, too," he said defensively. "They salted their sites and showed him some stuff they had supposedly just brought up. He found out about it . . . I don't know how."

"Must have chapped his ass," I said. "People doing something dishonest like that."

He gave me a blank look. "Well, there wasn't anything he could do, since he didn't want to be investigated himself. But he got to keep the stuff they showed him to make him think they were on the track."

I looked at Loftin when he said all this. He couldn't look back.

"Did you bring the state attorney's people in to scare Garvey, after he'd gotten a taste of the money?"

He nodded.

"Tell me about it."

"We needed a reason to quit working the wreck site— what he believed was the wreck site, anyway. When the agents came around, that was all the reason he needed."

"But you had another job, right?"

"Yes."

"The plane?"

He nodded reluctantly. "By that time, he was counting on the money. One dive and he'd have it."

"Did you take his truck?"

"I was going to meet him at a private dock over by Fort Walton."

"But he didn't show up?"

"No."

"What did you think had happened?"

He raised his hands helplessly. "I didn't know. Maybe he'd run off, or maybe something had gone wrong."

"Didn't occur to you he might be in trouble and that maybe you ought to call for some help?"

He shook his head slightly and tried to look like he was eaten up with remorse.

"Where's the truck?"

"Huh?"

"Where did you leave the truck?"

"It's in a garage. We were going to take it to New Orleans or Miami, leave it in the airport to make it look like maybe he'd left the country."

"I want it."

"Huh?"

"Phil Garvey is dead. I'm trying to put together some kind of an estate. I want his truck."

"When?"

"Right now."

He started to look at his watch but I cut him off.

"Tell your secretary to cancel your appointments. I want that truck right now."

He picked up the phone and pressed a button. "Louise, listen, cancel everything for the rest of the day and re-schedule, will you? Something just came up."

CHAPTER 34

LOFTIN DROVE AND I SAT IN THE PAS-
senger seat, comparing the ride of the Range Rover to my
truck's. This was smooth and a little mushy. My truck was
stiff and would handle much better off the pavement. This
baby was built for comfort—which, in my opinion, is about
as overrated as a college degree.

I said nothing, and neither did Loftin until we were east
of town, practically to Milton, and he turned off the highway, down a little section road that cut a line through some
planted pines. The sun angled down through the pines in
narrow shafts and it looked cool and restful in there among
the trees.

"What are you going to do next?"

"Pick up Garvey's truck," I said. "Sell it and give the
money to his widow."

He thought for a minute.

"If it's money you want . . . well, you've got the case."

"What case is that?" I said.

"You know what case."

"I don't know anything about a case. You tell me."

"It was in the plane."

"I didn't see anything in that airplane except bodies. Not pretty, I mean to tell you."

"You're lying."

I reached over and slapped him on the cheek. Not too hard.

"Watch your mouth," I said.

His face puckered and his knuckles went white on the wheel. We went another quarter-mile down the section road before he spoke again.

"There was a case on that airplane. It was packed with cash and securities and jewels." He was pleading, almost, for me to believe him.

"That so? Wonder what happened to it."

He opened his mouth to say something, then changed his mind. He turned off on another road.

"So what are you going to do after you get the truck?"

"I'm not sure."

"Are you going to the police?"

"Maybe."

He said nothing. His expression was a mix of fear, bewilderment, and just a little hope.

He made one last turn and pulled up in front of a barn, well weathered and long abandoned.

"Who owns this?"

"Culp."

We got out of the wagon and walked to the sliding door in the face of the barn. I pushed it open. The chrome from the Toyota's bumper looked dazzling in the gloom.

"Keys in it?"

"Yes."

"Okay, then. You and I have just one last little piece of business this morning."

"What's that?" He sounded hopeful.

"I'm going to whip your ass."

He took a step back and held his hands up in front of his chest in the submissive gesture of an animal that has lost a fight for dominance.

I stepped up and faked him by dropping my left shoulder. He took the fake and tried to cover up with both arms. I hit him over the ear with a cupped hand. Hard enough that he screamed and went down in a pile, clutching the side of his head. I kicked him in the stomach. He screamed again. Then rolled over on his side and vomited.

That was the entire fight.

"Good luck with the case," I said. "Hope it turns up."

I got in the Toyota and it cranked the first time. I pulled out of the barn past Loftin, who was kneeling now, a long drooling line of green mucus hanging from his lips, his arms wrapped tight around his chest, and a stunned look on his ashen face.

I drove back into town, feeling slightly stupid and ashamed of myself. Still, if Loftin never did a day of time, never lost his law practice, never suffered in any way for his little part in what had happened to Phil Garvey, he would remember this morning. Actually, he was lucky but didn't know it. I'd been tempted to carve my initials in his chest.

When I got back to town, I stopped at the newspaper office and wrote out an ad for Garvey's truck. He'd put less than fifty thousand miles on it, and he'd taken care of it the same way he took care of all his gear. So I asked for seventy-five hundred and figured I'd take six.

After I left the newspaper, I drove downtown to the little square where the bums congregated around the statue of the old Confederate cavalryman. They rested here between meals at the seaman's mission and drinks at the dives that traded on their despair.

I parked and walked through the park until I spotted one who looked reasonably clean and sober.

"You want to make an easy fifty?" I said.

"Oh, Captain," he said.

"Can you drive?"

"If you need a wheel man, then I'm your boy."

"You got a license?"

He took a shabby leather wallet out of his back pocket and showed me a current Louisiana driver's license.

"Come on," I said. "I'll have you back here in two hours tops."

He hung back for a moment. Men had been rolled in this park and a couple beaten apparently for the sheer hell of it. Word gets around.

"Straight goods," I said. "I'll pay up front."

I took out my wallet and handed him a fifty.

"Lead on, Master," he said, "and I will follow."

We got in Garvey's truck. In the closed cab I could pick up the faint scent of old, metabolized alcohol coming from his pores. But it wasn't too bad. He bathed, anyway.

I drove to the parking lot behind Loftin's office, gave the man the keys to my truck, and told him to follow me. He stayed right on my bumper all the way back to the river house. I left Garvey's truck under the low limb of the old live oak—no sense putting any more miles on it—and we drove back into town in my truck.

He told me his tale of woe in a sort of rambling, detached way. It was almost as though he hadn't been a player, merely a passenger in his life. I barely listened. At the end of the story, he said, "I could get me a ship in New Orleans, sure could. But I don't believe nobody ever gets no ship out of this hole."

I stopped in front of the bus station.

"You picking something up here?" he said.

"No. Dropping something off."

"What?"

"You."

He gave me a look.

"You can get a ticket to New Orleans and be there to-night. That fifty ought to cover your ticket. If it doesn't, come back out here and I'll give you what you need, plus a little for dinner. Otherwise, the park is about ten blocks, that way."

I pointed down the street toward the waterfront.

"Long time since I rode the Hound."

"Make up your mind," I said. "I'm in a hurry."

He thought for a second or two, then said, "I'll be a minute."

A little later he was back, leaning through the open passenger window.

"Thirty-eight fifty," he said. "One way. And I sure ain't interested in no round-trip."

"Good luck," I said. "Hope you find a ship."

"Bless you, friend," he said.

I nodded and put the truck in gear. He went back into the bus station and I drove back out of town.

My next stop was Garvey's shop. I still had my key, and when I let myself in the air in the place smelled old and stale. It was like going into an attic that had been closed up for years. It didn't seem right that Garvey's shop should smell that way. Seemed like it should have smelled of sweat and salt water.

I opened a window and turned on some lights, then went to work. I inventoried everything in the shop. Tanks, regulators, wet suits, fins, masks. Everything down to the lead weights you string on your belt and the Hawaiian slings you use for speared fish. Some of the gear was new and I made a column on a sheet of paper where I listed all of that. Some he used for rental, and that went in another column. I made a note about the condition everything was in. Except for some fraying on the occasional wet suit and a little chipped paint on some tanks, everything was in good shape, which was no surprise.

The first inventory took a couple of hours, and when that was done I started looking over the tools and heavy equipment. There was an air compressor that looked like it was in pretty good shape. I checked the desk and found the log. The compressor had slightly less than a thousand hours on it, and Garvey had, naturally, done all the maintenance. I found the number of a heavy-equipment dealer in the Yellow Pages, got a quote on a new machine, and made a note of the price.

I went through the rest of the tools, down to the precision gunsmith's screwdrivers that Garvey had used when he worked on regulators. I could use them myself.

It was late afternoon when I'd finished the inventory. I got the Yellow Pages out again and made a list of all the dive shops in the area, writing the numbers out in the margin, next to the names.

Then I made the calls and my pitch. I was representing Mr. Phil Garvey in the liquidation of his diving business. I was prepared to offer the entire inventory, which included . . . blah, blah, blah.

Three of the people I talked to were interested enough to make appointments to come by the next morning and look everything over. I told them I wanted bids by noon. Then I started on the desk and file cabinets. Fairly early in that game, I found the title to the Toyota truck. Phil had put it in his name and Rachel's. He'd done the same with the business. He'd also given her complete power of attorney, bless him.

It was dark by the time I had everything sorted into piles—throwaways, dead records, receivables, follow-ups. I figured Garvey still had a couple of thousand coming from customers who owed him for lessons or gear. And there would be some refunds coming from insurance policies that ran for another few months. Deposit refunds on the building and the phone. I put all that stuff in a box to take home with me. I could write the letters there.

There was one last thing I could do before I left. I picked up the phone and called the Outrigger. I asked for Pete and the voice said, "You got him."

I identified myself and he said, "Hey, how you been? Your buddy turn up yet?"

"Yes and no," I said, "if you know what I mean."

"Not exactly. But I ain't asking, either."

"Right now I'm taking care of some things for him. Stuff that needs doing badly, but that he isn't in any position to do for himself. You understand?"

"Perfect."

"I want to sell that boat. You have a line on any possible buyers?"

"How much?"

"Whatever's fair. You keep ten percent."

"Well," he said, "that boat is in good shape, so I could move it easy. I've had a couple of people ask me about it. I don't think there would be any problem at all with seventy or eighty K."

"Can you make it happen in a couple of days?"

"Only if everything is legal."

"Strictly legal."

"I'll do what I can. But I can't promise anything."

"Fair enough."

I hung up and called another number.

"Yes."

"Rachel, this is Morgan."

"Oh, hello, Morgan. How are you?"

I told her I was fine. Just fine. Then I ran down what I'd been doing and told her I would appreciate it if I could come by in the morning, before she left for the hospital, to get her to sign some things.

"Absolutely," she said. "I'll have coffee. Listen, Morgan, you didn't have to do all that, but it sure makes a difference to me that you did. I don't know if I would ever have gotten around to it. I know it can't have been fun."

"It was no problem," I said.

I put the box full of papers on the passenger seat of the truck. Then I turned out the lights, locked up, and went home. I hadn't done anything really hard. But I felt almost too tired to think.

About a mile from the river house, I pulled off the two-lane onto a road that wasn't much more than a pair of old wheel ruts leading down to a sinkhole where people had dumped old bedsprings and appliances. I took the little Ruger rifle from behind the front seat. I kept it wrapped in an oily towel along with a couple of full magazines. I fitted one of the magazines into the rifle, jacked a round into the chamber, and pushed the safety on. Then I wrapped the other magazine back up in the towel and put it back behind the seat.

I stepped off toward the river house through the gum trees and gallberry bushes. There was just enough light left in the sky that I could see twenty or thirty feet ahead of me, but it was fading and the woods would be totally dark by the time I reached the river house. That suited me fine.

My senses, dulled from an afternoon spent working like a clerk, came back to life as I moved through the woods. I smelled the wet, rank earth as my feet uncovered it and I picked up the sounds of birds and small animals that had heard me first and were moving to get out of my way. A mosquito next to my ear seemed to whine as loud as a police siren. Even in the gloom I picked my way easily through the trees. By the time I reached the edge of my lawn, I felt entirely alert.

I stayed back in the trees for fifteen or twenty minutes, waiting and watching. No sounds came from the vast old house. Nothing moved. But I decided to give it a little longer. I didn't think Culp and his associates would give up that case, and its contents, without a fight.

When I decided, finally, that the house was most likely empty, I crossed the yard running in a crouch. When I went through the rooms, the Ruger was through each door ahead of me. Nothing.

I carried the rifle with me when I went out to the old mule barn and hit the weights for an hour or so, just to burn off some of the frustration. I showered and warmed up a little chili for supper.

After I'd finished eating and cleaned up, I went into my reading room and did the work I'd brought with me from Garvey's shop. I rebilled everyone who was overdue. Instructed insurance companies to cancel policies and send refunds. Terminated the lease on the building. I put together a pile of the things that would require Rachel's signature. It was past midnight when I had everything in shape and went to bed. With the Ruger in easy reach.

CHAPTER 35

A HALF-HOUR BEFORE DAWN, I WAS UP and dressed and waiting in the trees with the Ruger, watching the house and listening for the sound of a vehicle on the blacktop or, better, the pressure of tires on the shell-covered drive. Yesterday, I had thought of this as the Indians' sacred time. Today, it recalled the stand-to ritual that the soldiers on the Western Front went through every morning of the First World War, when they would man their trenches and look east into the sunrise, waiting for the German attack that almost never materialized. Nobody came for me at the river house, either.

I took the papers by for Rachel to sign. She went through them carefully, reading everything before she put her name on the line. But I could tell it wasn't easy and that she was working to keep her composure. We were both relieved when the last paper was signed and it was time for me to get out of her house.

The three dive-shop owners came by and looked over the inventory at Garvey's shop, examining everything and trying not to give anything away with their faces. They all made bids. The highest was for a little more than I had expected and I took it. The man said he would be by with a cashier's check and a U-Haul in the late afternoon. We set a time.

I called Pete at the Outrigger.

"I got a live one," he said. "He knows the boat and he's hot for it. But he wants to survey it. He's got someone lined up but I need to know where the boat is."

I told him.

"When can he look at it?"

"Anytime. I can do it today, if he's available." I gave him the number at Garvey's shop and told him to call me.

"Let me check on it. I'll be back to you in a short."

I watched while the man in the white short-sleeved shirt with three ballpoints in the pocket went over *Second Shot.* He said nothing and he made no notes. I felt an irrational sort of resentment. Who the hell was *he* to be inspecting Garvey's boat?

When he was finished, he stood on the dock with his face slightly flushed and a few beads of sweat popping like small blisters from his forehead.

"It's in perfect shape," he said. "Hull, trim, fittings, electronics—everything. I can't guarantee the engines unless I test a sample of the oil, but I'll bet you wouldn't find enough metal in that crankcase to make a filling for a mouse tooth."

"Take the sample if you want. Or check the engine logs. Garvey had the oil analyzed every couple of hundred hours."

"I'm not surprised."

He left with the logs, and a couple of hours later I had

a sale. An hour after that, the U-Haul left the lot behind Garvey's shop with everything except a couple of half-empty cans of WD-40 and a Sierra Club calendar.

I had two checks to turn over to Rachel, with the truck sale still to come. Then there were the insurance refunds and the other little items, like the telephone deposit, that would trickle in over the next couple of months. A few more loose ends and, once they had been tied up, the books would be closed on Phil Garvey.

But the books were still open on Vernon Culp. I wondered, as I watched the U-Haul pull out of the lot and into traffic, what was keeping him.

He knew that I knew. He also knew, though maybe not with absolute certainty, that I had the case with a million in bearer bonds, that much again in cash, and who knows how much in uncut stones. Even if he couldn't be absolutely sure—if there were a chance I'd left the case inside the airplane on the bottom of the Gulf—he had to make a try for it. If it went right, he would have the case, and its contents, and be shed of me. A twofer. He had to try for it. I was depending on him.

Probably, he was rounding up talent and putting together his team. But he'd be in a hurry. I was depending on that, too.

Nobody followed me out of town back to the river house. I parked on the dump road again. Walked through the woods carrying the Ruger again. Found the house totally empty again.

But there were three messages on my answering machine. Tom Pine, Nat Semmes, and Jessie Beaudreaux all wanted me to call. Tom and Nat could wait. I called Jessie.

"How are you?" she said.

"I'm fine," I said. I told her what I'd been doing.

"Is there anything I can do to help you, Morgan?" she said. "I was pretty good with a shotgun once."

And hated it, I remembered. But it was true, she had been good. But that had been an accident; a case of being in the wrong place at the wrong time.

"No," I said. "But thank you for asking."

"And thank you, sir, for turning me down."

"My pleasure."

"You want me to come over there tonight, fix us some shrimp, maybe?"

It sounded good. The house felt lonely as a coffin around me. But I managed to give her a prudent answer.

"Better not."

"Like that, then?"

"Could be."

"In that case, be careful. Or have I said that already?"

"I can't hear it enough," I said.

"'Bye."

"Good-bye."

I made coffee and sat on the front step to drink it. The night was warm and clear with just enough wind coming out of the south to keep the bugs down. The river was low and moving so slowly that it didn't make a sound. But I could smell it and somehow sense it.

All things considered, I was feeling pretty good. A little itchy, maybe, waiting for Culp to make his move. Seemed like it had to be soon.

I kept the Ruger close but I didn't think they would be coming this early. Later on, probably, hoping to surprise me.

Fat chance of that, I thought, and decided I would take a position out in the trees, a couple of feet back from the edge of the lawn. I knew the spot I wanted. A place that gave me a good view.

And a fine field of fire.

I was thinking about another cup of coffee—no reason to sweat the caffeine, since I'd be up all night anyway—and had just about decided it was time when the phone rang. I'd carried the little handset out to the porch with me. I pushed the button to open the connection, hoping that it wasn't Semmes or Pine calling.

"Hello."

"Morgan, thank God."

"Hello, Rachel," I said.

"They've got Rick," she said. "And they say they'll kill him."

Chapter 36

Rachel seemed in control of herself.

"They said to make sure you brought the case with you," she said. " 'No case, no kid,' was what he said, and I believe he meant it."

"I've got the case in the cab of my truck," I said.

I thought, as I sat across from Rachel at her kitchen table, that it might be time to call Pine.

"I need a decision from you," I said. "You have to make it."

"All right," she said.

"Do you want to call the law, or do you want me to handle it?"

"I—" She shook her head and then ran the fingers of one hand through her hair. "I don't know. What happens if we call the law?"

"I'm not sure. Tom Pine would do his best for you as long as it was in his hands. But that might not be very long. Kidnapping is a federal crime, so he might have to turn things over to the FBI. It might get real big, real quick."

She thought for a while. Everything in the room seemed utterly still.

"That means lots of people could be involved, doesn't it?"

I nodded. She wasn't looking for answers.

"There would be people who didn't know Rick, or really care about him. They'd have other things on their minds, wouldn't they? Headlines. Promotions. Turf wars. That's the way it works, isn't it?"

I nodded again.

"I don't care about anything except Rick."

I said nothing. Waited for her to go on while she looked at me with her face compressed into a knot of pain. I wanted to look away, at the dishes drying next to the sink or the crayon drawings held on the refrigerator door by magnets.

"What do you care about, Morgan?"

"I want to get Rick back," I said.

"And that's all? You don't care about seeing them caught and punished? You just want to get Rick back?"

"That's right."

"You lied to me once, when I asked you about what was troubling Phil. Remember?"

I nodded.

"This Loftin person was suing him and it was on his mind. I called you and you told me you didn't know anything."

"That's right."

"Are you lying now?"

I shook my head.

"Because if you plan on going in there like some kind of cowboy, if you're thinking about taking any kind of risk with my child, then I might as well call the FBI right now. Tell them about that case and make you give it to them."

"I understand."

"I have to be sure, Morgan. I have to be sure you're not lying to me."

"I'm not," I said. I couldn't think of anything to say, other than that, to convince her.

She stared at me.

"Will you do it exactly the way they want it done?"

"Yes."

"And what about you?"

"Me?"

"You're not worried about what they might do to you? Once you get Rick back?"

"No," I said. That wasn't a lie, either. It wasn't bravery or heroism or any of that. Past a certain point, you just lose interest in yourself.

She looked at me for a long time and her face changed, slightly, with the relief that comes when you've made your decision, good or bad, and are willing to live with it.

"All right, Morgan," she said. "All right. Here's what they want you to do. Please do it exactly the way they want it. For Rick."

I nodded.

"Promise me."

"For Rick," I said.

They wanted me to be waiting by a pay phone, in the lot of a little mom-and-pop grocery on the highway north of town. They wanted me there at one in the morning, alone. And they wanted me to have the case with me.

I got there a few minutes early, pulled up close to the phone, and rolled down the window so I could hear it ring when they called. The store was closed and the lot was empty. There was no traffic on the highway.

I looked up and down the blacktop. There were plenty of places where someone could be sitting in the pine and jack oak, glassing me through a set of binoculars or, for that matter, an 8x scope. Even though the store was closed, the parking lot was still illuminated by a pair of old street-lamps in a feeble attempt to deter burglars. A good, modern scope could easily gather enough of that diseased yellow light for a shot. You wouldn't even need one of those expensive night-vision jobs that show everything in lurid, watery green.

The back of my neck felt cold and a vein in my temple jumped like it had been touched by a wire.

I looked at my watch. Ten minutes to one.

Either they would shoot me now and hope that I had the case with me and didn't have any backup or—they wouldn't. I closed my eyes and tried to make myself think about a long, wild river in Alaska, gorged with cold green water and full of large wild steelhead. It was one of those places I'd told myself I had to see sometime before I died. Could be that this was as close as I would ever get.

The phone rang. I stepped out of the truck and my legs felt heavy. I walked around the back past the tailgate as the phone rang a second time and the skin danced along the top of my spine. The phone rang a third time before I picked it up.

"Yes," I said.

"Okay, asshole," the furious voice said. I liked it that he was emotional.

I waited.

"You listen," the voice said.

"I'm listening."

"Do it wrong and we waste the kid," the voice said.

"I'll do what you say."

"You'd better."

I waited.

"You remember the barn?"

"The one where you hid the truck?"

"That's right."

"I remember."

"Can you find it again?"

"Sure."

"Then do it—fast."

He hung up and so did I.

I walked out of the field of yellow light to the edge of the parking lot where it was dark, unzipped my fly, and flowed. I could have held it. But I wouldn't have been able to see what I was looking for if I hadn't gotten away from the liverish glow of the lights.

I scanned the shoulder of the blacktop, fifty yards in each direction. Back again. Keeping the eyes moving. You never stare at one spot too long. It was one of the techniques that I'd learned somewhere along the way. Just one of many that made me "good in the woods," as people used to say back when it meant something.

I picked up the movement just as I had decided it was no good and was zipping up. Not much movement. A slight shift in the composition of the shadow line. Then another. What I guessed was that it was somebody putting down his binoculars and picking up his radio or his cellular phone. Letting someone down the line know what I was doing and that I was still alone.

I wanted them to know that. It would help the kid's chances.

I got in the truck and pulled out of the lot onto the blacktop. In fifteen minutes I was turning off the highway onto the section road I'd driven to recover Phil Garvey's truck. This time, I was after his son.

I intended to make this the last trip—one way or the other.

CHAPTER 37

I PULLED UP IN FRONT OF THE BARN DOOR. Cut the engine. Then my headlights. Stepped out of the cab. The night was still and quiet around me.

They took a while before they showed themselves. Making sure, I suppose, that I hadn't been followed.

I stood fixed to one spot of ground, waiting. And thinking that if they were in a hurry and eaten up with fear—which was likely—they could just go ahead and kill me where I stood, hoping that I had brought the case and everything in it with me, they way I'd said I would. They couldn't be sure I had, though, so the smart thing would be to wait until they had the case and all of its contents, then kill me. I was hoping that they were at least that smart. I told myself that you couldn't be dumb and loot a bank. Not completely dumb, anyway.

As reassurance it was a pretty thin blanket.

"Let's put the hands up," a voice said. Same voice I'd heard over the phone. It wasn't Loftin and it wasn't Jenkins. I wondered if it was Vernon Culp himself, the Don Trump and Charlie Keating of the Panhandle.

I put my hands up in a half-assed sort of way. Testing the air.

"All the way, asshole."

I put my hands up smartly.

There were three of them. Once they started talking, I recognized Loftin's voice. And Jenkins's. I still wasn't sure the third man was Culp.

Someone patted me down. Awkwardly. It wasn't something he knew how to do or liked doing.

"No gun and no tape recorder," Loftin said.

"Okay. You can put your hands down."

Before I could do it, Loftin hit me. It was a kidney punch, and the mercy was that Loftin didn't really know how to put his shoulder into it and follow through so that the punch had all his weight behind it. If he'd known, I'd have been too gimped to do anything for the next twenty-four hours and would have pissed blood for three days.

But the punch hurt. My vision tunneled and my breath left me and my legs sagged. I went down to my knees, and when I got there Loftin kicked me. In the ribs.

He was better at kicking than hitting. It felt like he'd split a rib on his first try. I felt another shaft of pain through my lungs and I saw small white explosions angling off in front of my eyes.

"Motherfucker," Loftin said. "Rotten cocksucker."

He really knew how to hurt a man.

He kicked me a little more but never hit the sweet spot again, like he did on that first kick. I'd been hurt worse outside a Fort Bragg bucket-of-blood beer joint on a Saturday night. But I'd been able to fight back then, while I had to curl up and take it now, like a kid trying to ride

out a drunken father's rage. It hurt my feelings as much
as anything. I wanted to peel Loftin like a snake and use
his hide for a belt. But I had to pretend I was in mortal
pain and let him kick. After a while, he quit. Convinced
by my act, I suppose, but also out of breath. Now would
be the perfect time to come down on him.

"Get up," he said, panting and spitting.

I stood up. It was hard not breaking his neck.

"How does it feel? Being on the other end."

I shook my head and tried to look pitiful.

"Not such a big badass anymore, huh?"

I looked at the ground and shook my head.

"I ought to pop you again."

"All right, that's enough." It was the voice I'd heard on
the telephone. Tired of Loftin's juvenile act. It did wear
thin in a hurry, as a matter of fact.

The man with the telephone voice stepped up close. It
was Culp. I remembered the face from the pictures over
newspaper stories. It was a long face, with a slightly
mournful mouth and the eyes you see on a dog that has
to find its own way of getting its dinner. There was something opportunistic about the eyes, along with something
fearful. I wondered if the eyes had had that look back when
he was pretending to be a shrewd banker.

"Did you bring it?" he said.

"The case?"

"Yes, goddamnit," he exploded, "the case. Did you bring
the case?"

"Just like you told me to."

"All right," he said with relief, like it was the first good
news he'd had in months.

"But there's one minor problem."

"Problem?"

"Yeah," I said. "It could be a problem. I'm sure you boys

can come up with a solution, the way you've planned this thing so far . . ."

"*What* problem?" he said, his voice rising.

"I brought half the money. You've got it now, and you've got me. If you want the rest of it, get the kid back to his mother. Safe. Then you'll still have me and I'll take you to the rest of the money."

"You sonofabitch."

I shrugged.

"We ought—" Loftin said. He didn't finish what he wanted to say because Culp gave him a look. But I knew what he'd left unsaid, and he was right. They should have. Just as soon as they'd checked to make sure I had, in fact, brought half of what was in the case. That was a lot. Enough, maybe, and certainly better than nothing. Prudent men would have known it was time to cut their losses or, in this case, sit on their winnings.

Would have been a real shame for me if they had been prudent men. But I felt confident. I was counting on greed, which is as close to a sure thing as you can get in this world. Sloppy, irrational greed. The kind that keeps the casinos in business and the lines running out into the convenience-store parking lots when the lottery gets up to fifty or a hundred million. These boys would never settle for a ham when they could have the whole fat hog.

This time Culp hit me. Flat-handed across the face. I imagined that, in his time, he'd hit women that way. That left Jenkins. He still needed to get his licks in.

"I told her I wanted you to bring the case and everything in it."

"And she told me," I said. "I just decided to do it this way. You can still get the other half. But the kid goes home first."

"We've got you," he said, putting all the menace he could manage into his voice.

"Yes," I said. "You do." This was another part of my gamble. They could try to beat it out of me. But you have to be hard to deal out torture. These boys were too soft.

"*Goddamnit*," Culp said. "Where's the other half?"

"Where's the boy?"

"He's in there," he said, waving his hand impatiently at the barn. I thought about trying for the gun. But Loftin had one, too. And probably Jenkins.

"I want to see him," I said.

"First, *we* see the case."

"In the truck," I said. "Behind the seat."

They took it out, opened it, and examined the contents in the weak beam of a plastic drugstore flashlight. The feeble yellow light played over the bearer bonds, currency, and uncut jewels. Paper and stone. No scissors.

"Exactly half," Culp said. "You don't take shortcuts, do you?"

"Let's see the kid," I said.

He stayed six feet behind me as I walked over to the door of the barn and opened it. Loftin and Jenkins were another six feet behind him. No chance of grabbing Rick and heading for the trees. And no need, either. I'd get him back home the easy way. These boys wanted that other half.

Rick was lying on a blanket that had been spread over a pile of hay broken loose from old bales. He was covered by another blanket. His head was still wrapped in six feet of white gauze, so it stood out like a searchlight in the dark barn.

"Rick," I said softly, "it's Morgan Hunt."

"Hello, Mr. Hunt."

I bent down close to him. He was shivering. It wasn't cold.

"You all right, sport?" I said.

"Yes sir," he said, trying to sound like he meant it. "How is my mom?"

"She's fine. A little bent out of shape since you turned up missing."

"I'm sorry."

"Not your fault. Anyway, we're going to get you back to her real shortly now."

I looked up at Culp and his partners when I said this. Culp had the old nothing-ever-goes-right-for-me look on his face. But he nodded.

"You thirsty?" I said.

"Yes sir," he said. "Real thirsty."

They'd taken a very sick kid, which was bad enough, and then hadn't given him any fluids. I'd known hard cases in jail who would have thought to give the kid something to drink while they waited for their payoff. Probably would have brought him a hamburger, too. I hoped, more devoutly than ever, to get a chance at these boys myself.

"There's a water bottle behind the seat of my truck," I said, looking at Jenkins.

Jenkins didn't move.

"Get it," Culp said impatiently.

I took Rick's small, trembling hand and gave it a squeeze. "We'll get you something to drink and then we'll get you out of here and back to your mom. You'll be home in two hours."

I looked at Culp.

He nodded but he wasn't happy. Why, *why* did things like this keep happening to him?

It just wasn't fair.

CHAPTER 38

I WATCHED FROM A THICK NEST OF PAL-
mettos across the road from the little mom-and-pop grocery as Rick waited in the parking lot for his mother. Culp
and Loftin crouched a couple of feet behind me, holding
their pistols in one hand and swatting mosquitoes with
the other. They were hopeless in the woods. Both of them.
No surprise there.

Jenkins waited in the shadows of the building, closer to
the boy, so he could grab him if anything went wrong. I
had called Rachel from a pay phone and told her what to
do. Culp had told me that they would kill the boy, and
me, if they saw the first sign of law. I told him that I
understood and that Rachel did, too. We wanted the boy
back, I said. Nothing else.

"Understand this," Culp said. "I'm in a place where I've
got nothing to lose. Not a goddamned thing."

I'd told him I understood.

So I watched from the palmettos as Rick sat with his back
against a gas pump, waiting for his mother to come pick

him up. He was too weak to stand. He looked small, insubstantial, and, with the gauze wrapped around his head like a turban, badly damaged. I wondered idly what Phil Garvey would do if he were suddenly resurrected and could get his hands on Culp.

There was no traffic on the highway. Anyone driving past wouldn't have been able to see Rick anyway. The angle was wrong. We waited. Culp and Loftin swatted the swarming mosquitoes. I left them alone. They didn't drink much.

A pair of headlights showed in the distance, followed by the sound of an engine winding out. Then the sound of hard braking as the vehicle slowed to turn into the parking lot. Rachel's little Cherokee stopped short enough to raise dust and she was out of the car like it was on fire, running to Rick and picking him up and holding him for a long time in her arms, then holding him out to look at him in the weak light. She looked at him for a long time and touched him delicately around the face and head. Then she hugged him again, looked around the parking lot to see if anyone else was there, and then put him in the front seat and buckled his seat belt across him. She stood over him for a minute, listening as he told her something. Probably what Culp had told him to say—that they still had me and that if she sent anyone after them they would kill me. They would, anyway, of course. They had to. But they were counting on her to be too much the hysterical mother to realize that. They were playing for time.

Rachel got back in the wagon and pulled out of the lot, onto the highway, heading back the way she had come.

"All right," Culp said, his voice low and furious, "let's go get the rest of it."

*   *   *

I sat in the backseat of a Japanese four-wheel-drive wagon with my hands wired behind my back. Loftin sat next to me, holding a pistol. Culp sat in the passenger seat; Jenkins drove.

I gave directions.

"Keep it slow," Culp said. "Last thing we need is to get stopped for speeding."

"I know that," Jenkins said. "Jesus."

"Just be careful," Culp said.

"Listen—"

"Everybody relax," Loftin said from the backseat. "Just relax."

"Relax, shit," Culp said.

The boys were having a tough time keeping an even strain. We rode along in edgy silence.

"What would have happened if I hadn't come along and found that case?" I said, sounding like someone trying to break the tension at the house party that had gone bad.

"We were looking for another diver," Loftin said.

"That shouldn't have been any trouble," I said. "There are divers all up and down this coast. Go over to Morgan City, you can find one of those boys who works the oil rigs. Something like that would have looked easy for him."

"Had to be the right man," Loftin said.

"What made Garvey right?"

"He wouldn't have made trouble."

"Trouble?"

"Yes, *trouble*. Once he'd been paid, we'd have never heard from him again. He'd want to get as far away from us as he could get and stay there. He wanted money for his kid. One-shot deal. He was desperate, but he wasn't greedy."

"And one of those rig divers might have come back for

more, once he saw what was down there and figured things out?"

"That's right."

"So you wanted Garvey because you knew he wasn't a blackmailer?"

"That's right. It would have worked, too, if he hadn't fucked up."

Died, in other words.

"The fuckups started a long time before that," Culp said bitterly.

"You mean me, right?" Jenkins said.

"Now that you mention it," Culp said.

"Maybe if I'd had a GPS that worked. I fly airplanes—I don't do electronics."

"Maybe if you hadn't panicked, been in such a big god-damned hurry to get out of that plane that you couldn't take time to go back and get that case. The whole thing was about that case. Without it—"

"Right," Jenkins said. "Sure. And with it, if I got picked up by anybody else, where was I? Down in Raiford, waiting my turn in the electric chair."

"Sure," Culp said. "And what difference did it make? You'd been paid."

"That case was a lot safer in the plane than it would have been floating around on the Gulf with me. And we found it."

"Luck. You opened up that raft and found the loran."

"Right. I did. *Me*. After the GPS went bad. *Your* man couldn't bring it up."

"Wouldn't have been any need," Culp said, with a little less heat and more regret now. "None at all, if you'd brought it out with you."

Jenkins sighed and drummed the wheel with his fingers.

"It's done," Loftin said. "Nothing we can do about it."

"Now *that* is a big help," Culp said.

We rode on, along the empty blacktop, in silence. I told Jenkins where to turn, and after a while we were at the end of the narrow, shell-covered drive that led up to the river house.

"Stop here," Culp said. "And cut the fucking lights."

Jenkins stopped the car. Cut the lights.

"Turn off the engine."

Jenkins did what he was told.

Culp rolled down his window and we could hear the night sounds.

"What now?" Jenkins said.

Culp ignored him and turned in his seat to look back at me. He pointed the pistol at my face and everything inside of me turned to cold, foul water. I understood why people pissed their pants. It wasn't the first time.

"This is your place?" he said.

"Yes."

"And the other half of it is here?"

"Yes."

"What else is here?"

"Nothing."

"You haven't set us up? There isn't a SWAT team waiting in the trees?"

"You had the kid and you said not to call anyone. I did what you said. The kid's mother wanted it that way."

"What about you?"

"I wanted it that way, too."

"Why?"

"I wanted the kid safe."

He looked at me, sighting down the barrel of the pistol, and I was reminded of the way Semmes had looked at Loftin through the gunsight he made with his fingers.

"Either you're a good liar or an incredible asshole."

I didn't say anything.

He studied my face. I wondered if he actually thought he could read something there. Maybe he fancied himself a stud at poker.

"All right, you two," he said, "get out. Go up to the house and look around."

"What . . ." Loftin said.

Culp cut him off.

"Do it," he said. "Do it right now."

There was authority, of a sort, in his voice. Enough to get Jenkins and Loftin moving, anyway. They knew their place and they needed strength. Culp had enough for both.

When they opened the doors, the lights inside the wagon went on and I could see all the fury in Culp's face. A lifetime of slights and frustrations, need and pain, showed in its lines and angles. It was the face of a man who believed he had been born to destiny and then been cheated out of it. The sort of face you saw across the table from you at every meal you ate in prison.

Loftin and Jenkins closed the doors softly, like hunters going into the woods early and taking care not to startle their game. The light went out. I couldn't see Culp's face any longer, but the muzzle of the pistol was still plainly visible, like the flat head of a snake that has coiled on your chest while you were asleep. When you woke up, it was there, inches away, tongue flickering to test the air, and there was nothing you could do about it.

"What's with you, anyway?" he said. "What the fuck is with you?"

"What's with you?" I said.

He said nothing for a moment. Sighed softly and twitched. "Simple. I'm here for my money."

"Your money?"

"Mine."

"Seems like you stole it."

He laughed like an old con listening to a Bible-beater making his pitch.

"Let me tell you something," he said. "Stolen money is fifty bucks that some street punk gets when he hits the local convenience store. I've danced with ladies at the country club whose grandaddies stole a hundred times what was in that case you dragged up from the bottom of the Gulf. I've had drinks with men who bought themselves a seat in the Senate with money that they stole, or their daddy stole. And you know what? They were having a little drink with me because they wanted me to contribute some of *my* money to their cause. I never asked exactly what that cause was and they never said. We both understood. Of course, when the time came, they didn't have the balls it took to come through. You show me serious money and I'll show you stolen money. Every time."

CHAPTER 39

CULP HAD TALKED HIMSELF OUT. I IMAGined that he was thinking about all those bad breaks that had reduced him to this, to coming out here at night with a couple of incompetent sidekicks to reclaim his getaway stake. Wasn't that long ago that he'd been able to arrange a quick flight up to Washington on his own jet for lunch with some tame congressman. Take his wife with him and send her on to New York to drop a little money on clothes and jewelry. Then fly out to Aspen for the weekend to do some skiing.

Now this. Pure wormwood and gall. Killing me was about all the pleasure that was left to him in the world. Just as soon as he had the money.

The sky brightened slightly. False dawn.

"All right," Culp said. "Why don't you show me where you hid my money?"

He opened the door, and when the light came on I could see that his face had lost its tension. He looked deeply tired, almost beaten. He was going through with it because he couldn't think of anything better.

He came around the wagon and opened my door. He might have been tired, but he was still careful to stay back a few steps and to keep the pistol pointed firmly at my chest.

"Be a good boy, now," he said.

I got out of the truck awkwardly. More awkwardly than necessary, in fact.

"Lead on," he said, once he'd closed the door.

I started up the drive like a mutineer on his way to the firing squad.

"Real easy, real slow."

I shuffled obediently.

I gave myself the first twenty yards to get my night vision back. After that I would be looking for any chance. Or maybe taking one that wasn't even there. He needed me alive to get his hands on the money. He might hesitate just enough.

The false dawn had faded and an oily dark had settled back over the woods. I ran this drive every morning and I could do it blindfolded. I stepped carefully over a live oak root that bulged up through the ground. I was thinking about the thousands of times I'd heard men in a column, weighed down with rifles, packs, and radios, trip over roots like that and go down cursing.

He didn't go all the way down but he staggered a few steps, and that was all I needed. I was off the driveway and into the woods, running crouched, as fast as I could with my hands wired behind my back. It wasn't all that fast.

He shot. Once. Twice. I heard the crack of one round as it passed over my head. Close. But they always shoot high, the rookies do, especially at night. I kept running, dodging around the thick trunks of pine trees and keeping low.

When I'd gone about a hundred, maybe a hundred and fifty, yards and was sure he couldn't see me anymore, I rolled onto the ground and slithered up close to a blow-down. I knew the tree. Had dropped it myself after a lightning strike killed it. I knew all the trees in these woods. That was about all I had going for me.

Their hands were free and they had guns. I knew the woods.

I could hear them shouting and arguing.

"Get a light, get a goddamned *light*," Culp screamed.

"What way did he go?"

"That way, goddamnit. Now get a goddamned light."

"Here. There's only one."

The boys hadn't done a very thorough equipment check. Garvey would have chewed their asses for that.

"Give it to me."

"What do we do now?"

"Let's just get the fuck out of here. We've got half of it."

"No. We're not leaving here until we have all of it. He's not going anywhere with his hands tied."

"All right. But the sun will be up in a few minutes. Let's just wait."

"And give him time to get to the highway? Christ. Come on. You two work up in that direction. I'll make a big circle down toward the main road. He probably went that way. Just make sure he doesn't try to get to the house and use a phone."

I could see the thin beam of the light moving off, away from me. I waited. They were giving me a straight shot at the car. But there was nothing I could do with it when I got there except try to drive it with my teeth.

I stayed put.

I watched the light as Culp moved further and further away from me, swinging out toward the main road. It was the right move, even if he was going a little too fast. After a while, I lost the light. About that time, I began to hear the other two.

One of them was coming straight for the blowdown, almost like he knew I was there. It would be the logical place, with the ground so clean under the big pines that there was almost no other concealment. I felt my pulse pick up to a gallop, and everything in me wanted to get up and run. I still had a margin of fifteen or twenty yards to work with, and at night he probably wouldn't hit me if he did shoot.

I wanted to run . . . but what you want to do is usually what you absolutely shouldn't do. I pressed myself harder against the ground, so hard that the rib that Loftin had cracked when he kicked me felt like a jagged edge of glass cutting at my flesh. My eyes watered.

But I could see well enough to make out his shape as he came out from behind one of the big pines, both hands on the pistol like they teach it these days. Good technique, I suppose, but I wasn't sure about it in dark woods. I'd want one hand free for balance. Problem was, I didn't have any free hands. Or a pistol.

He took three or four steps and swept the area ahead of himself with the pistol. When the pistol had gone through its arc, he took another three or four steps. Swept the area again with the pistol. Good form. But bad eyes.

It took him almost ten minutes to come across a clear space that had been made by the shade of the old pine that was now lying on the ground waiting for me to buck it up with the chain saw and burn it in my fireplace.

I didn't move. Barely breathed. But I felt like I was lying wide open in the sunlight, wearing a bright-pink clown suit. Any second he would see me. Would he shoot?

He was ten feet from me. It was Loftin. Eyes searching the woods twenty or thirty feet out in front, his big front teeth biting down over his lower lip, breathing loud enough for me to hear it. It seemed like he should have heard me. My breathing. My heartbeat. The ringing in my ears. But he never looked down.

I saw movement at the top of the clearing. Jenkins, moving just like Loftin, only a little more erratically, checking behind him and back toward the house.

Loftin came on. Two or three steps at a time. Sweeping the area ahead of him with his gun and with his eyes. He was eight feet from me. Then five. If he looked down, he would see me. He couldn't help it.

He stepped up on the blowdown. Then over it. I couldn't see him now, but I could still hear him. Three steps and pause. Three steps and pause.

I was watching Jenkins as he came on. Moving more and pausing less and looking over his shoulder, back in the direction of the house. To make sure I hadn't gotten behind them, I suppose.

I didn't think Jenkins knew where Loftin was. I was sure that Loftin didn't know Jenkins was behind him. A lot of men had been killed at night by people on their side. Stonewall Jackson, for one. And a couple of men I'd known who'd never become legends, just names on a wall. And thousands, maybe millions, of others in wars nobody remembers. Night raises the panic factor to insupportable levels. You lose track of where the other people are. Of where you are. Of where your enemy is. You're scared. You can't see ten feet in front of you, but for some reason you feel as though you're standing under stage lights, visible to anyone within a mile. You imagine yourself in the sights of a dozen different unseen rifles. When you're surprised or startled, you can't help yourself . . . you shoot.

Loftin was ten feet on one side of the blowdown, Jenkins fifteen feet on the other, when I kicked a dead branch on the tree so hard that it snapped with a sound that, to an agitated mind, could have only been a shot.

The still air around me suddenly erupted. Each of them was shooting. I could see the muzzle flashes from Jenkins's pistol, so intense in the dark woods that the light seemed to go straight through the lens of my eye and into my brain.

Jenkins became an indistinct shape in my vision. For a moment I thought I had been blinded and lost him, and then I realized he was down. He'd been hit. I could hear Loftin coming back toward the blowdown. He was moving quickly.

He almost stepped on me as he came over the tree. I whipped my leg and caught his just below the knee. He went down, face first, hard on the ground. I moved like a crab, but much faster, and had my legs around his neck like scissors. I locked them down tight and I could hear him strangle. He clawed at me but couldn't reach anything vital. His fingers were desperate, clutching wildly at my thigh. Then, in just a few seconds, they began to go limp. I wanted to squeeze harder so the next sound would be a decisive, final pop, and I would feel his fingers go inert.

But I backed off. Just a little. I could see the gun. It was too far for him to reach it. But to make sure, I moved a yard or two, dragging him like a scorpion with a fresh kill. I waited until he was gasping and his fingers were moving again. Then I tightened the pressure for a second to show him I could do it anytime I wanted.

"You have about thirty seconds," I whispered, "to twist that wire off my wrists. If you don't do it, I'll break your neck."

He made a sound. There were no words in it.

"Thirty seconds," I said, and tightened the grip just a little for just a second.

I could feel his hands moving, reaching for the wire. We were tangled up like a pair of ancient wrestlers locked in a mortal hold.

I could feel his fingers on my wrists, groping at the wire where it was twisted.

"It's too strong."

"Thirty seconds."

"I can't."

"That's a lick on you, then. Either you unwrap that wire or I break your neck."

"No . . ."

"Do it."

I could feel him straining. Hear him sobbing. The wire seemed to give.

"I can't."

I locked down on his neck.

His hands worked harder. Frantic now, like the hands of someone trapped underwater, clawing for the surface.

The wire seemed to be giving.

"You got it now," I said. "Come on."

He strained and I felt myself straining with him. He seemed to collapse just as my hands came free. He started to say something, but before he could get the words out I clamped down on his neck and held the pressure until he went limp.

I rolled away from him. Got the pistol in my hand, then rolled back, snug against the blowdown. I pulled back the slide on the pistol, saw the gleam of the chambered round, made sure the safety was off, and then listened for the sound of Culp moving.

Nothing.

I searched the woods ahead of me for a sliver of reflected light.

Nothing.

If he'd run for the wagon, he could be there by now. But if he'd come to the sound of the shots, he could be ten feet away, waiting for me to stand and give him an easy target.

Pressed against the earth and the blowdown, I listened. It was the quietest time of all in the woods. The sacred time. If he was there, I might be able to hear him. To sense him. I strained to pick up some sound, some presence.

The only sound was Loftin gasping for air. I wished, then, that I'd held the pressure a little longer and killed him. Right now he was in the way.

I thought about breaking another branch to startle Culp into revealing himself. But it wouldn't work again. My hands ached as the blood flowed into them and feeling returned.

If he'd gone for the car, I thought, I would have heard it by now. If I waited a little longer, it would be daylight. But if he was close, and watching, he would still have the advantage.

Loftin was moving. Twitching and clawing first at his throat and then at the ground.

I made up my mind the way you do when things are like that. You make your best guess and then you say, "Okay, then, the hell with it. If I'm wrong, I die."

One thing you always know is that running away never rattles someone the way charging him will. Run away as fast as you can, and you still give him time to get off a whole magazine. Run at him and you close the gap before he can fire more than a couple of shots. The range is closer and that's a point for him. But if you come hard, you might rattle him and throw off his aim. What you want to do is open the range, but what you need to do is close it. Always assault an ambush, even when what you want to do is run like hell. *Especially* then.

I took a breath and vaulted the thick tree trunk, screaming like a madman in the dark, still woods.

Culp fired instantly, but it went high.

He was right in front of me, right where I'd thought he might be. The worst place he could be. I was still yelling, still moving, heading right for him. But he was ten long steps from me, standing straight up, with the pistol gripped in both hands and leveled right at me. Perfect combat stance with his knees slightly bent, his feet planted, his arms locked out in front of him for an easy kill shot. No deflection and point-blank range.

I knew I was dead.

CHAPTER 40

H E SHOT HIGH, JUST LIKE THEY ALL DO. Not very high—I heard the crack of the round over my head, maybe only a couple inches. But high enough. He was a banker.

I ran straight into him, and his gun. The impact carried us both to the ground. It felt good. Everything suddenly felt good.

We rolled around on the ground for a few seconds. Culp clawed at me like a pinned animal, snarling and desperate and without any hope or strategy. I waited for the right opening and got a hold on one of his arms. I used my weight, and his, to pop the arm out of its joint. He screamed, but the sound died quickly when I got an arm around his neck, used the other arm to apply some pressure, and cut off his air. I'd done it to Loftin but had backed off. This time, with the woods around me in those last few moments of quiet and calm before the sun comes up and the day begins, I was going to finish. You seldom get to put your hands on your true enemy and feel the life go out of him. There was a wild, undeniable, terrifying joy in it, and as the seconds passed Culp went limp and sagged in my arms.

He was on his knees and I was over him, putting the pressure into my hold, squeezing the life out of him. I could feel it; feel the urgency of his resistance diminish until all that was left was a kind of quivering hold on existence, a last, feeble, biological spasm.

I broke the hold. I couldn't do it. Culp sagged to the ground and I picked up the gun and walked to the blow-down. I sat down and shook, like I was soaked and freezing, for a full five minutes.

I was moving again, like a sleepwalker, when I heard tires on the shell surfacing of my drive. I had wired Culp and Loftin together. Left hand to right. Accounted for all the pistols and unloaded two of them. Birds were singing all around me, but it might have been radio static. I was waiting for Loftin and Culp to come around enough that I could march them up to the house, where I would make a phone call.

I stopped and listened to the sound of the tires. Then the slamming of a car door.

I moved through the woods quickly, checking back on Loftin and Culp even though they weren't going any-where. Not for now, anyway. Not any more than Jenkins.

The car was a sheriff's cruiser. Tom Pine was standing next to it, holding a blunt, ugly, police-model shotgun.

I told Pine everything while we waited for a meat wagon and another cruiser to take the prisoners in.

"Busy night," he said. "I'd be wore out, if it was me."

"I am."

"One thing," he said, sounding merely curious, in a bored sort of way.

"What's that?"

"How come you're here? You took the case with you when you went to ransom the kid, right?"

"Right."

"So how come you're out here? I don't suppose you were just showing them your big, beautiful house."

"I told them that I'd kept half the money out here. I figured if I gave them all of it, up front, they wouldn't have any reason to turn loose the kid. My deal was, once the kid was back with his mother, we'd come out here and get the other half."

Pine nodded ponderously. He was leaning against the hood of the cruiser, arms folded across his massive chest. He was chewing a toothpick and enjoying the morning. We could have been talking about the fishing.

"So did you keep half?"

I didn't say anything.

"I'd have to figure that you did. I mean, they would know how much was supposed to be in the case, more or less, and unlike a lot of the dudes I do business with, they would know how to count past their fingers and toes. They wouldn't have come out here unless they'd believed you."

"I see your point," I said.

"So the other half of it is here?"

"Could be," I said. "I'll know before you finish your report."

He shook his head slowly side to side. "Oh mercy. You know, Morgan, if you were a real badass, first-degree hard case, and all of that, then you could of just gone ahead and killed these boys right here in the woods. Claimed self-defense. You wouldn't have got no serious argument from anyone. The kid would have said that these were the creeps that snatched him. So you would have been clear. You could have said there never was any money."

"I know."

"Now you gone and created a situation for yourself."

"How long will it take you to get your report in order?"

He thought for a second or two.

"Late afternoon, I expect. I never was a burner on the paperwork."

"Plenty of time," I said.

Rachel Garvey shook her head decisively. "No way," she said. "Give it to the law."

"It'll go to the government, and they'll put it in an escrow account where it will draw some kind of anemic interest against the day when they finally settle all the claims against Culp's bank," I said. "Lawyers will have gotten most of it when the dust finally settles. It would still be down there in that plane if Phil hadn't gone after it. Seems like you've got a stronger claim than the lawyers."

"I don't care."

"It'll pay a lot of medical bills. Pay for college."

"I don't want it, Morgan."

"All right."

"Will *you* keep it? Your claim is as strong as Phil's."

I shook my head.

"See there?"

I had the rest of the contents of the case in my truck, but before I delivered the bonds, stones, and currency to Pine, I went by Semmes's office.

He listened to my story, and when I finished he shook his head and looked out the window at the bay, shimmering and blue in the light of a clear spring day.

"The woman has more brains than either you or Garvey, you know that."

I nodded.

"I sometimes believe that found money might be one of the great curses of these poor, dismal times. I haven't seen a jackpot yet."

"No?"

He shook his head again. "Drive over to that Creek Indian bingo operation in Alabama sometime."

"No, thanks," I said. "I don't like the neighborhood." It was a mile or two from Holman prison.

"Right neighborhood for it," Semmes said. "What used to be a race of warriors is now reduced to selling to what used to be a race of pioneers chances at the great, glittering jackpot. The pioneers come in chartered, air-conditioned buses and they buy their cards with their retirement money. The only thing thicker than cigarette smoke in that hall is the desperation. I don't know what the winners do with their money. Now and then one of the losers will go berserk and kill himself. The Creeks make some money— honest money, I suppose you could call it—and they spend it on alcohol programs for the tribe. It makes a nice, sweet symmetrical circle, the way I see it."

I nodded. But Semmes was just warming up.

"Consider how it would have been if Garvey had been looking for genuine Spanish treasure."

"Huh?"

"Spain hasn't been the same since it made plunder the national policy. It mistook gold for wealth and wound up poor and weak."

"All right," I said, "I'll give you that. But Rachel Garvey isn't Spain. She's a woman with two kids, one of them very sick. Seems like she could use the money."

"I agree. And I think we can get her a piece of it."

"I thought . . ."

"A *clean* piece," Semmes said, holding up his hand. "Give me a few minutes."

I waited while he made some calls. It turned out that the government paid a reward to anyone who helped recover money hidden from the people cleaning up after bankers like Culp. Our cut would come to 10 percent.

"Now you have to take the rest of the money to Pine," Semmes said.

"I hate to do that."

"Believe me, Morgan," Semmes said, "you'll walk out of Pine's office feeling like you just stepped out of a suit made of anchor chain."

"If you say so."

"I do," he said. "And by the way."

"Yes?"

"Hell of a job."

Pine was glad to see me and to take the money off my hands.

"You wouldn't have never been able to rest," he said.

"I guess."

"Listen, my man, 'cause I am speaking the truth. Culp and them would have screamed about how you had that money until somebody listened. You'd have been laying up at night, figuring new ways to lie. That's how Culp lives. Might be all right for him. But you ain't made of it."

"Right."

Pine swung his leg out from behind his desk and kicked the metal case, which was lying on the floor, with the toe of one of his size-fourteen boots. The case went sliding across the tile floor and stopped in the corner.

"I'm tired of talking about it. It's just money. Let's talk about something important."

"Like what?"

"Tomorrow."

"Tomorrow?"

"Bet your ass. Tomorrow is Saturday. Ain't we going fishing?"

I drove from Pine's back to the river house. It looked good, with the green out all around it, but unoccupied and sterile. I had a dozen different things on my list, including a load of custom-milled cherry flooring, but I didn't feel much like doing any of them.

So I got a beer and sat on the step and watched the river. It was low and dark and there was something so reliable and restful about it that I decided it was good for another beer.

The phone rang just as I got back to the step and had settled in. I got back up and went back inside. It felt like a chore.

"Morgan," Jessie said, "are you laying around on your ass feeling sorry for yourself?"

"How did you guess?"

"No guessing about it. I *know* you, man. I been knowing you and you don't change. But I've got a plan. Why don't you take me swimming down at the beach, and when it gets dark we can come back here and I'll fix something to eat?"

"I'll be there in fifteen minutes."

"Try for ten."

CHAPTER 41

We swam for a long time and then sat on the beach, watching the small curling waves and the busy shorebirds.

"So what's troubling you, chief?" Jessie said. "Can you get a bead on it?"

"Seems like it could have turned out better," I said.

"That ain't it."

I wanted to ask her why, if she already knew what it was, she had asked me in the first place. But I didn't. That's the way she approaches things.

"You know what it is?"

"I'll bite."

"It's over. Your friend is dead, but that's not your fault, and it's not even why you're feeling low. You just don't like that it's over and there isn't anything more you can do for Garvey or for Rachel. You did more than most anyone could have. And things were fine as long as you were looking for him or afterward taking care of things for her. Selling the boat or going after the boy the way you did.

Doing that, you were in your glory. Now it's done and you don't have anything to think about except how he's dead, she's got that sick boy to look after, and you got nothing to do but sand boards and pound nails."

"I don't mind pounding nails," I said. "Hell, I *like* pounding nails."

"Maybe, once you get started doing it. But a lifetime of it would look like another stretch on the farm to you. But don't worry about that, okay, *cher?*" She seldom called me that, using that old Cajun locution. Only when she was trying to get through to me. Like now.

"All right," I said. I meant it. I felt better already.

"May not look like it now. But something will come along."

We went back to her house and stood together in her big glass-and-tile shower, soaping each other until we couldn't stand it any longer. Then we fell into her big bed under a slowly turning ceiling fan and stayed there for what must have been two or three hours. I even slept a little, for what seemed like the first time in days.

She made jambalaya and we ate on the porch. While we were cleaning up, she said, "How about a party tomorrow night?"

"Absolutely," I said. "Pine's coming over to go fishing. Can you call Phyllis?"

"Sure. And Nat Semmes and Bobby. And Rachel, if she'll leave the boys. I'll boil up some shrimp. Whole tub of them."

Tom and I filled a stringer. He used a cane pole and crickets, which he said was the way God meant for bluegill to be caught. We quit early, cleaned the fish, and then Tom went with me to the mill to pick up my lumber and then helped me unload it and stack it. Phyllis came in her own car.

Nat and Bobbie came a little later and brought Rachel with them. She took me aside and told me that she was having Phil cremated and that when Rick had recovered enough she wanted to take the ashes out into the Gulf and scatter them. Would I come?

I said I would.

She didn't say another word about it. Any of it.

Jessie had hurricane lamps set up on the porch. Semmes had brought some wine that he said was good. I said I believed him. Bobbie asked me for a tour of the house and I took her around, showing her what I had done and telling her what I had planned.

"You do good work," she said. "Nat doesn't know which end of the hammer to hold. Can I hire you sometime?"

"Can you afford me?"

"He works for nothing," Nat said.

"Then I can afford you."

Jessie brought out the shrimp and we sat around a table, peeling and eating, drinking Semmes's wine and talking. Pine ate more than anyone, by a lot, and Phyllis kept after him, saying that he might be bulletproof but he wasn't coronary-proof. Pine said he didn't believe in that stuff and, anyway, if he couldn't scarf a few shrimp and drink a little wine on Saturday night, then life wasn't worth living.

It went on like that, and at one point, when everyone seemed to be talking at once and laughing at once, I looked across the table and saw Jessie smiling. Not at me, necessarily, just smiling. Then I looked past her at the dark space that was the river and the long, blurred line of dark pines on the opposite bank. It was a fine mild night, spring on the coast, and the fragrance of wisteria was on the air. It felt good to be alive.

With some people, it doesn't take much.

234